WHISKEY GINGER

PHANTOM QUEEN BOOK 1 - A TEMPLE VERSE SERIES

SHAYNE SILVERS
CAMERON O'CONNELL

ARGENTO
PUBLISHING

Shayne Silvers & Cameron O'Connell

Whiskey Ginger

The Phantom Queen Diaries Book 1

A Temple Verse Series

ISBN 13: **978-1-947709-12-6**

© 2018, Shayne Silvers / Argento Publishing, LLC / Cameron O'Connell

info@shaynesilvers.com

For updates on new releases, promotions, and updates, please sign up for my mailing list on **shaynesilvers.com**.

CONTENTS

STALK US ONLINE

To get a free copy of **FAIRY TALE** (a prequel novella with Nate Temple), news updates, book release alerts, and other secret bonus content from the Temple Verse...

SIGN UP for SHAYNE'S NEWSLETTER:
  www.shaynesilvers.com/l/219800

And... FOLLOW and LIKE:

Shayne's FACEBOOK PAGE:
  www.shaynesilvers.com/l/38602

Cameron's FACEBOOK PAGE:
  www.shaynesilvers.com/l/209065

We respond to all messages, so don't hesitate to drop either of us a line. Not interacting with readers is the biggest travesty that most authors can make. Let us fix that.

BOOKS IN THE TEMPLE VERSE

CHRONOLOGY: All stories in the Temple Verse are shown in chronological order on the following page

PHANTOM QUEEN DIARIES

WHISKEY GINGER

COSMOPOLITAN - *PREORDER NOW! - JUNE 19, 2018*

OLD FASHIONED - *PREORDER NOW! - JUNE 26, 2018*

DARK AND STORMY - *PREORDER NOW! - JULY 10, 2018*

FEATHERS AND FIRE SERIES

UNCHAINED

RAGE

WHISPERS

ANGEL'S ROAR

BOOK #5 - *COMING SUMMER 2018...*

NATE TEMPLE SERIES

FAIRY TALE - FREE prequel novella #0 for my subscribers

OBSIDIAN SON

BLOOD DEBTS

GRIMM

SILVER TONGUE

BEAST MASTER

TINY GODS

DADDY DUTY (Novella #6.5)

WILD SIDE

WAR HAMMER

NINE SOULS

BOOK #10 - *COMING SUMMER 2018...*

CHRONOLOGICAL ORDER: TEMPLE VERSE

FAIRY TALE (TEMPLE PREQUEL)

OBSIDIAN SON (TEMPLE 1)

BLOOD DEBTS (TEMPLE 2)

GRIMM (TEMPLE 3)

SILVER TONGUE (TEMPLE 4)

BEAST MASTER (TEMPLE 5)

TINY GODS (TEMPLE 6)

DADDY DUTY (TEMPLE NOVELLA 6.5)

UNCHAINED (FEATHERS... 1)

RAGE (FEATHERS... 2)

WILD SIDE (TEMPLE 7)

WAR HAMMER (TEMPLE 8)

WHISPERS (FEATHERS... 3)

WHISKEY GINGER (PHANTOM... 1)

NINE SOULS (TEMPLE 9)

COSMOPOLITAN (PHANTOM... 2)

ANGEL'S ROAR (FEATHERS... 4)

OLD FASHIONED (PHANTOM...3)

DARK AND STORMY (PHANTOM... 4)

SHAYNE AND CAMERON

Shayne Silvers, here.

Cameron O'Connell is one helluva writer, and he's worked tirelessly to merge a story into the Temple Verse that would provide a different and unique *voice*, but a complementary *tone* to my other novels. SOME people might say I'm hard to work with. But certainly, Cameron would never...

Hey! Pipe down over there, author monkey! Get back to your writing cave and finish the next Phantom Queen Novel!

Ahem. Now, where was I?

This is book 1 in the Phantom Queen Diaries, but books 2-4 will launch within a 30 day period starting June 2018, tying into the existing Temple Verse with Nate and Callie. This series could also be read independently if one so chose. Then again, you, the reader, will get SO much more out of my existing books (and this series) by reading them all in tandem.

But that's not up to us. It's up to you, the reader.

What do you think? Should Quinn MacKenna be allowed to go drinking with Callie? To throw eggs at Chateau Falco while Nate's skipping about in Fae? To let this fiery, foul-mouthed, Boston redhead come play with the monsters from Missouri?

You tell us...

CHAPTER 1

*T*he pasty guitarist hunched forward, thrust a rolled-up wad of paper deep into one nostril, and snorted a line of blood crystals—frozen hemoglobin that I'd smuggled over in a refrigerated canister—with the uncanny grace of a drug addict. He sat back, fangs gleaming, and pawed at his nose. "That's some bodacious shit. Hey, bros," he said, glancing at his fellow band members, "come hit this shit before it melts."

He fetched one of the backstage passes hanging nearby, pried the plastic badge from its lanyard, and used it to split up the crystals, murmuring something in an accent that reminded me of California. Not *the* California, but you know, Cali-foh-nia—the land of beaches, babes, and bros. I retrieved a toothpick from my pocket and punched it through its thin wrapper. "So," I asked no one in particular, "now that ye have the product, who's payin'?"

Another band member stepped out of the shadows to my left, and I don't mean that figuratively, either—the fucker literally stepped out of the shadows. I scowled at him, but hid my surprise, nonchalantly rolling the toothpick from one side of my mouth to the other.

The rest of the band gathered around the dressing room table, following the guitarist's lead by preparing their own snorting utensils—tattered magazine covers, mostly. Typically, you'd do this sort of thing with a dollar-bill, maybe even a Benjamin if you were flush. But fangers like this lot

1

couldn't touch cash directly—in God We Trust and all that. Of course, I didn't really understand why sucking blood the old-fashioned way had suddenly gone out of style. More of a rush, maybe?

"It lasts longer," the vampire next to me explained, catching my mildly curious expression. "It's especially good for shows and stuff. Makes us look, like, less—"

"Creepy?" I offered, my Irish brogue lilting just enough to make it a question.

"Pale," he finished, frowning.

I shrugged. "Listen, I've got places to be," I said, holding out my hand.

"I'm sure you do," he replied, smiling. "Tell you what, why don't you, like, hang around for a bit? Once that wears off," he dipped his head toward the bloody powder smeared across the table's surface, "we may need a pick-me-up." He rested his hand on my arm and our gazes locked.

I blinked, realized what he was trying to pull, and rolled my eyes. His widened in surprise, then shock as I yanked out my toothpick and shoved it through his hand.

"Motherfuck—"

"I want what we agreed on," I declared. "Now. No tricks."

The rest of the band saw what happened and rose faster than I could blink. They circled me, their grins feral...they might have even seemed intimidating if it weren't for the fact that they each had a case of the sniffles —I had to work extra hard not to think about what it felt like to have someone else's blood dripping down my nasal cavity.

I held up a hand.

"Can I ask ye gentlemen a question before we get started?" I asked. "Do ye even *have* what I asked for?"

Two of the band members exchanged looks and shrugged. The guitarist, however, glanced back towards the dressing room, where a brown paper bag sat next to a case full of makeup. He caught me looking and bared his teeth, his fangs stretching until it looked like it would be uncomfortable for him to close his mouth without piercing his own lip.

"Follow-up question," I said, eyeing the vampire I'd stabbed as he gingerly withdrew the toothpick from his hand and flung it across the room with a snarl. "Do ye do each other's make-up? Since, ye know, ye can't use mirrors?"

I was genuinely curious.

The guitarist grunted. "Mike, we have to go on soon."

"Wait a minute. Mike?" I turned to the snarling vampire with a frown. "What happened to *The Vampire Prospero?*" I glanced at the numerous fliers in the dressing room, most of which depicted the band members wading through blood, with Mike in the lead, each one titled *The Vampire Prospero* in *Rocky Horror Picture Show* font. Come to think of it...Mike did look a little like Tim Curry in all that leather and lace.

I was about to comment on the resemblance when Mike spoke up, "Alright, change of plans, bros. We're gonna drain this bitch before the show. We'll look totally—"

"Creepy?" I offered, again.

"Kill her."

CHAPTER 2

I figured I had a little time before they made a move, so I shrugged off my thick woolen peacoat and hung it on a nearby chair as the band advanced.

No sense ruining a perfectly good coat on these amateurs.

You probably think I'm insane for taking on four vampires at once, but I'd grown up in South Boston and had seen my fair share of fights, with the scars to prove it; by now, I knew how to read a dangerous situation—and this didn't cut it.

I mean sure, Mike and his band of Gothic Beach Boys were vampires. They'd killed people. But that didn't make them tough, it simply made them killers. One look at their twitching fingers and shifty eyes told me all I needed to know about my chances.

These posers had never been in a real scrap in their lives.

In fact, it was painfully obvious they had no idea that attacking as a group—even if that group happens to have preternatural reflexes—hinged on somebody getting the party started. They had, on the other hand, figured out that—no matter how good your odds are of jumping someone and leaving them a bloody mess on the floor—whoever goes first has the highest probability of taking a lick or two.

Of course, I wasn't about to wait around for that.

"Mike the vampire," I muttered under my breath as I drew my contingency plan from where it hung at the small of my back. The kiss—that's what you call a cluster of vampires, by the way—halted as one and stared at the multi-colored monstrosity I held in my hands. I cocked it a handful of times and smiled.

Then I pulled the trigger.

I left a few minutes later with the paper bag in hand. On my way out, I passed one of the concert staffers rushing down the hallway. You know the type—the crew members dressed in uniform shades of black who are always chittering away into their headsets and running around before a show starts—the ones who can't stop looking at their clipboards.

"They should be out here by now," he muttered as he passed by.

"Oy!" I called. The staffer turned, and I realized he was just a kid, really. Probably fresh out of high school, his cheeks still laden with baby fat. I sighed, then shot him in his poor, innocent face.

"What the hell, lady?" he yelled, raising his clipboard—told you so—to shield himself from the stream of water spewing from my Super Soaker 2000. He spluttered and tumbled backwards, completely doused in holy water.

"Sorry, boyo," I said as I headed towards the stairwell that led to the alley outside. "Had to be sure they wouldn't snack on ye." I slung the water gun's strap over my shoulder and slid it out of view beneath my coat, choosing to ignore the steady stream of curses being directed at my back. Still, I felt bad for the kid. I could only imagine his terrified reaction when he finally walked into that dressing room; the skin on Mike's face had only just begun growing back by the time I left.

*O*nce outside, I took a deep breath of the crisp winter air, holding it in for as long as possible, ignoring the faint odor of trash wafting down the alleyway. I cursed inwardly for putting myself in such a shitty situation; I put on a tough front, but things could have gone a lot worse if any of the vampires had been the least bit scrappy. I finally felt my heartrate begin to slow.

"Seems like you did us a favor," a man said, stepping out of the *God-*

damned shadows.

"Jesus Christ!" I yelled, whirling.

"Whoa!" The vampire held up both hands in surrender, his eyes wide, staring down the nozzle of my water gun with a grimace on his face that took a moment to fade. He tilted his head a fraction, looking past the nozzle to me. "Truce?"

Here's the thing about vampires: I hate them. Have for years. They're like cockroaches. I mean I get it: they're simply scuttling around doing what they need to do to survive just like the rest of us. But that doesn't mean I don't feel the urge to squeal and stomp the second I see one. Unfortunately, in my experience, vampires are almost as hard to kill as cockroaches, so— when a fanger offers me a truce—I usually take it.

"Truce," I said, lowering the weapon.

"Super Soaker, huh? That's a new one," the man said, drily.

I shrugged, deciding it better not to tell the strange vampire that every undead precaution I'd taken before coming here came straight from *The Lost Boys*, circa 1987—I'd left my garlic necklace at home; it hadn't really gone with my outfit.

"Well," he said, stepping into the light, "we appreciate it, in any case."

"We?" I asked, glancing warily down both sides of the alley.

"Oh, don't worry, I'm the only one of our number that remains. Once we heard their screams, we decided it was best not to interfere. You left them alive, I trust?"

"Aye," I said, after a moment's hesitation, uncomfortable with the vampire's casual reaction to what had gone down in that dressing room. I mean, who listens to the sounds of tortured screams and thinks "I'll just leave them to it?"

Fucking vampires, apparently.

"Excellent," he said. "I believe our…lesson would be a little redundant, in that case. We couldn't allow them to go around pretending to be what they are. I'm sure you understand." The vampire smiled a perfectly ordinary, if a bit too white, smile.

That was the trouble with vampires; their fangs were retractable—which meant he and his kind could pass for human most of the time. Very pale, nocturnal humans—completely indistinguishable from your average late-night radio DJ, the stripper who always gets off a few hours before the rest of the girls, or the nurse who prefers the night shift...basically, don't trust anyone who sleeps while everyone else is awake, people.

Of course, that didn't mean this vampire was exactly average. In fact, he gave off an older, more alien presence than Mike and his bandmates. It didn't help that he loomed over me, which meant he had to be pretty damn tall; at six-foot, I was well above an average woman's height, and I wasn't used to being looked down on, literally or figuratively.

I didn't like it.

I realized he was taking my measure as well, arching an eyebrow at whatever it was he saw. I briefly considered saying screw it and dousing him anyway for being such an annoyingly tall, ancient breed of cockroach, but decided it wouldn't be worth the trouble. Until, that is, I caught him staring into my eyes the same way Mike had earlier in the evening.

The vampire gaze.

It was a handy parlor trick in a vampire's arsenal, sort of like hypnosis on crack—I'd seen a cop point his gun at his best friend under its influence. Of course, the fact that it didn't work on me at all meant he was wasting both our time. "Are ye done?" I asked.

He blinked rapidly, then tried to cover up his surprise with a charming smile and a shrug, as if to say I couldn't blame him for trying. I'd seen men at the bar do the exact same thing after grabbing a girl's ass as she walked past. A few guys had pulled the same shit on me, once or twice; I'd done my best to make sure those sorry bastards never breathed through their noses again.

What can I say?

I'm big on boundaries.

"Ye know, where I come from, that could be considered breakin' terms," I said, casually pumping my Super Soaker.

"And where *do* you come from?" he asked, clearly intrigued by my ability to ignore his date-rapey attention. Apparently, being a vampire didn't make him any less male.

"Wrong question," I quipped.

He frowned. "What?"

I turned and headed towards the street. "Getting' colder."

"Wait! Who are you?"

7

I reached inside my peacoat, pulled out a slick purple orb and tossed it over my shoulder. The water balloon broke behind me, releasing a spray of holy water. I heard the vampire behind me hiss as he danced backwards.

"Ice cold," I called as I turned the corner, took hold of what lay inside the brown paper bag, and promptly became invisible.

CHAPTER 3

*M*y name is Quinn MacKenna, and I'm a black magic arms dealer. If you don't know what that means, don't worry, you aren't the only one. Basically, when the real monsters that go bump in the night need something, they call me. Of course, by monsters, I mean Freaks —that's the preferred term, though I'm not sure how politically correct it is in comparison. Freaks come in all shapes and sizes, ranging from your average citizen with supernatural abilities to fabled creatures from folklore and fairy tales.

That's right, I do believe in faeries.

I even know a few.

Those who aren't faeries or Freaks are known as Regulars. I do business with them, too, but your average Joe wouldn't know a mythological artifact from a toaster oven.

Take the priceless relic I'd managed to snag from the Blood Man Group as payment for a late-night delivery of A-Positive blood crystals from a lab outside Shanghai, for example: the thick metal band dangled from my thumb, nearly big enough to slide over two of my fingers.

The Ring of Gyges, as it was popularly known, had originally been fitted for a Greek king, centuries before Christ was born. It wasn't supposed to exist—just another handy metaphor used by Plato to explore morality. And yet here it was on my finger, and here I was, invisible as fuck.

The vampire I'd ditched a few moments ago came tearing out of the alleyway, searching fruitlessly for me. I held my breath and remained as still as I could; vampires didn't rely on only one sense to hunt. He tensed, sniffing the air, but eventually wandered away towards the nearest major intersection, muttering obscenities in a language I didn't speak—Dutch, maybe?

I twirled the ring a little, waited another minute or two just to be safe, then returned it to its sack; I managed not to stroke it and call it My Precious, but it was a close thing. Then I made a call.

"This is Jimmy," the man who picked up said.

"Evenin' Jimmy."

"Quinn? Jesus Christ, how'd you even get this number? This is my private cell."

"Not important. Tell me, have ye ever been to the House of Blues?"

"Not important she says," Jimmy muttered, his thick, gravelly baritone barely audible. I listened to him fumble around for something. "Alright. Yeah, House of Blues. The concert hall next to Fenway?"

"Yeah, that one. Listen, ye should swing by."

"Are you serious, Quinn? You called me to invite me to a concert?"

I rolled my eyes, but realized he couldn't see it. "For a detective, you're a bit daft, ye know that? Just run on down and make sure everything is on the up and up. I won't be there...but I was there, if ye know what I'm sayin'."

Jimmy's curses accompanied the sounds of what I assumed was him grabbing his coat and keys. "Fine. Anything I should watch out for in particular?"

"Ye still wear that crucifix your Grammy gave ye?"

"Of course I—oh, God damn it, Quinn! Why?"

"Might not want to bring Him into it, if I were ye. Not right away, anyway," I said, grinning. "And because it never hurts to be prepared. Have a good night, Jimmy." I hung up, chuckling, and ordered an Uber to pick me up and drop me off a few blocks north at a friend's bar.

I know, I know, I was being lazy. Thing is, while Boston had a fairly solid public transportation system, I preferred to avoid crowded buses or trains. One, because people. And two, because carrying priceless artifacts on the orange line would be asking for trouble.

I would have preferred to cruise around in my own car—a '69 Mustang Mach 1 so sexy that I should have had to pay a sin tax to drive it—but she wasn't currently drivable, and I didn't have troll insurance. So, here I was, waiting on the corner for the car to arrive, crossing my fingers that Jimmy would get to the concert hall in time to mitigate any damage the vampires might cause.

Collateral damage wasn't really my thing.

Fortunately, Detective Jimmy Collins was beyond reliable, not to mention an old friend—a Southie survivor who'd done two stints in Iraq before getting out and joining the local PD. He and I hadn't seen each other lately outside Mass, but occasionally I helped him out and fed him tidbits of information; he'd gotten a reputation, not to mention a promotion, for offering solutions to cases that never made sense to anyone else.

Jimmy didn't really buy into the whole Freak business, but he'd seen enough weird shit happen here in Boston to know that it never hurt to keep an open mind. And of course there was that ongoing thing going on between us that kept creeping up; I hadn't realized it, but I'd missed our witty banter.

My driver's car pulled up, emergency lights flashing as I ducked inside. I watched him fiddle with the GPS. He pulled off into traffic, and I settled back to enjoy the ride, when someone suddenly slammed a hand on the hood of the car.

The driver slammed on his brakes.

A man's face popped up behind the windshield, his hair an ashy shade of brown with faded streaks of sun-bleached highlights, his blue eyes wide and panicked. He pointed to the Uber sticker on the rear window and yelled through the glass, "Hey! I'll give you a hundred dollars, cash, to take me to this address." He brandished a phone and the location it displayed.

"Oy!" I yelled back. "Get your own ride!"

The man didn't seem to hear me and flashed a crazy wide grin the moment the Uber driver nodded. "Sorry," the driver said sheepishly, glancing back at me, "but a hundred dollars is a hundred dollars."

I cursed and prepared to lash out at the man the moment he joined me in the back, but he hopped up front, instead. "Damned Candy Skulls," he muttered. "This is why I can't have nice things…"

I had a moment to wonder if he was on drugs before he brightened and flashed the driver a crisp hundred-dollar bill, pulling it taut between his hands. "Anyway! Hi ho, silver! I'm on vacation, I've got a date, and I'm in a rush. So, tell you what, I'll give you another hundred if you can get me there in five."

The driver put in the address, wordlessly, and took off, tires squealing. I fell back into my seat and grunted. The man spun, seeming to notice me for the first time. "Oh, shit! I didn't realize anyone was back there. My fault."

"You're right," I said, "it is your fault! Who d'ye t'ink ye are, hijackin' me car like that?"

The man grinned and extended a hand. "The name's Nate Temple."

I eyed the hand in disdain. "Listen here, ye bastard, I don't care who ye are, that doesn't give ye the right to throw money at people like that. It's not me fault you're runnin' late."

The man chuckled and got comfortable in the front seat, lounging back with a sigh. "Yeah, well, I lost track of time and forgot I couldn't...well, nevermind. Listen, I'll be out of your hair in no time, don't worry."

I glowered at him, but decided not to argue. It's not like I was in that much of a hurry—it was the principle of the thing, really. I'd grown up lower middle-class, and lavish displays of wealth like that always rubbed me the wrong way. Spoiled brats like this asshole were almost as bad as vampires, in my opinion.

Almost.

The driver whipped over, pulling up alongside the curb in record time. "Two minutes to spare!" Nate cried. "Excellent. Thanks!" He passed over two hundred-dollar bills and slid out of the car and shut the door, but then doubled-back and rapped on my window. The driver glanced at me. "Want me to roll it down?"

"Are ye fuckin' serious? Absolutely not," I hissed.

Nate rapped again, hard enough to shake the glass, this time. The driver winced and rolled down the window, anyway. I cursed, exasperated, and whirled on the Uber-crasher. "What d'ye want?"

Nate raised his hand up. "Thanks for being a good sport. High five?"

I stared at him, slack-jawed.

He waited, patiently, refusing to leave until I slapped his palm. I had to hand it to the guy; he had balls. I only wish they weren't on the other side of a metal door.

I'd have loved to test them with the tip of my boot.

"Fine," I growled and high-fived the bastard. Nate jerked his hand back as if I'd zapped him, staring at his palm, eyes narrowed. A woman stepped out onto the sidewalk from the restaurant next door, waving. She had short-cropped, all-white hair which stood out beneath the lamplight. "Nate!" she called.

"Get us out of here," I said to the driver. "Now, or I swear I'll leave a review so scathin' that your own ma won't talk to ye for a month."

The driver did as I asked, and I watched Nate and his companion greet each other on the street, the former seeming to forget all about me—his attention clearly devoted to the stunning woman in front of him. I sighed in relief and studied my own tingling palm, praying I'd never run into that bastard again.

Because he obviously had some magic to him judging from the reaction of our high five. And something about that name...

CHAPTER 4

$\mathcal{T}$he line outside the pop-up bar was epically long despite the chilly weather. This late in the evening, that usually meant everyone still outside would be sorely disappointed, since it was likely the place would stay packed until close. But I wasn't the type to waste my time in lines; I ignored the crowd altogether and headed straight for the door.

"I'm sorry ma'am, but you'll have to get in line," the bouncer said. He was a big, beefy guy I didn't recognize with a lot of scruff on his face. I had no way to gauge how old he was, but I was guessing he was younger than I was; he had one of those pure, guileless faces that let me know exactly what he was thinking.

"Is Ryan workin'?" I asked, tucking my hands in my pockets for warmth. "Let him know Quinn is outside. He'll come and get me."

"Ryan's behind the bar tonight, miss. And, as you can see, we're pretty slammed."

I heard a few people grumbling behind me and a few calls from the back that I couldn't make out...but I doubted any of them were polite offers to join them in line. I leaned in close. "Listen, I don't really care that you're new. I've had a long night, and if ye don't get the fuck out of me way in the next five seconds, I'll have to make ye. And I'm sure ye don't want a scene in front of the bar, so..." I leaned back. "Your call."

The bouncer's expression contorted into something much less friendly. But, bully for him, he didn't explode or get in my face like an amateur. Instead, he reached for the walkie-talkie mounted on his shoulder. "I need someone out here, now. We've got a guest who doesn't want to get in line." He released the walkie. "I don't know why you model types always think you can just walk in everywhere you go," he muttered, clearly irritated.

A short, handsome man in his late forties poked his head outside a moment later. I knew from past experience that the suit he'd worn to work would be immaculately tailored—but he'd already taken off the jacket and rolled up the sleeves of his dress shirt, his tie pinned by a thick gold bar that caught the light when he leaned past the bouncer to see who was causing all the trouble.

"Quinn!" he bellowed, pulling me into a hug I most certainly did not ask for, his face ending up mere inches away from my chest.

"Christoff," I replied, hands still in my pockets. He drew away quickly, an apology written all over his face; Christoff knew how I felt about the invasion of my personal space, but had a hard time remembering it in the heat of the moment—something about being Russian, I assumed. I nudged him. "I'm here to see Ryan."

"Oh yes, come in, come in. That will be all, Hank," Christoff said to the bouncer before hooking an arm around the small of my back and guiding me through the door. Hank, meanwhile, stared over Christoff's shoulder at me like I was some sort of diseased animal he couldn't wait to put down. I blew him a kiss, then fought my way through the crowd.

Inside, I spotted Ryan O'Rye, true to the bouncer's word, busting his ass behind the bar; I watched him take three orders without even making eye contact. He simply thrust his right ear forward to catch everything they had to say before working his particular brand of magic—and believe me, it was magic. There were wizards out there who couldn't even bake a cake, let alone mix a proper drink.

"Go on upstairs," Christoff barked up at me in his thick, Russian accent. "I will take over for Ryan for a few minutes. It is good for guests to see owner doing some good, honest work." He thrust his shirt sleeves a little further up his arms, although the bulging muscles of his biceps didn't allow for much maneuvering.

I followed Christoff's directions to the back, where a flight of stairs led up to the office he shared with Ryan, his bar manager. I paused at the bottom of the stairs, taking in the décor of Christoff's pop-up bar—the type of bar which changed every few months to reflect things like the holidays or popular cultural phenomena.

What I saw left me literally speechless.

CHAPTER 5

*R*yan had barely made it through the door before I accosted him. "Really, Ryan?" I asked, gesturing towards the décor through the windows that overlooked the bar.

He shut the door and sighed. "Not my idea."

"Well, whose was it then?" I scoured his face for a clue. "Wait, Christoff?"

Ryan rolled his eyes and mimicked his boss' accent, "In Soviet Russia, we support our country when things go horribly wrong, because if we do not, everyone is killed in sleep."

I snorted. "Still, I think the St. Louis Arch on fire was a little much," I said, pointing out Christoff's grainy security camera footage on the far wall. "And is that a dragon?"

Ryan nodded. "The damn thing is wrapped in aluminum foil, even. I don't know who sells him this stuff. But hey, a few cars did blow up by the Arch last month, and then there was the YouTube video a few years back of that billionaire and the dragon that everyone was calling a hoax, until it disappeared from the internet forever." Ryan shrugged.

The alleged terrorist attack Ryan was referring to had happened only a couple months back. The thing is, there hadn't been any casualties, so the media coverage should have been minimal. But St. Louis seemed to be a hotbed for all kinds of weird phenomena, and people were starting to notice. Personally, I wished somebody had targeted Busch Stadium, instead.

Go Sox.

"Right, the billionaire…" I echoed. Honestly, I'd never seen the video of the dragon from a few years back—so, real or not, I couldn't say. It struck me as yet another one of those irritating internet sensations that get people all riled up for no good reason.

"Anyway," Ryan continued, "turns out anti-terrorism drinks appeal to all kinds of people. We even get politicians stopping by, looking to show support," he said, sneering. "They have a bad habit of buying rounds and insisting we put it on their nonexistent tab."

"Maybe ye can write it off on your taxes?" I joked.

Ryan sighed. "I swear, if I have to make one more Bomb Pop shot, I'm going to lose my shit."

I winced. "That seems in poor taste."

He threw up his hands. "Right?!"

"I know a guy who can cut ye a good deal on poisons?" I offered. "He has all the classics: bubonic plague, polio, even smallpox. All guaranteed to come with a side of autism."

Ryan laughed and shook his head. "It hasn't gotten to that point. Yet." He collapsed on the couch by the door. "So, did you get it?"

I tossed him the paper bag.

"You're a saint. I—hey, Quinn?"

"Yes?" I asked absently, glancing at the various camera angles present on the monitor, looking for any other crazy decorations. A "Stand for St. Louis" sign hung over a mural of the Arch shrouded in flames and smoke. American flags were plastered just about everywhere else, except for the smaller room in back, which had a chrome dragon's head mounted over the less-trafficked cocktail bar.

"Why is there blood on this bag?"

I blinked, turning back to him. "D'ye really want to know?"

Ryan sniffed the bag, then held it at arms-length like it contained dog shit, or something equally foul. "Let me rephrase my question. Why is there vampire blood on this bag, Quinn?"

I snatched the sack from him, took out the ring, and set it on the desk. "There, ye ninny."

Ryan looked as though he might say more on the subject, but let it go in favor of studying the ring on the table. He rose from the couch and glided over to the table. I noticed that he moved much more smoothly now, the way he sometimes did when he was really in the groove behind the bar. But then many of the Faelings—creatures born in the Fae realm that had, for whatever reason, wandered into our world—were known to be excessively graceful when they wanted to be.

"Did you test it?" Ryan asked.

I smirked. "I did."

"And?"

"Works like a charm. Well, like an artifact, at any rate," I clarified. I had to be specific when talking about merchandise; charms were a unicorn of a different color, and I didn't want Ryan getting the wrong idea.

"Price?" Ryan asked, his face as close to the ring as he could get without actually touching it.

"Entry?" I asked, hopeful.

Ryan snorted. "Not unless this thing also grants wishes."

"Ryan!" I groaned.

"Quinn!" Ryan responded, mockingly. He straightened and met my eyes with his own, and I saw something inhuman flash behind them. "We've been over this. It's dangerous."

I bristled at that. "And?"

"And I know you can take care of yourself, but that's in your world. In mine..." Ryan shook his head and studied his hands for a few moments. Tiny lights flared up within them and began to disperse around the room. Fireflies. They danced above our heads for a few seconds before landing in various parts of the room...parts which suddenly caught on fire.

I watched the room burn around us, the smoke billowing up, with mild annoyance. "Are ye done?"

Ryan rolled his eyes and snapped his fingers, the illusion—what Ryan's kind called glamour—dispersing immediately. I reached out and flicked one of his pointy-ass ears.

"Ow!"

"Put those away."

He self-consciously ran his hands over his ears, which quickly resumed their usual size and shape. "Look, all I meant to do was show you what my people can do. Not only the illusions. Among my kind there are some who can make the illusions real. What if they catch you sleeping and burn a house down around you? It wouldn't be magic then, Quinn. Just fire."

What he meant was that I wouldn't be protected. I didn't look much like a Freak—unless you thought exceptionally tall, leggy redheads were particularly freakish—but I sure wasn't a Regular. You see, magic doesn't work on me. Never had. I mean, sure, I could see it. Hell, I could taste and smell it. But anytime someone pointed magic of any sort in my direction, it crashed against an invisible barrier, fizzled, and died. Sadly, that didn't mean I was immune to glamour, and I'd never put it to the test against grammarie—a form of Faeling magic that allowed its user to do truly improbably things. From what I understood, grammarie disregarded not only logic, but physics.

Which is why, deep down, I knew Ryan's concerns were justifiable. Still, there was a whole other world out there, a world with different rules, ones that defied science and imagination. Who in their right mind would pass that up? Besides, I had another reason for wanting to go to the Fae realm, a reason I couldn't talk to Ryan about. He was a friend, but he was also a Faeling—a creature out of a storybook, with questionable allegiances.

My trust didn't extend quite that far.

Suddenly, the sound of wood sizzling and popping, coupled with the acrid odor of smoke, assaulted my senses. I could practically feel the fire singeing the fine hairs on my forearms. I punched Ryan's arm. "What did I just say?"

The sensations disappeared immediately as he rubbed his shoulder. "Okay, okay, fine…You know I'm only trying to protect you."

"I don't need your protection, Ryan O'Rye," I said, glaring.

He flinched.

"But," I amended, "I do appreciate ye tryin'." I strode past him, took up the ring, and tossed it to him. "The ring for a favor to be determined later."

Ryan caught it and hissed between his teeth as it settled in his palm. "But not entry," he clarified.

"Not entry."

He nodded, and the pain in his face faded.

"Now," I said, "where does a girl go to get a drink around here?"

CHAPTER 6

a series of heavy-fisted knocks at my door woke me up the next morning. I cradled my head as I blindly stumbled out of bed, the night before a faint blur. I remembered having a few drinks down at the bar before heading home, settling early on a whiskey cocktail with champagne in it that Ryan had dubbed The Fifth Horseman. I seemed to recall it tasting great at the time, but now even the faintest idea of it made me a little sick to my stomach.

I bypassed the door for the bathroom in my desperation to find the Ibuprofen. Vampire gazes and Fae illusions I could handle. But hangovers? A girl could use some help. I tossed back a couple tablets and scowled, bleary-eyed, at the door, which refused to shut up.

"I'll kill ye," I whispered at it, then shuffled forward, peering through the peephole. Jimmy Collins stood on the other side of the door, his dark face warped, but still recognizable. I cursed my luck; he *would* show up the morning after I'd had three or four too many, when I looked my roughest. Oh well, what was the quote? If he couldn't handle me at my worst...

Yeah, right, as if *this* was as bad as it got.

I sighed, then unlatched and turned the various locks on my door—you could never be too careful in my line of work—and threw it open. "What do ye want?" I asked, staring from beneath my bangs—a tousled mass that completely obscured one of my eyes.

Detective Jimmy Collins, Boston PD, stood self-righteously in my doorway, chest puffed up like he was about to deliver a sermon or sing from a hymnal—the man had the voice of an angel and knew it.

"Oy, Jimmy, ye should sing me a song. But," I said, raising a finger to his lips to interrupt whatever he'd been about to say, "it should be a quiet song. A lullaby. From out here. Goodnight, Jimmy."

Jimmy slammed his hand against the door to stop me from shutting it, ignoring my ridiculous suggestion. "We need to talk," Jimmy said, his tone disapproving.

"Well then *you* need to whisper." I wandered back into my apartment, letting Jimmy invite himself in. "And close me curtains," I added, before curling up on my couch in the fetal position, tucking my knees into the massive sweater I'd slept in.

Jimmy sighed and did what I asked. I felt more than saw him wander around the room, closing curtains, only to settle into the loveseat on the other end of the living room. I cracked open an eye, then stared at him in surprise; he looked like he'd been up all night, his clothes disheveled and wrinkled, his eyes tired and bloodshot. He retrieved a little notebook from his suit jacket.

"That's cute. Do ye get those as stockin' stuffers?" I asked. "Ye know, instead of socks? Little notebooks and handcuffs and mugs that say 'Best Detective'?"

He ignored me, which was a shame; I genuinely wanted to know. "Quinn MacKenna," he began, "where were you last night between eleven and midnight?"

I groaned. "Damnit Jimmy, is this payback for me callin' ye late last night? I swear I won't do it again if ye let me go back to bed."

"Answer the question," Jimmy said, his tone cold.

"I don't remember," I replied, honestly, baffled by the situation. "Wait, when did I call ye?" I asked.

"You called my private number," Jimmy said, lips pursed, "at 10:47."

"Well then," I replied, doing as much mental arithmetic as my screaming brain would allow, "between eleven and midnight, I would've been headed to a friend's bar. I got an Uber." I decided to leave out the details regarding the other passenger temporarily appropriating my ride; I expected Jimmy might find it funny, which would only piss me off.

Jimmy's hard expression grew a little less severe. "Can you prove that?"

"And why would I need to prove anythin' to ye, Jimmy Collins? What is this even about? Ye never said."

Jimmy hunched forward. "Quinn, last night you called me and told me to go to a crime scene. A crime scene which I had no reason to know existed. A crime scene I am now responsible for. Which is why I'm here, now, in the wee hours of the morning instead of in my bed, fast asleep."

"Oh, please," I said, exasperated. "Those vampires are a bunch of babies. It was just a little holy water. Their skin'll grow back, I swear. Eventually."

Jimmy's eyes widened in surprise. "Vampires?"

"Oh, Jesus, Jimmy. Yes, vampires. Bloodsuckers. Freaks. Why do ye think I called ye in? I wanted ye to make sure they wouldn't do anythin' stupid. "

Like take a bite out of the staffer I'd doused with holy water, for example.

Jimmy reached into his pocket and tossed a small pile of photographs on the table. "They won't be doing anything, stupid or otherwise, ever again, Quinn."

I glanced down at the photographs and pressed a hand to my mouth, my stomach rolling. "Oh, fuck me."

"Officially," Jimmy said, snatching them up, "you never saw those."

It took me a solid minute to process what Jimmy had shown me, my eyes pinched closed as if I could put all those images in a box and toss it into the deep, dark recesses of my subconscious.

Instead, I dwelled on them, the photos telling a story I didn't want to hear, but felt compelled to listen to.

Mike and his bandmates had been hung upside down and staked to the walls. Not only staked, I realized, but pinned. Like butterflies—their wrists and ankles stretched and held to the wall by thick slivers of wood. Pools of blood had collected beneath each corpse.

I barely made it to the bathroom before throwing up.

Jimmy waded in and held my hair back like we were in high school all over again. I wanted to tell him to stop and let me get sick in peace, but couldn't get the words out. Oh well.

Guess he'd end up seeing me at my worst, after all.

When I finished, he flushed the toilet and leaned against the sink, looking nothing like the boy from my childhood. Back in high school he'd been thin and rangy, tall and athletic enough to play varsity ball—at least until he'd torn his ACL his senior year and enlisted in the Marines. He'd put on serious muscle since; he was built more like a linebacker now than a point guard.

For all that, his face hadn't changed much—a few lines here and there and a battered look in his eyes that never entirely went away. But behind those eyes was a totally different person, someone I didn't always recognize. That's what happens sometimes, though; I'd become the kind of person who fought Freaks head-on with children's toys, and Jimmy had become the kind of person who could look at a bloody crime scene without blinking.

People change.

I took the hand towel he offered me and dabbed my mouth and forehead. Not surprisingly, I felt a lot better. "Go fuck yourself, Fifth Horseman," I muttered.

"What?" Jimmy asked.

"Nothin'. So," I said as I settled with my back against the tub, "what now?"

"Now you show me your phone, so I can cross you off the suspect list."

"And then?"

"And then you help me figure out who did this."

"Alright." I turned on the bath faucet. "But first I'm goin' to shower. And ye, Jimmy Collins, are goin' to take a nap on me couch before ye fall over." I waved away his protest. "There's no point arguin'. Besides, whoever or whatever did this won't be found before dark—that's when the Freaks come out to play. Ye should know that by now."

"You think it was a Freak?" Jimmy asked. "Not some religious nut targeting vampires?"

"Religious nut?" I asked.

"They were crucified upside down, Quinn."

I felt my stomach shift uncomfortably.

"What part of I'm about to take a shower do ye not understand, Jimmy?" I asked as I wobbled to my feet, turned on the hot water, and threatened to remove my sweater. "Or is it police procedure to interrogate a woman while she's less than decent?"

Jimmy rubbed the bridge of his nose, then walked out.

"Fetch me a towel, too, while you're out there!" I called.

He groaned.

I grinned.

CHAPTER 7

I used a second towel to dry my hair as I walked Jimmy through what had happened the night before. Well, some of what happened. I glazed over a few things, like the exact nature of my exchange with the vampires. The legality of what I'd done was questionable at best, and I wasn't in the mood for a lecture, let alone a trip downtown in the back of a cruiser.

"So, when you left, they were all alive?" Jimmy asked, when I'd finished.

"Aye. I mean, they were huddled in a corner whimperin', but they were alive."

"And why were they whimpering, again?"

"We had a water gun fight. I won."

Jimmy gave me his best cop stare—a flat, no nonsense look—like the one a mother gives when she asks a question she already knows the answer to, like "did you do the dishes?"

"Quit playin' bad cop with your eyes, Jimmy. Ye know it won't work on me. Besides," I added, "t'isn't me ye should be tryin' to pry information from, all I did was give a few vampires a much-needed christenin'."

Jimmy scratched at the coarse goatee he'd grown since becoming a detective. It made him look distinguished, not to mention older; with his ridiculously smooth skin, he always looked ten years younger when he shaved. "Well," he replied, finally, "it doesn't help that you're my only lead. I mean who else can I turn to who can help solve my multiple vampire homicides? God...did I just say that?" He rose and started pacing the room. "I hate you sometimes, you know that?"

I smirked, knowing he didn't mean it. If he did, he'd have dipped out the moment he knew I wasn't his suspect. Of course, I could handle a little hatred if it meant he planned to keep marching around in my apartment; even after pulling an all-nighter, the man looked like he could save children from a burning building, his pent-up energy riding the air like a living thing. Like a fire I wanted to huddle around. I started to say something to that effect, but then realized I hadn't brushed my teeth after my brief encounter with the toilet bowl.

"Anyway," I called from the bathroom, once I'd had a few moments to collect myself, "there was a kid goin' to check on the vampires, one of the concert employees, who should've seen 'em after I left. I made sure he was soaked in holy water, just in case."

"Yeah, I talked to him," Jimmy replied, flipping the pages of his notebook. "He's the one who pointed me in your direction, actually. Said I was looking for a giant, soulless ginger...woman who thought it was fun to try and drown people." Jimmy chuckled. "Luckily my partner wasn't there to hear your description, or we'd be doing this at the precinct."

"Ooh," I said as I ducked out, foaming at the mouth with toothpaste, "would ye have handcuffed me, Jimmy?"

Jimmy glanced up from his notes and frowned. "Not unless you were under arrest."

I blinked, then scowled at the impish expression that appeared on his face. "I see how ye are," I said, pointing at him with my toothbrush for good measure.

"Anyway," he continued, "the concert employee said the door was locked and his key wouldn't work. By the time he got security to open it, the band was...well, you saw. I got there a few minutes after the first two uni's called it in, which made them extra suspicious, I might add."

I rejoined him in the living room. "So why d'ye ask what I was doin' between eleven and midnight?"

"That's the slimmest window we could come up with between when the band was last seen and when they were found. Our forensics team couldn't give us a time of death. Not even a ballpark. I've never seen them look that confused—not even on the Lollipop case."

26

I winced at the reference. That had been the first, and only, time Jimmy had ever called me in to help on one of his cases in a hands-on capacity.

And the last, if I had anything to say about it.

But, considering the fact that I'd accidentally roped him into a case with its own host of unanswered questions, I supposed that made us even.

"That makes sense," I admitted, finally. "Half the blood they had in 'em wasn't theirs to begin with, and they probably had the vitals of corpses even before they got shish-kabobbed. Speaking of, ye may want to warn your people not to let daylight hit their skin, or they may be in for a wee bit of a surprise."

Jimmy's eyes widened in surprise. He checked his watch. "It shouldn't matter right now. We loaded them and shipped them to the morgue before dawn." He scribbled something in his notebook. "Still, I'll call our medical examiner. Better to be safe than sorry. Anything else I need to know?"

"That's pretty much all I can tell ye," I confessed. "My experience with fangers is limited. I learned most of what I knew from watchin' movies."

"Seriously?"

I shrugged. "They're surprisingly spot on. Except for Twilight. Sparklin' vampires are a load of fuckin' gobshite."

"Well, can you give me anything else to work with? Like who might have wanted them dead? You said you didn't think it was a religious killing."

"Not even a Shepherd could've done 'em that fast, no. And they wouldn't have gone about it like that, anyway." Shepherds were basically the Vatican's take on special forces—priests and other do-gooders who took on evil when it graduated from metaphorical to literal. I'd never met any of them, but I'd heard rumors of an old, rundown safehouse somewhere in Boston.

"So who, then?" Jimmy asked.

"There was a fanger outside, in the alley, come to think of it. Quite a bit older, judgin' from how he acted," I said. In my experience, the older a bloodsucker was, the more likely they were to be irredeemable assholes. "He didn't seem too pleased by the fact that Mike and his vampire band had decided to go around tellin' people they were vampires," I explained. "Too much exposure. That's a big no-no for us Freaks, ye see."

"Right..." Jimmy stared down at his notebook as if unsure what to write.

"Do ye need me to spell 'vampire' for ye, Jimmy? I know ye were shit in school," I offered.

Jimmy threw one of my couch pillows at me. I caught it and tucked it to my chest, drawing my knees up, my plush bathrobe parting to expose my freshly-shaven legs. Jimmy's eyes followed the motion, lingered on my thighs, then flicked back down to his notebook. He cleared his throat. "What'd he look like?"

"He was a fuckin' giant. Six inches taller than me, at least, I t'ink. Dark hair. Pale, but that isn't surprisin'. Dark clothes. Honestly, other than the height, he looked pretty much the way most of 'em look." I shrugged.

"So I should put an APB out for 'vampire' and wait?"

"Aye, although, personally, I don't t'ink he's your Freak." I realized Jimmy was staring at me. I'd forgotten how intense his gaze could get when he listened, really listened—how sometimes the brown of his irises disappeared altogether.

"Whoever, or whatever," I went on, choosing to ignore my flushed cheeks, "murdered the band was able to take out a room full of vampires without leavin' a trace in the space of time it took to go get security to bust open a door..."

I could see Jimmy was struggling to comprehend what I was getting at, so I tried to put it in terms he could understand. "Vampires are fast, right?" I said. "They're fast, ruthless hunters that can't be killed easy. Whatever killed 'em didn't simply do it quick. It did the job thorough. Then it hung 'em, like trophies, like it wanted ye to know what they were." I let that sink in for a moment. "I t'ink ye should leave this one alone, Jimmy."

"Why? Because they were Freaks?" Jimmy asked, a vein in his temple throbbing. "Because it's dangerous? That's not how the justice system works, Quinn, and it's sure as shit not how I work."

"I know that, Jimmy," I replied, gently tossing the pillow back at him. "T'ing is, justice will win out sooner or later. Only, it'll be more...final, than what ye and your folk have in mind."

It was a tough thing to admit to a cop, but I knew I was right. In Boston, crimes like this got handled discreetly, well before Regular law enforcement could get involved. Jimmy sticking his nose into it would only lead to trouble, for both of us.

Jimmy thrust his notebook back in the pocket of his suit jacket. "That will be all for today, Miss MacKenna. Thanks for your help. I'll be in touch."

I sighed, rose, and went to the window, pulling back the curtains to stare out at a gray January morning. I waited for Jimmy to leave before sliding my forehead against the cold window pane. It felt good. Much better than

Jimmy's silent judgment had, anyway. In the end, this was why I kept my distance, content to flirt and fantasize, but little else; no matter how attractive I found him, I couldn't be with someone who refused to play by the rules of my world.

Jimmy wasn't wrong for wanting justice—I knew that. But how were you supposed to convict a creature you could barely contain? Where would you put it once you did? Sure, Jimmy had the moral high ground, but he couldn't see that he stood on a deserted island, surrounded by sharks.

Still, I knew better than to dwell on it.

I had better shit to do with my day.

CHAPTER 8

I met Ryan for brunch at *The Druid*, a stellar Irish bar in the heart of Inman Square. The sun had come out a bit, so I wasn't surprised to find him near the window, sipping a dark, frothy beer. He didn't see me right away, but a few other patrons did. The catty, jilted expressions of more than a couple women stalked me as I settled down across from him.

"Hey, Quinn. Glad you could make it."

"Stop lookin' happy to see me," I replied, crabbily.

"What?"

"Try to look miserable. Otherwise that blonde by the door is goin' to claw me eyes out the second ye head to the bathroom."

Ryan grinned. "The sorority girl in the red sweater? Or the dirty blonde soccer mom in the corner with the green blouse?"

"Both? Either." I untied my scarf and draped it over my purse, which I'd hung on the back of my chair. "This is why I can't do brunch with ye, ye realize."

That was only partially true. Granted, Ryan being so popular with the fairer sex was annoying, but the real reason I hesitated to spend time with him was the fact that he moonlighted for the Faerie Chancery—a motley collection of Fae riffraff who had settled in Boston over the centuries, whose members allegedly ranged from the beguilingly charming to the utterly repulsive. Ryan, who trended towards the former, was the sort of person I could rely on in a pinch, but not the kind of guy I routinely spent my downtime with.

Except for the occasional brunch, of course.

Because brunching alone is just sad.

Ryan held up his hands as if there were nothing he could do about the female attention. I rolled my eyes. "Ye could maybe, ye know, tone it down a wee bit?" I waved at his face, a smooth-skinned, chiseled thing; Ryan looked like a young, square-jawed Matt Damon, accent not included.

"This *is* my face, Quinn. I mean, minus the ears."

"Oh," I replied, dumbfounded. Honestly, I'd always assumed he'd used glamour to make himself more attractive—plastic surgery on steroids. I studied the Faeling for a moment, noting the tight curve of his jawline and the wide expanse of his cheekbones.

I had to admit I could see the appeal, but there was something else there, something dispassionate that said, "I won't be there when you wake up." Some women, admittedly, went for that sort of thing, but I'd never been one of them. Besides, I suspected I could take him in a knockdown, drag out fight.

Definitely not my type.

"You'll just have to make yourself uglier, then," I said, finally. "I can push ye down the stairs? Maybe break your nose?"

Ryan pursed his lips.

"There, much better," I said, grinning. "Keep that up."

"I ordered for you." Ryan took a liberal sip of his beer and dabbed at his mouth with his napkin.

"Irish breakfast?"

"Uh huh. I don't know how you eat that junk and stay so thin."

"Practice. I've been trainin' for this me whole life. Besides, I'm runnin' class today with Sensei out of town. You're welcome to come, ye know. We could work on breakin' that nose of yours?"

Ryan rubbed absentmindedly at his neck, which had taken a bit of a beating the last time he'd come to one of my classes on a whim. "I think I'm good."

The waitress arrived with our food, her attention so fixated on Ryan that she bumped into a fellow waiter. Drinks flew as water glasses wobbled and crashed. Lemonade spilled all over Ryan's lap.

Before the waitress could so much as apologize, we were surrounded by a small contingent of women with napkins, each of them murmuring words of encouragement. Ryan waved them off, grinning ear-to-ear. "Don't worry about me. It missed me completely. See?" He rose slightly and pointed to his jeans, which were as dry as could be.

The waitress set down our food and apologized as the women wandered back to their tables. I frowned at the Faeling across from me. "That hit ye full in the crotch," I said. "I saw it."

Ryan grimaced. "Yeah, it did."

I grunted, realizing Ryan had used glamour to make it seem as if his jeans were dry. Which meant he was sitting in a pile of lemonade. I considered handing him my napkin, then thought better of it.

His crotch could probably benefit from a soak.

"So," I began, "what is it ye wanted to talk to me about?"

Ryan poked at his salad. "It's about the ring," he said, tossing his napkin on his empty plate. "I never told you why I needed it."

"Ye know I don't ask those sorts of questions. Not me policy."

In fact, my policy was pretty much the opposite: don't ask questions you don't want the answers to. You could argue the hardest part of being an arms dealer was finding and securing the goods I trafficked, but that wasn't the case. The toughest part about dealing in illicit goods, in my experience, was ignoring my conscience. In order to make that easier on myself, I routinely played both sides, I always protected confidentiality, and I never pried into my client's intentions—to say I worked in a moral grey area would be an understatement.

"I know. Plausible deniability," Ryan said. "I get it. But you need to know, I think. I want you to know. Just…in case."

"In case what?"

"In case something happens to me. Not," he amended, palm raised, "that I have any reason to suspect something will happen to me. But still."

"Alright," I said, "I'm listenin'."

Ryan studied the table for a moment, frowning. "Have you ever heard of a spriggan?"

I shook my head.

"Well, even among my people, spriggans are rare. They used to be more common, but after the changeling raids ended and the Christians started consecrating their graveyards, they sort of faded into obscurity." Ryan polished off his beer and leaned forward, oblivious to the various sets of kohled eyes tracking his every move. "A few weeks ago, I found one wandering outside King's Chapel. I'm not sure how he got here—although I have a few guesses. There have been...boundary issues, lately. But what concerns me most is that he's, well, old."

"Why is that a problem? Is he dangerous?" I asked, concerned about what that might mean; among Freaks and Fae alike, old often translated to powerful.

"More to himself than to others. He's *old*, Quinn. Like nursing home old."

"Wait, d'ye mean he's senile?" I asked, eyes wide.

Ryan thought about it for a moment, then nodded. "Yeah, something like that."

"Well, that isn't good."

Ryan shook his head. "It's not. But for the most part he's harmless. Spriggans are strong, but they aren't very enterprising. The problem is, I can't convince him to stay out of sight. He likes to wander, especially around cemeteries, even though he can't get in."

I frowned, considering how people might react to seeing a Faeling touring the city. Depending on his appearance, it could cause quite a stir... unless you had the means to make him invisible. "So," I said, catching on, "that's why ye needed the ring."

"Exactly. I can't keep an eye on him all the time, so I needed to find a way to keep him out of sight. When you said you had a client looking to make a trade for the Ring of Gyges, it seemed like the perfect solution."

"And?" I prompted.

"And I would like to introduce you. I don't think he's dangerous, but if something happens to me, I want to be sure someone knows how to track him down. For his safety as much as for everyone else's."

I checked the time on my phone. "When did ye have in mind?"

"Can you swing by tonight, before we open?"

"Aye, but why haven't ye brought him to the Chancery? Surely they'd know what to do with his kind."

Ryan sighed. "It's not that simple. The Chancery isn't so much an organization as it is an enforcement agency. It exists to keep our kind in check and make sure we don't get outed to the world. They don't care about social issues, like taking care of the elderly. To them, he'd be a liability."

Did that mean they'd lock the spriggan up? Or worse? I realized I'd never really questioned the Chancery's purpose; I'd always thought of them like the DMV or the IRS—there to be a pain in my ass and little else. "Wait, how do they plan to keep ye lot from outin' yourselves around the world?" I asked. "I thought the Chancery was based here in Boston?"

"It is, because this has become our home," Ryan explained. "But every Fae knows not to cross the Chancery, no matter where they ended up."

"Sounds a wee bit medieval, if ye ask me."

Ryan grunted and shook his head. "You have to understand, most of us can't return to Fae. If the world, even the Freaks, of other cities and territories found out we were here, they'd try and force us out."

"Why? What's wrong with the lot of ye? Other than the fact that ye keep stealin' their women," I teased.

"We're different," he said, ignoring my joke, then held up a hand. "Yes, I know, so are you. But even Freaks develop ideas about what's normal and what isn't. So we keep a low profile. A few communities know we're here, but the majority know only that Boston is off limits. That keeps most out."

"And the ones it doesn't?"

Ryan shrugged. "A few werewolf pack incursions. The Sanguine Council sent in a few hitters the other day that we chose to ignore."

I wondered, idly, if the fanger I'd met in the alley had been with that crew. From what I'd gathered over the years, the Sanguine Council was a governing body made up of Master vampires—sexist, I know—who allotted and controlled various territories. Like Queen Cockroaches.

"So that's why..." I muttered, drifting off. Honestly, I'd always wondered why there were so few factions in play here in Boston; most of my business was done with individuals looking for something specific, like the deal I'd done with Ryan. "Oy, what about that rogue necromancer from last year?" I asked, perking up. "Where was the Chancery then?"

Ryan hesitated. "I wasn't part of that decision, but from what I understand, the Chancery thought there was too much media attention already, and they didn't want to get involved and risk exposure."

I ground my teeth, but nodded absentmindedly. There had been a lot of coverage; the wealthy son of a prominent politician can't go missing overnight without getting some sort of media coverage. Then his death, his resurrection, and the subsequent blackmail...the Lollipop case I'd worked with Jimmy had been one hell of a nightmare.

"Alright, well, I have to stop by Desdemona's," I said. "I promised her I'd drop in and say hello. I'll need to be goin', or I won't have time to grab a change of clothes and meet ye tonight. You'll have to get the check."

Ryan's eyes flashed. "Would that be a favor?"

Ryan, like most Faelings, treated favors like currency. And, as of last night, he owed me a significant one—one that he would love to pay back as quickly as possible. I got up, wound the scarf around my throat, and pinned him to his seat with a withering glare. "Considerin' ye invited me to brunch under the pretense of makin' me babysit a potentially dangerous creature, I dunno if ye wanna be playin' the favor game with me right now, Ryan O'Rye."

Ryan flinched, then nodded.

"Be sure to leave a big tip," I said, with a wink that earned me several scowls from around the room. I considered tousling Ryan's hair on my way out, but decided that would be excessive.

Everything in moderation, people.

CHAPTER 9

I tossed my bag against the wall, removed my shoes, and clapped twice to get the classes' attention. They fell in according to their experience and various belt categories—a small contingent of brown belts, a few blues, and one purple. The only other black belt in the room besides myself, Jenny, stood at the front of the class, staring pointedly over my shoulder at another late arrival.

"And who's that, then?" I asked her as I approached.

"Don't know. Haven't seen him before."

The newcomer wore a pair of sweatpants and hoodie, neither of which were typically seen in the dojo. The man paused outside the sparring area, hands tucked away in the pockets of his hoodie, studying the decor.

"I'm sorry," I said, stepping forward, "but this is an advanced class. The beginner's classes are on Tuesdays and—"

"Thursdays, yeah, I know." The man nodded amicably. "I read the website. But I'm not exactly a beginner, and the website also said you'd take anyone, regardless of skill level. So, I figured I'd check it out."

I exchanged looks with Jenny, who shrugged. "Well, the t'ing is," I said, mulling it over, "the Sensei's out of town this week, and I can't sign ye up, so…"

"How about I sit in for a class? Just to observe," he offered.

I gave the newcomer a once over, considering his compromise. I had to admit he looked very at home in a dojo; even beneath the hoodie I could tell he was fit and a little edgy—the edges of a tattoo licked his throat and he sported a high and tight haircut. Military, maybe? A cop? Servicemen often gravitated to dojos like ours for one reason or another, though they rarely stuck around for very long—their egos typically couldn't take being lumped in with snot-nosed little kids whose parents were only too glad to drop their spawn off for a class or two every week.

Before I could respond, I noticed Tanya, the sole purple belt, had raised her hand. I rolled my eyes. "I'm not your high school math teacher, Tanya. Ye don't have to raise your hand."

"Oh, right." Tanya's hand sunk back down to her side. "I was just gonna say I know where Sensei keeps the waivers. He's had walk-ins before."

"Well, then," I replied, sighing as I eyed the clock above the door. "I suppose that's fine, so long as he signs. Are ye alright with that?" I asked.

The man nodded. "The name's Jacob, by the way."

"Get Jacob a waiver, would ye?" I asked Tanya, who nodded and sprinted off. "Alright," I called out, clapping my hands once more, "spread out and work on your own. Jenny and I will keep an eye out."

While Jacob and Tanya finished up the paperwork, the rest of the class dispersed, each individual progressing slowly through their kata forms. I paced the room, correcting the occasional misstep, or pointing out a minor angle adjustment.

Eventually I padded over to the newcomer, Jacob, who was watching discreetly from the back of the room, wearing a skeptical expression. "Not what ye were expectin'?" I asked.

He shook his head. "I'm not sure what some of the moves are for. The kicks and thrusts make sense, but some of that looks pointless," he said, looking pointedly at Tanya, who was waving her hands away from her face like she was very slowly fighting off a wave of bees.

Frankly, I had to admit that—from an outside perspective—the class resembled untrained dancers executing a sloppily choreographed routine. But I knew better. "Tanya, come here!" I called. Tanya turned around, surprised. She shot Jacob a guarded look, which surprised me, but hustled on over anyway.

I smiled, trying my best to be reassuring; for some reason Tanya had always been shy around me, so I was a little less brash whenever I spoke to her. I didn't want to scare the poor thing off. "Alright," I said, "show us the movement ye were just workin' on."

Tanya fell back into a basic stance, her weight anchored evenly between her staggered feet, and began thrusting her palms away from her face in slow motion. I reached out for her hair at the same speed, trying to grab it with first my left, and then my right hand, but her palms efficiently diverted both from doing so.

"So, defensive techniques," Jacob said, sounding bored. "I guess that makes sense."

Tanya frowned at him.

"Turn around for me?" I asked Tanya.

The instant she did, I struck.

I reached out, snatched her by her shoulder, and tried to yank her around. Reacting completely on instinct, Tanya grabbed my hand and slammed her foot down on my own, pinning it in place. The strikes that followed were so fast that—had I not been prepared for them and reacted accordingly—I might have paid dearly for my little demonstration: her left elbow shot back towards my stomach and then launched up towards my face at the precise moment I doubled up. She disengaged smoothly, then fired off a back kick that hovered mere inches from my face before she stepped away to face me.

The whole display took about six seconds.

I glanced over at Jacob, who still seemed a little incredulous. I rolled my eyes, wondering what it would take to impress this guy. "Show him again, Tanya. But slower. Walk him through it."

Tanya danced through the movements again, explaining the kata—one of the very first she had ever learned—as she went: the grab and stomp to pin the assailant in place, the elbow to the solar plexus to drive the air out and force the attacker forward in time to meet the next elbow, which would shock and disorient the attacker long enough for the victim to step forward, deliver a strong back kick to their assailant's face, and then...

Tanya shrugged. "Depends how much damage I want to do."

I turned to Jacob and explained that, in theory, Kenpo was all about reaction—that its function was primarily one of self-defense. In practice, however, the easiest way to feel secure was to make sure the attacker was too maimed to hurt you or anyone else, ever again.

The best defense was a strong offense, in other words.

"What if it was just someone asking for directions?" Jacob asked, smirking.

"Then they should've used their words, not their hands," I replied, shrugging.

Jacob's smirk faded, his expression thoughtful. "Do you spar during the advanced class?"

I noticed Tanya's face had paled considerably. "We do," I responded. "But there's no one here I'd pair ye with, at your level."

Jacob nodded absentmindedly before meeting my eyes. "I'll spar with your best, then, and go easy."

CHAPTER 10

*J*enny bowed to Jacob, her opponent, then pulled her long blonde hair into a functional ponytail. I'd considered teaching the presumptuous bastard a lesson myself, but she'd insisted. "I like pinning the cute, cocky ones," she said, when I told her what he'd said. She and I had exchanged looks, a laugh, and that was that.

A girl likes what she likes.

I checked to make sure they were ready, then called for the fight to begin and backed away, keeping a close eye on both; it was my job to track points and watch for any illegal strikes.

Jenny adopted a balanced stance and worked her way from one side of the mat to the other, her forearms weaving as she maneuvered her guard in response to Jacob's slight body language cues. His own stance was surprisingly mobile, his hands high by his face, one leg slightly forward, both knees slightly bent.

"Muay Thai?" I asked, my curiosity getting the better of me.

Jacob almost smiled, but then focused his attention back on Jenny. He poked out a punch, but she simply slid out of reach, careful to maintain her distance until she knew what he was capable of.

Unfortunately, he didn't give her that kind of time.

The side of Jacob's foot arced towards Jenny's head with surprising speed, missing only by a hair as Jenny danced away. True to the Muay Thai style, Jacob let his momentum carry him until he was facing her once again.

At least he didn't seem bored anymore.

I took a second to glance at the crowd, all of whom seemed eager for a blow to land. I had to admit, so was I; fights like these always got my blood up. But then I noticed Jenny hesitate out of the corner of my eye, like a startled deer caught in the headlights, frozen in place. That's when Jacob launched himself at her, shoulder pressed against her thighs as he rose and twisted, bringing her down in a motion so smooth it might have been called art had it not ended so violently.

Jacob was mounted over her hips before she could react, one hand pinning both her wrists up and behind her head, the other raised over her face and balled into a fist, the implication clear.

"Enough," I said.

Jacob glanced at me, shrugged, and rolled off.

Tanya, who stood a few feet away, approached as Jacob waded into the small crowd of students—many of whom were too shocked to be congratulatory. I frowned, ignoring the nagging sensation that I'd missed something.

"I'm sorry," Tanya said once she was within earshot. "I wanted to say something sooner, but while he was signing the waiver, he kept asking about fights here. It sounded like he was itching for one."

I patted her shoulder. "Don't ye worry about it," I insisted. "Some men are like that. Besides, Jenny's a big girl, she can handle gettin' tossed around a wee bit." As if to prove it, I padded over and offered Jenny my hand. Casual conversations began to bubble up as the class realized what time it was. "Not like ye to freeze," I remarked as I drew Jenny to her feet.

She turned away. Embarrassment, maybe? His takedown had been smoothly executed, but Jenny should have seen it coming. I decided not to press. "Alright class," I yelled, "that's all for today!"

"You didn't see his *face*," Jenny whispered as she brushed past me. I frowned after her, but—before I could follow and ask what she meant—I found Tanya at my elbow once more, looking down at her feet, her brow furrowed.

"Was there somethin' else?" I asked.

She nodded. "Yeah. He, uh…well, he asked me a bunch of other questions. About you. I thought you should know."

I scowled and quickly scanned the crowd, but couldn't find Jacob among the sea of black gis; he must have already left. I turned and shrugged. "Men are like that, too," I said, wryly. "I t'ink it's best to avoid 'em whenever possible." I winked and was gratified by Tanya's small, tight-lipped smile.

Especially because that meant she couldn't see the alarm bells going off in my head.

CHAPTER 11

*B*y the time I made it to my aunt Desdemona's townhouse, I'd managed to shake off the icky feeling I'd left the dojo with after learning I had a potential stalker on my hands. It helped, of course, that I was headed to my childhood home; if I hoped to feel safe anywhere, it was here.

The townhouse was one of those reclaimed colonial buildings that Boston is known for: brick on stone on brick, the glass and white window trim older than most presidents. I'd grown up in it, trading in sets of furniture over the years, slowly conforming to Dez's eclectic, precolonial tastes.

As I crossed the threshold, I spotted the picture of the two of us looming over her mantle—her dark, classically pretty features a fierce contrast to my thick red mane and a face that most found more fascinating than attractive. We wore classic ballgowns, modeled after women of a different era—Dez a refined Scarlett O'Hara, myself a young, bratty Mary Kate Danaher.

Dez really liked her old movies.

I'd always hated dresses, but I'd sat for the portrait at Dez's request. Its twin hung in the master bedroom, except in that portrait my mother sat in my place, her smile bright and welcoming—only a few years removed from the day she died and the day I was born.

Desdemona, my mother's best friend, had adopted me shortly thereafter, insisting I call her my aunt to avoid confusion; we looked nothing alike, after all. Still, despite not being blood relatives, somehow, I'd inherited both her accent and her stubbornness.

In fact, she and I had gotten into an argument about that very painting, which I'd planned on taking for myself when I moved out. Dez had refused to part with it. "Your ma was me best friend in all the world," she'd said. "I want to keep her memory close, Quinn."

When I'd asked why her relationship with my mother trumped mine, she'd tugged my ear. "Because ye have more of her in ye than ye know, and ye can find it without me help. Besides, I paid for it."

I smiled at the memory as I left the living room and headed towards the stairs. "Dez, it's me!" I called.

"Quinn! Come in, I'm in the guest room upstairs."

I followed the sound of her voice and the telltale pounding of a hammer. The guest room, which had once been my room, had recently been converted to a workshop—except Dez hated that term for some reason and continued to call it a guest room out of pure obstinacy, as if I could still stay the night so long as I didn't mind sleeping in a room full of knickknacks and sawdust.

I found her bent over the thick worktable, covered in paint of every color, tinkering with her latest project. I couldn't tell what it was, but she was clearly invested in it, so I did what any good family member would do and pretended to care.

"Very nice," I said.

"Oh, shut up," she replied, not bothering to look up. "Ye don't even know what it is, ye silly t'ing. With all the trouble in Italy...ye know, with the Vatican bombin' and all that, Patricia thought we should try and sell a few new pieces and send the proceeds as charity."

Dez, a staunch Catholic and former member of the IRA, had long ago chosen Charity as her preferred virtue—her way of giving back to atone for a past she refused to talk about. Lately, she seemed especially compelled, often working into the wee hours on one project or another. Of course, it didn't help that Patricia—one of those high-minded, heavy-handed converter types—was Dez's next door neighbor, and the sort of woman who prided herself on her ability to organize little, artsy ways to give back to the community. But, considering I didn't exactly spend my evenings in a soup kitchen ladling cream of mushroom into the cups of the unfortunate, I supposed I shouldn't throw stones.

Maybe just a little shade.

"That's sweet of ye," I said.

"Well, it's sweet of *ye* to come see me today," she said. She unhooked the apron she wore over her clothes, removed the mangled shirt she'd tied over her head to cover her hair, and faced me, smiling. "Now, come give your aunt a hug."

"Is that me shirt?" I asked incredulously, pointing at the stained and shredded piece of fabric in her right hand.

"Why, it may be," Dez said, turning it about in the light as if she had never before seen it. "Oh, I am so sorry, Quinn. I hadn't realized..."

"Ye hadn't realized ye were usin' me t-shirt as a bonnet? The t-shirt I got from the concert I went to when I was sixteen that ye grounded me for? Well," I said, folding my arms over my chest, "you'll have to forgive me if I don't believe a word of it."

Dez glanced up at the ceiling, put on her most innocent face, and proceeded to thoroughly wipe her grimy hands clean with my t-shirt.

"I'll kill ye," I growled.

She laughed and tossed the shirt at me as I chased her around the room. She squealed. "Quinn! Be careful, there's plastic on the floor!"

I caught her by the waist a few seconds later, laughing. "I swear on me power that if I ever catch ye with one of me t-shirts on your head again, I will toss ye out a window, ye miserable old bag."

Dez swatted at me. "Set me down right now. What's this 'on me power' nonsense, then?"

I lowered her to the ground, chuckling. "I heard it from a wizard."

"And what was his name?" she asked, clearly upset to learn I'd been consorting with wizards. Dez was aware Freaks existed—both she and my mother had encountered a few back in Ireland years ago—but she knew nothing about what I did for a living, or who I did business with. I knew she wouldn't approve, of course, but mainly I kept it a secret to avoid her having to worry about me.

Or that's what I told myself, at least.

"Harry," I said, after a second's hesitation. "Of the House Gryffindor, First of His Unfortunate Name, The Boy Who Lived, Seeker of Snitches, and Father of Gingers."

"Well, ye tell this Harry to leave ye alone and leave his oaths to himself. I won't have me own niece listenin' to the likes of him and his dirty no good..." The rest of what she said faded to a dull mutter that was vaguely offensive, but mostly amusing.

You see, there were two things Desdemona disliked more than anything else in the world: magic, and books that weren't written by John or Luke. Technically, the Harry Potter series fell into both camps, which is why I'd used him as my scapegoat. I couldn't tell her that several months back I'd had to handle a hostage situation alongside Boston PD and, in the process, had met a spectacularly inept wizard—a wizard who, unfortunately, wouldn't be around to make oaths ever again.

"D'ye know a man came by the other day, lookin' for ye," Dez said, interrupting my thoughts.

"A man?"

"Aye, a man. Although I must say he looked a little off. He walked funny, like somethin' was wrong with his leg. I offered to help him back to his car, but he put me off. Still, seemed nice enough."

"I didn't give anyone this address, Dez. Ye know I wouldn't. Besides, I haven't lived here in years."

Dez shrugged. "Well, anyway, he said ye should keep an eye out for him. Didn't leave a name, though. Said he'd be in touch."

"That's all ye found out? Some answerin' service ye are."

"Don't ye take that tone with me, Quinn MacKenna," Dez shot back. "Are ye hungry?" she asked, shifting tones seamlessly. "I made stew."

I felt my stomach recoil at the thought of more food after my fattening Irish breakfast. As much as I liked to joke with Ryan and stuff my face when we got together, I kept a pretty close eye on my diet and hit the gym religiously—it paid to be fit in my line of work. It also paid to be a decent shot, a superb hand-to-hand fighter, familiar with various types of weapons, and able to tie lots of knots. Basically, I'd inadvertently spent my entire adult life preparing to do what I did for a living.

That, and win gold in the Zombie Apocalypse Olympics.

"No," I said, finally, "I think I'm alright, I can't stay long." I could see she was disappointed, so I added, "I honestly didn't feel well this mornin'. Keepin' me food down might be a struggle."

"Because ye were out drinkin' all night, I'd wager," Dez said, pointing at me with an accusatory finger.

"Of course not, it's probably mornin' sickness," I joked.

Dez froze. "What?" She reached out and snatched both my arms, her grip painfully tight. "What did ye just say, Quinn?"

I tried to pull back, but Dez wouldn't budge. "Easy there, Dez. It was just a joke, I swear."

"Swear it on your power."

I laughed, thinking she was teasing me for my comment earlier, but she didn't join in. She simply stood there, staring at me. She looked...sad. No, not sad. Grief-stricken. I relaxed and bent down a bit, so she didn't have to strain her neck to look up at me. "I swear it on me power, Dez. A joke. Nothin' more."

Dez let go of my arms and stumbled into the table. I tried to catch her, but she shooed me away. Once steady, she rose and clasped my arm, much lighter this time. "Ye mustn't scare me like that, Quinn."

"Oh?" I asked. "Shame on ye, Desdemona Jones. T'is the twenty-first century, I'll have ye know. I can go and have meself a baby if I want one." I refrained from mentioning the fact that the idea of raising a plant, let alone a tiny human, filled me with anxiety.

"I know that, dear..." she replied, drifting off for a moment to collect herself. "It's just the last person I cared about who got pregnant was your ma, and t'ings didn't go as planned after that. I'm sorry. I lost me head there for a second."

It all clicked into place—of course she was concerned. My family had a long history of troubled pregnancies, according to what my mother had told Dez. I'd basically joked about having cancer, as far as my aunt was concerned. "Oh, right," I said, fighting off the urge to curse, "I should've realized—"

"Don't ye worry, dear," Dez said, patting my arm.

"So..." I said, glancing over her shoulder at what she'd been working on —an assortment of wood and paint and glass. "How 'bout ye tell me about this project you're workin' on?"

"Don't ye have to be somewhere?" Dez asked.

"I can spare some time."

CHAPTER 12

I ended up making it to the bar only a few minutes late, which, it turned out, was still a few minutes earlier than Ryan had expected me to show. I frowned at him as he finished tidying up, folding plastic wrap over tubs of fruit and placing them in the knee-high refrigerators that lined the base of the bar.

"Don't look at me like that," Ryan said, his back turned.

I scowled.

"Don't look at me like that, either."

I rolled my eyes. "So, where's the little guy?"

Ryan grunted. "He's in the storage warehouse around back. I wouldn't call him that, though."

"And why not? Is he big?"

Ryan craned his head toward the ceiling and the glinting tin foil dragon that loomed over us, mulling over my question. "Depends on the lighting," he replied, finally.

I frowned. "And what's that supposed to mean?"

Ryan chuckled. "It's hard to explain. You know, it's funny, but I never actually met a spriggan in Fae. My father did, though. Back then he was serving in the palace guard, putting in his hundred years."

"His what now?"

Ryan picked up a glass to polish as he explained, "It's basically like compulsory military service; you pull your century working for a royal house and then go on about your business. Some Fae like the benefits and stick around, some don't."

I took a seat at the bar. I had a dozen questions, but I didn't want to interrupt Ryan's story. He never really talked about his time in Fae, not his family or the truth behind his exile. All I knew was that, about thirty years ago or so, he'd been thrown out of Fae for some slight or other. I'd even heard a rumor or two that he'd killed another Faeling—but when I brought that possibility up, he'd laughed like it was the funniest thing anyone had ever said. Apparently, homicides were far more common—not to mention socially acceptable—in Fae. According to Ryan, getting kicked out for killing one of your own there would be the equivalent of getting life without parole for shitting on your neighbor's lawn.

I still had no idea if he'd been pulling my leg or not.

Thinking back on it, I realized I knew very little about Ryan, really; I'd only met him a few years back, after an unfortunate run-in with a troll under Paul's Bridge whose name, incidentally, had also been Paul.

"My father," Ryan continued, "enjoyed it. Something about being a guard made him proud. Patriotic, maybe, I don't know. Anyway, one day, when I was young and stupid, I told him I wanted to be a member of the Royal Guard. I thought he'd be all for it, you know? It felt kind of like rooting for your dad's team without caring about the sport. That, and I think part of me wanted to surpass him; he was a guard, so I decided I wanted to be a Royal Guard. Instead, he flipped."

Ryan chuckled and exchanged one glass for another. "The Royal Guard were nothing like the palace guards, my father explained, after the flogging. They were more like Manlings, creatures to be feared, without question." Ryan winked at me, but then his expression grew distant. "Apparently, he'd seen one. Came across it by accident one night. A nightmarish creature which scared him so much that he forbade me from speaking for a year rather than risk me enlisting to serve alongside it."

"Hold on. You're sayin'," I said, keeping my voice low, my expression earnest, "that there's a spell out there to get ye to shut up for a whole year?"

Ryan flung his dishrag at my face, ignoring my laughter. "I'm saying, Quinn, that my father saw a creature that horrified him that night. And that soon you'll have the same opportunity."

Well, shit, when he put it like that...

Maybe "little guy" *wasn't* the best nickname.

CHAPTER 13

*E*xcept, damnit, he *was* a little guy.

Really not much taller than a small child, the spriggan had a comically large head perched on a slender neck—the physics of which would have excited quite a few biologists. His skin was flabby and wrinkled, his eyes dopey, lips thin. His earlobes dangled down to his shoulders and his nose was a bulbous protrusion. He looked like, I kid you not, a sock-loving house-elf.

"I'd introduce you," Ryan was saying, "but he hasn't told me his name."

"Dobby," I said, immediately.

"What?" Ryan asked.

The spriggan's eyes shot over to me and a slow, languid smile spread across his face. He ambled over, completely ignoring Ryan, who had inadvertently tried to corral the little creature and stop him from approaching, and halted a few feet away.

"Uh, hello there," I said, unsure what else to do or say. Frankly, I was always this awkward around tiny humans; I'd given up altogether on making friends with people who had children, lest they try and introduce me.

"Seems like he likes you," Ryan said, his brows knitted together.

How the hell could he tell? Did he have a tail wagging back there that I couldn't see? I leaned around to look, then jerked back guiltily as the spriggan tested the air with his hands, like a mime. His eyes were closed. Finally, he grunted, and—in the most masculine, leonine voice I have ever heard—said, "Well, hello there, my lady."

Ryan laughed at the expression on my face, but shut up immediately when the spriggan spun to face him. I realized the creature was wearing clothes from the children's department. His Avengers sneakers lit up, spewing tiny flashes of red and blue as he marched towards Ryan, pointing at him. "You, little Fae, shall call me Dobby." The spriggan glanced coyly over his shoulder at me. "The lady has spoken."

"Um, I'm not sure if you even know what that name even means," Ryan began, "besides—"

"The *lady* has spoken."

Ryan's mouth gaped for a moment, then snapped shut.

"Excellent work, Dobby," I said, grinning. "I can never get him to shut that trap of his."

"Trap?!" Dobby yelled, eyes wild, teeth gnashing together. The lights of the warehouse dimmed and then suddenly went out. I could feel movement in the oppressive darkness—something massive skulking just a few feet away. Boxes thumped together as an immense weight settled atop them, their boards cracking beneath the strain.

"It's not a trap," Ryan said, his voice oddly calm. "That's an expression Manlings use."

Dobby's voice rumbled in response, echoing from the rafters, "Expression?"

"Yes. Think about it, what comes out of a mouth can be a trap, yes?" Ryan asked.

The silence was broken by a horrible, lumbering sound, like logs careening down a hillside. A moment later, as the lights flickered back on, I realized that the sound was Dobby's laughter.

"Mouth! Trap!" Dobby—having transformed back to his tiny, vaguely hideous self the instant the lights returned—said, pointing at his mouth, grinning. He sauntered off, singing, "It's a trap!" in a thick baritone before slipping on the Ring of Gyges and disappearing from sight.

CHAPTER 14

I plopped down, pressed my forehead against the wood of Christoff's desk, and tracked the swirling pattern of the office's large area rug with my eyes.

Eventually, I shut them entirely.

"Please tell me ye didn't give a batshit shadow monster a ring to make himself invisible?" I groaned, a moment later.

"I didn't give a batshit shadow monster a ring to make himself invisible," Ryan replied immediately, as if he'd been waiting for my reaction.

I glanced up in surprise.

"*We* gave a batshit shadow monster a ring to make himself invisible," Ryan equivocated, grinning at me. "Except, he isn't batshit. He's—"

"Got the temperament of a wee child?" I accused.

"Excitable," Ryan finished, with emphasis. "But so far it hasn't been a problem. I don't let him go out alone at night and, in daylight, he's harmless. Just a quirky little old man who happens to be invisible."

"And if he decides he wants to go out for a night on the town without supervision?" I asked.

"It's Boston," Ryan said, clearly amused by my reaction to the situation. "The city is well lit at night, and smart people stay away from the places that aren't. At worst, someone sees something they can't quite explain, and it gets chalked up to local superstition."

"No," I said, "at worst, Dobby, the Big-as-a-House Elf, goes and murders half the city while invisible." It probably should have reassured me that Ryan was acting so calm, but frankly I couldn't trust him to be impartial; both Faelings and Freaks tended to underestimate the danger they represented to society. It was a matter of perspective.

And Ryan was too close to see the writing on the wall.

Ryan shook his head, laughing. "Well, apparently he doesn't mind listening to the *lady*," Ryan pointed out, "so maybe you could use that to keep him from eating people."

"He eats people?!" My eyes widened.

Ryan waved that off before I could freak out too much. "It was an expression, Quinn."

I breathed a sigh of relief, then scowled at him. "Do ye know how many Freaks I've met, personally, that eat people?"

"Oh," he replied, "Yeah, that's fair. My bad."

"Ye know what...I need a drink," I admitted, stretching. Between this morning's interrogation, my filling brunch, my brief stint as a second-rate Sensei, and meeting a spriggan, I'd had a pretty full day; a little nightcap before heading home would be ideal—anything to avoid dwelling on the shadow monster living in Christoff's warehouse.

I had enough nightmares to worry about.

"Sure thing," Ryan said, hopping up off the couch, "I'll run on down and make you a—"

"If ye even t'ink the word 'Horseman,'" I growled, "I *will* tell Dobby to eat ye."

Ryan raised his hands in surrender, but couldn't suppress a chuckle. He was about to ask what I wanted when my phone rang, Wagner's "Ride of the Valkyries" dun-dunning loud enough to attract the attention of a few of the bar staff downstairs. Ryan glanced over my shoulder at the caller ID and laughed.

"Saved by the bell," he said before heading downstairs.

"Hey, Dez," I said as I picked up the phone.

Her screams were the first thing I heard.

CHAPTER 15

*G*unshots were the second.

"Dez?" I said, too shocked to be panicked. "Dez! Are ye there?!"

I felt more than saw Ryan run back up the stairs and stand beside me—so focused on what I could hear that I'd shut my eyes. It sounded as if the receiver were colliding with something, like a microphone tumbling down a flight of stairs. Eventually even that stopped, and I heard someone pick up the phone.

"'Ello, is this Quinn MacKenna?" A man's voice asked. He had a Londoner's accent, a garbled Cockney dialect that sounded like he was trying to swallow his words whole as he spoke them.

"Put Dez on the phone," I growled.

"Oh, I'm afraid Desdemona—it is Desdemona innit? Right. I'm afraid Desdemona is indisposed. Now, please tell me this is Miss MacKenna? I'd hate to have to ask this nice lady to give me your number a second time."

"What do ye want?" I asked, grinding my teeth to stop myself from lashing out.

"Straight to the point, no threats? How refreshing," he said. "So, it seems last night you took somefin that didn't belong to you. From what I understand, there was some miscommunication involved...but I'm sure you can imagine how very unhappy I was to find out that my ring had been promised to someone else, not to mention the fact that it had been taken. Now, I dealt with the double-dipping bloodsuckers last night, but that still leaves me short a ring."

The ring. The bloodsuckers. I felt a pit open up in my stomach as I realized I was talking to the man who'd murdered Mike and his band, the man Jimmy was looking for.

And he had my aunt.

How had he even found her?

"She doesn't know anythin'," I said. "She's an old lady. Just let her go."

"Well, now, I don't think I want to do that. Besides, she seemed awful spry when she shot at me a minute ago."

I frowned. Since when did Dez have a gun? Dez hated guns, almost as much as I loved them—that, along with my taste in music, had been our sole points of contention. I shook my head, deciding I could dwell on that later.

I needed to focus.

"You'll be wanting your ring back, then?" I asked, after taking a few steadying breaths. I shot a warning glance at Ryan—whose expression had turned murderous—to stop him from speaking. I couldn't risk giving the Englishman an excuse to hurt Dez. Playing along was my only option.

For now.

"Oh no. No need for that, Miss MacKenna," the Englishman replied. "See, there's some merchandise here in Boston that I'd hoped to get my hands on, and a ring like that could come in very handy indeed. But then, lucky for me, I found out about you. Seems you're quite the expert in getting your hands on things that don't belong to you. So I had me an idea. It goes like this. You use that ring you nicked to fetch what I need, bring it to me, and I'll let this lovely lady go without a scratch, no questions asked. What do you say?"

I ground my teeth. He'd taken Dez hostage to blackmail me into stealing something for him? Talk about taking things to the next level for no reason. "I have a phone, ye know," I said, finally. "If ye wanted me to get somethin' for ye, all ye had to do was reach out like everyone else."

"Oh, but I'm not like everyone else," the man said, chuckling. "See, I'm not a fan of asking, dearie. Leaves too much room for a misunderstanding. Asking implies that you could say no, which really isn't how things stand. So, what'll it be? From one professional to another, I think you should take the deal."

I heard Dez's muffled scream in the background.

"Fine," I hissed. "What is it ye want me to steal?"

He talked. I listened.

CHAPTER 16

*T*he next morning I found myself following a man carrying a steel briefcase down Beacon Street in the middle of the afternoon. Fortunately, he wasn't moving quickly; tailing someone is much harder when they are moving significantly faster than everyone else on the street.

Everyone knows when they are being chased.

The briefcase I'd been told to steal was handcuffed to his left arm, which you'd think would draw attention—I mean, how often do you see men sporting handcuffs as jewelry—but didn't. I figured there was some sort of spell involved; if I took my eyes off him, even for a second, he became almost impossible to relocate. A nifty trick for evading unwanted attention.

Fortunately, I wasn't the only one keeping tabs on him.

"The mark is on the move," Ryan said, his voice a tinny buzz in my right ear.

"Oh, for Christ's sake, Ryan, do ye have to keep callin' him 'the mark'?" I asked. Ryan had been in my ear for a couple hours now, clearly embracing his role as lookout. I swore to myself that if he made one more spy movie reference, I was going to shoot him.

"The mark is headed towards the park," Ryan said, ignoring me entirely.

And now he's rhyming.

"I see that, ye silly bastard," I grumbled.

Despite my reservations, the Faeling had insisted on coming. My guess

58

is he felt guilty for sending me after the ring in the first place. I considered letting him off the hook and claiming it was all part of the job, but that wasn't strictly true.

This was Dez we were talking about. Family. I'd worked hard to make sure no one could ever trace me back to her or use her as leverage like this. That's part of why I rarely visited, these days, if I was being honest; I preferred to think of her safe and sound, tucked away in her guest room, doing charity work.

"You sure you don't want me to call in reinforcements?" Ryan asked, for perhaps the seventh time. He meant the Chancery, or at least a few of its members. It was tempting; I could only imagine what sort of resources they had at their disposal to hunt down blackmailers. But I couldn't risk it.

"Has he made me?" I asked, ignoring the Faeling as I pretended to window shop, doing my best to appear inconspicuous. I strolled along the opposite side of the street, glancing sidelong at the man, letting him control the pace.

I'd opted for the bored, trophy wife look: a slim beige overcoat, a black turtleneck tucked into a pair of black leather pants, knee-high boots, and a pair of Burberry sunglasses I'd bought for the occasion, the frames and lenses comically large. I looked ridiculous in them—like some kind of freckled alien—but I was certain no one could see my eyes beneath, least of all the person I was tailing.

"Now look who's using the lingo," Ryan quipped. "But no, I don't think so. As far as I can tell he's making his way to the Amtrak station, which would be consistent with what the English guy said."

The Englishman, the kidnapper, had given me the relevant details the night before: follow the man with the briefcase from his Riverside hotel to the Back Bay Station and, at the first available opportunity, steal the briefcase.

According to him, how I went about stealing the briefcase was entirely up to me. When I asked what the man was doing with a briefcase hand-cuffed to his arm and what was in that briefcase, I'd been politely told to mind my fucking business. I got the same answer when asking about who else might also want the briefcase and what the man might do to stop me from taking the briefcase.

Basically, I was going into this blind.

"Did ye check the train departure times?" I asked.

"Yeah, pretty sure he's taking the train to St. Louis. It's the only one departing that makes any sense."

"Wait," I stumbled a little, the heel of my boot catching a break in the pavement, "ye mean the man with the briefcase permanently attached to his wrist is headed to the most recent terrorist capitol of the United States?"

"Oh...shit," Ryan said. "Quinn, please tell me we aren't about to try and steal a bomb?"

"We aren't," I replied.

Ryan sighed in relief.

"We're about to steal a briefcase...that might have a bomb in it," I said, using Ryan's tone from the night before. Frankly, the possibility bothered me at least as much as it did him; he wasn't the one standing thirty feet from the guy with the briefcase attached to his arm.

"I hate you sometimes, you know that?" Ryan said, finally.

"Get in line."

A large Greyhound bus pulled up to the light, momentarily blocking my view. I hurried up the street, hoping he'd pop out in front of the bus. "Ryan, I've lost visual."

"He's still there...wait, no, he ducked down an alley on that side. I can't see him from up here."

"I'll cut across."

"I'm coming down," Ryan said. I could hear him retrieving the fold-up lawn chair and preparing to leave the roof, cursing.

"Don't," I said. "Stay there and keep an eye out in case he pops back up. If I need ye, I'll let ye know."

More curses from Ryan followed, but I was already moving. I jogged across the intersection as soon as the walk sign flashed, hands burrowed in my pockets, shoulders hunched, as if I were cold and hurrying to find the nearest boutique and get warm.

I couldn't afford to blow my cover.

I saw the alley as soon as I made it to the other side of the street. It was one of those service alleyways, the ones you always see trucks pull into to drop off food and such, which meant it was wide but—with tall buildings on either side—not particularly well lit. I had just poked my head around the corner when I heard Ryan's voice in my ear.

"Quinn! He's behind—"

I didn't bother listening to the rest, what with the metal barrel of the man's gun pressed into my spine hard enough that I could feel it through my coat.

"Get inside alley," the man said with an accent I couldn't quite place. Something Slavic that would turn all his w's into v's, from what I could tell.

"Don't you dare go down that alley, Quinn!" Ryan yelled, his voice loud enough in my ear to make me cringe.

"Listen," I said, "I don't know who ye are, but I'm sure ye know it's not polite to tell people what to do at gunpoint." I began to turn, hoping to catch a glimpse of his face, but he jabbed me with the gun before I could get a good look. I heard the sound of footsteps on metal stairs and Ryan's labored breathing before he hung up, probably by accident. Either way, it seemed like I was on my own.

"Alley, now, or I shoot and walk away."

Oh, good. More threats. I decided I'd had enough of this nonsense; I couldn't risk telling the Englishman to go fuck himself, but I wasn't about to let this guy tell me what to do. "Alright, fine," I said, calling his bluff. "Go ahead and shoot."

"What?"

"I told ye to shoot me," I repeated. "You shoot an unarmed woman in the middle of the street and see how far ye get, even with your spell. Go on, then."

The pressure on my spine eased, then disappeared. "Why are you following me?"

"Can I turn around?" I asked.

"No. Answer the question."

I sighed, but decided to go with the truth. I didn't have a ready lie available, and, frankly, I was too emotionally fried to bother. "I was sent to steal your briefcase," I admitted.

Silence, then something truly horrific happened: he chortled. I know it may not seem as terrifying as I make it out to be, but have you ever heard an Eastern European laugh maniacally? It ranks right up there with a cackle of hyenas surrounding you in total darkness and, well, cackling.

"If you can get briefcase off," the man said, after his laughter died away, "it is yours."

CHAPTER 17

*H*is name was Serge Milanovich.

"I am from Belgrade," he'd explained in broken English after we'd left the alley. "The people who put briefcase on my arm say they will pay me a lot of money to deliver briefcase to New York City. They fly me from Berlin in private plane, but there was snow, and we land here, in dangerous city where no one goes. And now I take train to St. Louis, but already there is someone following me."

Now Serge sat at a picnic table across from me, cradling his face with his hands, the briefcase perched in his lap. Children too young to be at school chased each other in the playground to our right, bundled in winter gear. Somewhere, I hoped, Ryan stood watch; I hadn't heard anything from him since I'd left the street.

"They did not tell me this would be dangerous. But then people I work for give me this gun and say be careful. And last night a man breaking in my room." Serge looked up at me, his eyes desperate. "I cannot get briefcase off. I have tried." Serge held up his wrist to me, displaying what I had mistaken for a handcuff, but which was actually a manacle made out of silver.

Seriously, silver.

"Won't ye be in trouble with your employers if ye lose the briefcase?" I asked icily, still unhappy that he'd gotten the drop on me, not to mention the jab to the lower back with the loaded gun. Honestly, I'd hoped he'd be a little less willing to talk and a lot less pitiful; if he hadn't reminded me of a flea-ridden puppy from a Sarah McLaughlin commercial, I'd have gladly taken my frustrations out on his face.

Serge shook his head. "I do not care. They cannot expect me to give my life, even for the money they have promised." He reached out and clasped his hairy hand over my arm. I frowned down at the offending meathook until he let go.

Something about this situation, about Serge, nagged at me. I frowned, studying the man. Frankly, I couldn't imagine anyone less conspicuous than he was; Serge wore a black track suit, had more hair on his face and chest than on his head, and was three shades swarthier than anyone I'd ever met. Why use him as your mule? Or was it simply because he came from an impoverished area and needed the money?

"Let me see," I said, finally, holding out my hand. Serge's eyes widened, but then he—very carefully—placed his manacled wrist in my hand. When nothing happened, he let out a gasp of surprise, but tried to cover it with a cough.

"What happened to the last person to touch this, Serge?" I asked. When he wouldn't look at me, I tugged on his wrist.

Hard.

"They fell and did not get up," he admitted, wincing. "But," he stammered, "I did not know if it would happen to you—"

"Shut it, ye liar," I hissed, ignoring the man's guilty expression. I studied the manacle. It had no seam that I could see. No clasp. No keyhole. "How did they even get this on ye?"

Serge shook his head. "I was asleep."

"Well, I'm not sure if I can get it off ye without some proper tools. Maybe a blowtorch—"

"No!" Serge hissed, pulling his hand back and cradling it.

"It's a binding," Ryan said, leaning over my shoulder.

I whirled to face him, but he was too busy staring down Serge to react to my glare. "A what?" I asked heatedly, once I realized he wasn't planning on elaborating further.

"They bound it to his body," Ryan explained. "It's a spell. A pretty simple one, but effective, and hard to counteract. A wizard could undo it." He flicked his eyes at me, and I could tell he thought that little tidbit of information meant something, but I had no idea what. Instead, I spun my wheels, trying to think if I knew any wizards who owed me a favor.

"Fortunately," Ryan said, interrupting my thoughts, "you won't need one. You just have to break the seal."

"Oh? And how do I do that?" I asked. I held up my hands. "Ye know I don't have any magic of me own."

Serge tracked our exchange with his eyes. He didn't seem quite sure what to make of Ryan, but smiled eagerly at the sound of being freed. I couldn't blame him, I realized; the thought alone of being chained to anything made my blood boil.

"In this case," Ryan continued, "all it means is that you'll have to make sure the metal isn't touching any part of his skin. Once you do that, it should fall right off. Like I said, simple. Well, simple for you, anyway."

Serge shifted in his seat to regard me, his face thoughtful. He held out his wrist once more. "Please," he begged. "I want to go home."

I sighed. "Fine," I said, taking hold of his wrist. I wrapped my hands around the metal and adjusted it until none of Serge's skin touched the cylinder. A light flashed—like the strobe of a massive camera—and the manacle expanded to the size of a dinner plate. Serge withdrew his arm, leaving me with a thin silver disk attached to a briefcase.

"Oh, that is good," Serge said, rubbing his wrists. He rolled his neck, his eyes twinkling with what I thought was excitement, but soon realized was a faint flickering light, like green flames broiling behind the sclera. "It has been so long..."

And that's when I learned why you shouldn't take briefcases from strangers.

CHAPTER 18

*S*erge leapt away from the picnic table and tore at the jacket of his tracksuit, ripping it off. Beneath, wrapped around the hairy skin of his stomach, was a belt made from the skin of some animal, strong and knotted over his belly button.

"Son of a bitch," Ryan swore. "Quinn, get behind me!"

I rose as Serge began to howl.

Seriously. Howl.

"And why I am gettin' behind ye?" I asked, hesitantly.

"He's a skinwalker. I'm such an idiot!" Ryan cursed. "I thought the silver was protecting him from Freaks, not protecting Freaks from him."

"And what the hell is a skinwalker?" I asked.

But, before Ryan could answer, Serge Milanovich transformed into a monstrous, bipedal creature that looked like a werewolf's demented cousin —something I only knew because I'd freed a few werewolves last year from an underground wolf-fighting ring to get even with a backstabbing client.

From what I'd seen while watching them tear into their former handlers, I'd learned werewolves were generally similar to their canine counterparts, only significantly bigger, and scarier. I'd even heard rumors that a few could land somewhere in between—part man, part wolf, only on steroids. But this was something else.

I watched in horror as Serge tore at his own skin, peeling it off in swathes to reveal a furred creature beneath that was neither man nor animal. There was no blood, which made the whole process seem rather like an orange haphazardly peeling itself—an image that would have made me laugh, only it was hard to find humor in anything with so many screaming kids nearby.

"Ryan, get everyone away from here!" I yelled, realizing that if things progressed any further, everyone would be in danger; just because I didn't much care for rugrats didn't mean I wanted to end up on the evening news for siccing a wild animal on a park full of kids.

He grunted. "Not a chance."

"Ryan O'Rye," I said, snatching his shirt collar and drawing him close, "I'll be havin' that favor, now."

"Oh, for fuck's sake—"

"You'll get everyone away from here, and you'll make sure no one gets hurt. And ye won't come back until you're absolutely certain everyone is safe. That's me favor. Now go!"

Ryan grimaced, then shook me off and ran around the Skinwalker-Formerly-Known-as-Serge in a wide arc, booking it over to the playground, shouting as he went, herding the horde of screaming children and panicked guardians towards the other end of the park.

I turned to face the nightmare Serge had become.

Just in time to see the hideous creature launch itself at me.

CHAPTER 19

I ducked a shoulder and rolled to my right, barely dodging the claws of the monster I'd helped create, though I still wasn't sure exactly how I'd managed that or why it was attacking me. A foul, musky scent permeated the air, like the inside of a hoarder's house—nothing but mold and cat piss.

"Jesus Christ," I said as I got back to my feet, dusting myself off in the process, "is that ye, ye filthy animal?"

The skinwalker snarled at me, spittle dangling from its gaping mouth. I noticed its teeth were cracked and popcorn yellow, and that more than a few looked sharp enough to do real damage. But what really bothered me was the creature's eyes.

They glowed a pupil-less, neon green.

"Now that's just ridiculous, Serge," I muttered.

"That is not our name." The voice floated freely in the air, almost like a ventriloquist's, hovering somewhere above our heads. The skinwalker's tongue lolled to one side as the disembodied voice spoke again, "He and I are one and we have no name. We are Us."

"D'ye borrow that from Hallmark?" I asked, poking fun at the beast, trying to buy time for Ryan to get everyone to safety. "Because I'm pretty sure that's Hallmark."

The voice hesitated before responding, "Who is this Hallmark? Tell us.

We do not borrow. We steal. We will kill this Hallmark and steal from him and what is his will become ours."

"Ah," I said, "because if ye take it, it becomes yours?"

"Yes."

"Ye know, Barney the Dinosaur would be very disappointed in ye."

"Then he too shall die. We shall eat him and we shall take—"

"Oh, shut up. T'was a joke, ye idgit."

The creature growled and gnashed its teeth, falling to all fours, the ridges of its spine visible beneath a thin sheet of mottled, matted fur. With remarkable speed, it galloped towards me, claws tearing divots in the grass.

I felt bad for whoever was in charge of landscaping.

Fortunately, all the time we'd spent talking had given Ryan ample opportunity to get everyone clear. Which meant it was safe to do things I wouldn't ordinarily do in a crowded park full of innocent bystanders.

Like draw a gun.

CHAPTER 20

I retrieved my Kahr CM9 from the compression holster at the small of my back, flicked the safety off, and fired three rounds as I threw myself backwards into the dirt. Luckily, the skinwalker went for my throat with its teeth instead of using its claws, which gave me more time than I expected to fire at its midsection—easily the biggest target.

The bullets disappeared, swallowed in its fur without a trace.

The skinwalker landed on top of me, growling. Its teeth looked even sharper up close, but what really killed me was the smell of its rancid breath. "Your mortal weapons cannot harm us. You cannot wound what is already dead," the voice said.

Well, shit.

"Plan B, then," I said. I shoved one hand over my ear, raised the other, and fired into the air, the barrel inches from the skinwalker's ear. It howled in pain and rolled away. I did the same, scrambling to my feet as the skinwalker whirled towards me. I kept my gun out and trained on the creature; I felt more secure with it in hand, no matter what the voice said.

"So," I asked, circling, "what exactly are ye?"

I wondered, idly, if there was some sort of etiquette primer out there somewhere that gave tips on how to handle monsters who planned to kill you. In my experience, the only trick that worked was to put them down quick, or to keep them talking. More often than not all I ended up with was a name and agenda to go with all the new scars, but occasionally—if I was lucky—they'd slip up and reveal a weakness.

Or, if I was unlucky, they'd try to bore me to death.

"We are the first of our kind," the voice said.

"Very helpful."

"We are legion. We are the hunted who became hunters. We are the formless ones. The nightwalkers. The—"

"Does this list ever end?" I asked. "Or d'ye keep goin' until I die of old age?"

"We are the first," the voice repeated.

"The first what?"

The voice didn't seem to understand the distinction. Honestly, I wasn't sure it understood anything I was saying. The creature's body language wasn't exactly easy to read. In fact, I was beginning to think the voice and the creature were separate somehow; the skinwalker had begun chewing at its shoulder in search of fleas in the middle of our conversation.

Suddenly, its ears perked up. A moment later I, too, heard sirens in the distance. "Looks like the police are on their way," I said.

"We will gnaw on their bones and take their badges and piss on their tires—"

I fired, twice, aiming for its eyes. It snarled and leapt at me, clearly unfazed, but this time I was able to anticipate its speed. I dropped my gun and stepped to the side, nimbly dodging its gaping jaws as it spun to snap at my leg. I reached out and, with a shout of triumph, took hold of its tail, yanking as hard as I could. The skinwalker yelped and tried to flee, but I held on, my forearms straining with the tension.

I watched with satisfaction as my unique ability began to take effect: Serge's features began to emerge as the magic that surrounded his body fled from our contact, his eyes returning to their unassuming shade of brown, clearly terrified. His teeth, square and uneven, looked comical in the skinwalker's elongated snout.

"What are you?" Serge asked, his voice breathy and labored.

A shout in the distance stole my attention. I turned, slightly, and Serge took the opportunity to shake me loose. I fell back on my ass as he took off, his gait somewhere between an out-of-shape middle-aged man in track pants and a furry, bipedal monster out of a Tim Burton movie.

He looked absolutely ridiculous.

"Boston PD! Hands up on your head, and get on your knees!"

I did as I was told, glad I'd already dropped my gun in the grass, or I'd probably be in a lot more trouble than I already was.

"What the hell was that thing?" I heard one of the officers ask.

"No idea," another responded.

"Well, why is she laughing?"

"She's probably in shock," was the reply.

For some reason, that made me laugh even harder.

CHAPTER 21

$\mathcal{T}$he interrogation room looked nothing like they did on TV. I'd expected a bare steel table and stone cellar walls to block out the sound of people screaming their confessions, but Boston PD seemed to have splurged for threadbare carpet and ergonomic swivel chairs. It was practically cozy. Inviting, even.

Probably a trap.

"Hello, Miss MacKenna," Jimmy said as he entered.

"Jimmy!" I said, beginning to rise, only to plop back down once I saw who he'd brought along.

"Miss MacKenna," Detective Maria Machado said as she entered behind her partner. Maria was a dainty Hispanic woman in her early thirties who prided herself on her immaculate make-up and even more immaculate case record; sadly, the only case she'd been unable to close had featured me as its primary consultant, which meant we weren't on the best of terms.

Frankly, I thought she was a bitch.

"Maria," I replied, frostily.

"Please call me Detective Machado, Miss MacKenna. Now, let's see what we have here..." Maria took a seat across from me, opened a folder on the table, and peered down at its contents for a full minute, frowning. "It seems you were found at the park with a registered handgun in your possession after several witnesses reported seeing a wild animal loose on the grounds. Why don't you tell me about that?"

Jimmy's eyes gave me nothing, so I shrugged and played on the drama of the moment, embracing the role of a woman who'd been attacked by a vicious, wild animal and had been very lucky to survive with only a few scrapes and bruises—that's what my official statement said, at any rate. Ironically, I could honestly say the truth would have seemed significantly more farfetched than my lie.

I mean, which story would you believe?

"Oh, you're right about that," I said, my voice a pitch higher than normal, my accent even more pronounced. "I was so scared! There I was, just mindin' me own business, when that creature came right up to me table, foamin' at the mouth. Ye should've seen the mongrel! As big as a horse!"

Maria's lips pursed, but she nodded. "This business you're referring to, did it have anything to do with the young man who escorted the rest of the bystanders to the other side of the park? Or the briefcase we found at the scene that you claim is yours?"

I fought to keep a smug expression off my face. I'd used my one phone call to get ahold of Ryan and warn him to steer clear, only to find out he'd used his Faerie glamour to alter his features over and over again while rescuing the bystanders. About now I figured the police were trying to weed through pointless sketches of men who looked nothing alike—fat, tall, skinny, short, etc.

"Why, Detective Machado, it sounds as if ye would rather talk about me personal life than what happened at the park." I sloped forward on my elbows. "Shouldn't ye be lookin' for suspects? Someone who might've let the wild animal loose? Or d'ye t'ink I had somethin' to do with it?"

"That isn't it at all, Miss MacKenna," she replied, but her expression said otherwise. Maria Machado didn't like me. I knew it, and she knew I knew it. Fortunately, that meant they didn't have anything to charge me with; if they did, I'd be in a cell already.

"Well, I've had a terrible fright, Detective, and I would appreciate it if you'd let me go home and recover in peace."

Maria met my eyes for the first time since she'd stepped in the interrogation room, and I fought the urge to scoot away from the table. That wasn't mere dislike in her eyes, it was hate—her upper lip twitched in contempt. What had I done to deserve that look? I glanced over at Jimmy once more, only to find him studying a worn space in the carpet, toeing it with his shoe; he couldn't look more disinterested if he tried.

"You're free to go, of course, Miss MacKenna," Maria said, finally. "Although, if you have anything you'd like to add to your previous statement before our forensics team finishes up at the scene, I suggest you tell us. I'd hate to find out you were impeding our investigation by being less than forthright."

"I wouldn't dream of it," I replied. "Have a good day, Detective."

She and I rose at the same time. I towered over her, which seemed to piss her off even more. She began flipping through the folder on the desk, speaking only once I had my hand on the door handle, "Naturally, we'll have to hold on to your gun, and the briefcase we found at the scene, until the investigation is complete."

I swiveled back around, but Jimmy was already boxing me out, his shoulders too wide to see past. He ignored my furious stare. "I think I'll see Miss MacKenna out," he said, guiding me towards the door.

Maria snorted.

"Jimmy, what the f—" I began.

Jimmy herded me out, shutting the door behind us before I could finish my sentence. "Not here. Come on," he said.

I trailed him, my temple throbbing. Losing my gun for a few days was bad enough, but without that briefcase I had no way to trade for Dez. I cursed inwardly, beyond pissed. Frankly, under the circumstances, taking my gun away was the smartest thing Maria Machado could have ever done.

Because otherwise she'd already be in the hospital.

CHAPTER 22

*J*immy abruptly shoved me inside a broom closet—or what I assumed was a broom closet; the two of us barely fit and I swore I could feel a broom handle pressed uncomfortably against my ass. I shoved it away and winced as it fell into what must have been a shit ton of buckets. Jimmy shoved his hand over my mouth, listening at the door.

"I'm goin' to kill that bitch," I hissed through his palm, my words garbled and warped.

"I'm going to pretend I didn't hear that," Jimmy said, releasing me.

"Hear me, if I see her anywhere near me or mine ever again, I'll—"

"You'll call me," Jimmy finished. "Because if she does, without cause, you could file a complaint. Which would be the first step. You know, before you threaten her life. The life of a detective. A detective that works for Boston PD." His tone suggested I was being irrational. I seriously considered eye gouging him.

"What's her problem, then?" I asked, still pissed, but willing to calm down if it meant finding a solution to my problem.

"She found out you called me last night," Jimmy admitted.

Did that mean she also found out *why* I'd called Jimmy? About the case he was working on? "Wait, does she think I had somethin' to do with the murders?" I asked.

"Not exactly," Jimmy replied.

I sensed he was holding something back, something he knew I wouldn't like. My eyes narrowed. "Then what?" I asked.

"She was...displeased with the idea that you have my cellphone number."

I frowned, then finally put the pieces together. "Oh, ye can't be fuckin' serious...all that animosity in there was because she doesn't want ye takin' me calls in the wee hours of the night?"

Jimmy clearly thought that question was rhetorical.

"I need that briefcase, Jimmy," I hissed. "I don't have time to deal with your fuckin' jealous partner." The ridiculousness of the situation was almost too much to handle; Maria's irrational jealousy was liable to get my aunt killed, at this rate.

"Do you need it for one of your clients?" Jimmy asked.

I shook my head, distracted as I plotted Maria's demise in my head. Poison, maybe? Something that couldn't be traced back to me. "Not exactly," I replied, finally.

Jimmy folded his arms over his chest, the middle button of his dress shirt barely holding beneath the strain. "Explain."

I took a deep breath and caught the scent of his cologne, realizing for the first time that I was alone with a very large, attractive man in a very dark, secluded closet. I cleared my throat and began to explain, haltingly, leaving out only a few details—like Ryan's involvement and Dez's attempt to fire on her attackers.

"You should have called me first, Quinn," he said the instant I was finished. I could tell he was pissed to be left out of the loop, but I didn't have time to put up with his self-righteous bullshit.

"And told ye what, Jimmy?" I demanded. "That a man kidnapped me aunt, and now he wants me to bring him a briefcase or she dies?" I shook my head. "I've seen how your people handle hostage situations, and I didn't much care for the outcome," I spat.

It was a low blow, and I knew it, but I was tired of having to explain myself to Regulars, especially cops, who refused to accept the fact that they were unequipped to protect people from the monsters—the real monsters. During the Lollipop case Jimmy and I had worked together, a kid had ended up dead—not because of the hostage negotiator's incompetence—but because the kidnapper always intended to bring the boy back to life as a thrall.

Necromancers were dicks like that.

But none of the cops besides Jimmy had given me the time of day, and in the end, that bumbling wizard and I had barely managed to prevent a zombie Apocalypse...which, of course, the mass media had blamed on radiation.

Radi-fucking-ation.

Jimmy's face was hard to read in the half-light that drifted in through the crack in the door, but from his silence I could tell I'd hit a nerve. "Damnit, Jimmy, I'm sorry. It's just," I struggled to put it into words, "there are parts of me world, of me job, ye can't understand. Ye can't survive unless you're willin' to play by our rules."

Jimmy took a deep breath and rolled his shoulders before opening the door, checking either side of the hallway to make sure the coast was clear. "Alright, let's go."

"Jimmy, I can't leave without that briefcase," I whispered, "and nobody'll believe—"

"No, they won't. But I do, and I'm tired of sticking my head in the sand while people are out there, getting hurt. Only, you should know you aren't going to like what comes next." Jimmy didn't pause to explain. Instead, he left me standing in the closet, taking off down the hallway at a brisk pace.

"Why won't I like what comes next?" I called, cursing as I rushed to catch up.

"Because you're gonna owe me."

CHAPTER 23

A half hour later, I sat in Jimmy's passenger seat, the briefcase—no longer secure in its evidence bag—cradled in my lap. I fiddled with the silver disc that remained chained to the handle, turning it in the light, running my hands over its impossibly smooth surface.

"You sure you should be messing with that thing?" Jimmy asked, flicking his eyes between it and the road in front of us.

"Nope," I admitted. If I was being honest, it was probably a really terrible idea, especially while he was driving. But it hadn't hurt me so far, and it was the only lead I could use to learn more about the man who was blackmailing me.

"Then maybe you should stop," he suggested.

"No t'anks."

Jimmy sighed. "And why not?"

"Because it's shiny?" I offered, flipping the briefcase over.

Jimmy grunted. "And it has nothing to do with the fact that you don't know how it works and you can't help poking at things you don't understand?"

I polished the shiny metal case until I could see my bright green eyes reflected in its surface. "None whatsoever. I'm a girl, remember? We like pretty t'ings."

Jimmy made to take the case from me, but I held it out of his reach.

"Leave it alone, nosy. You're drivin'. Besides, I'm pretty sure it's programmed to smite the unworthy."

"It what?"

"It'll knock ye unconscious, or some such. The skinwalker was a little vague on the details," I admitted, "But I don't want ye to get us killed because ye can't help pokin' at things *ye* can't understand."

"Whatever you say," Jimmy said, clearly skeptical. "Anyway, what's our next move?"

"Well, first I need to figure out what's inside this t'ing and where it came from. I don't want to hand it over without at least knowin' that much."

"I think you've got a few things mixed up," Jimmy said.

"I what now?"

"First of all, I said 'our' next move, not yours. And second—"

"Jimmy," I interrupted, "Listen, I appreciate ye gettin' me the briefcase and all, but I don't think you understand—"

"No, Quinn. I don't think *you* understand. I didn't pull the briefcase from lockup for you to hand over to some thug. The briefcase is in my custody. Which means where that briefcase goes, I go."

"Oh, for Christ's sake, Jimmy—"

"It's not up for debate, Quinn. I told you that you'd owe me. This is how you pay me back. You keep saying I'm out of my depth, but I'm not going anywhere, so you might as well get used to it." The muscles in his jaw tensed, the leather of the steering wheel creaking beneath his hand.

I glared out the window and willed the traffic to move quicker. Still, maybe this was for the best; if Jimmy got a real good look at my world, and didn't run screaming, maybe he and I stood a chance.

"You never did tell me," Jimmy said, trying to be conversational, "what got you started with all this?"

"What do ye mean?" I asked.

"I mean all of it," Jimmy replied, waving his hand in the air. "Whatever you call it. The Freaks. The deals you make with them. How did it start? Was there an application you had to fill out? What was the job interview process like?"

"I was recruited," I replied, trying to be as vague as possible. To be honest, I really didn't want to talk about it; it was a time in my life I'd worked hard to forget.

"You were recruited? Seriously? By who? And why?"

79

I considered how much to tell Jimmy—weighing how much he needed to know against how much I wanted him to. "It was a long time ago, Jimmy," I replied, finally.

"It's fine," Jimmy said, picking up on my tone. "I was curious, that's all. But I get it. There's some stuff people don't like to talk about. Can't talk about."

I glanced over and realized Jimmy probably understood—better than anyone—why someone might keep shit to themselves. Jimmy, after all, refused to talk about a lot of things: his overseas tours, his mom leaving during his eighth-grade year after his brother died, what it was like being the only black kid in a Southie Catholic school, or how it felt to lose his full ride with only a few games left in the season.

We'd met at that Catholic school, spending a whole year and change together before I got suspended my sophomore year for the umpteenth time, gave up on the whole religion thing, and opted for public school. We'd been close, especially for outcasts, both of us too mixed up to bother with undamaged people.

I also realized that, if I was going to talk about it with anyone, it might as well be Jimmy; I could trust him to relate, at least. "After I graduated," I began, "I traveled a bit. Lived in New York City for a while. Made some friends. I found out what I was while I was there, but it didn't really change all that much. I was still a wee girl in a big city who couldn't pay her bills. And so, when I ran out of money, I went home."

Jimmy snorted. "Bet Dez made you crawl back on broken glass."

"Aye, she did," I said, grinning, remembering how she'd insisted from then on that I pay rent, threatening to kick me out if I didn't keep my room clean or do my dishes. I'd lived in fear of her booting me out for months.

"So then what?" Jimmy asked, bringing me back to my senses.

I fidgeted a little with my jacket, drawing it tighter over my shoulders. "Then I met him. The bastard who recruited me. At first, everythin' seemed great. He put me up in a nice apartment, treated me well, showed me the ropes. Later, I found out he'd heard about me and my abilities from friends in New York. T'ings began changin' not long after. He got rough. Violent." I shivered, then straightened, determined not to let it bother me.

Jimmy clearly wanted to say something, but he didn't interrupt, which I appreciated.

"The whole time, though," I said, finally. "I was learnin', watchin' how he ran his business, who he bribed and who he threatened. He didn't just trade in artifacts, like I do. He ran guns, drugs. Ye name it..." I drifted off. There was more to the story. A lot more. Like the fact that he'd used me and my gifts to steal things from his competitors. Or the fact that he'd trained me to use those guns, even taught me how to cut his coke. In hindsight, it was obvious to see what a toxic relationship we'd had, but I'd been in love with the bastard, too wrapped up in our twisted romance to realize how much danger I'd been in.

"Anyway," I said, "one day everythin' changed. He pissed off the wrong people. The wrong Freaks. And they came for him. For both of us, really." I fingered the scar on my knee from when I'd had to jump from a burning window to a nearby rooftop. "I survived, he didn't."

Jimmy waited to be sure I was finished before asking, "Did they come after you again?"

"Aye, once or twice. They know better now."

"Because you kept sending their people home in body bags?" Jimmy joked, his smile wry.

I chuckled and shook my head. "Because now, when they need somethin', they know who to call."

CHAPTER 24

*T*he briefcase wouldn't open.

"Here, let me try," Jimmy offered, peeling back the cuffs of his dress shirt. He'd followed me doggedly into my apartment as if I'd planned to ditch him the second I got out of the car, but I wasn't complaining; I'd even jerked to a halt a few times, just to be obnoxious.

He hadn't found it as funny as I had.

"Seriously?" I asked, rolling my eyes.

"What?" he asked.

"Ye t'ink that because you're a big strappin' man that ye can open it when I couldn't? I'll have ye know I'm perfectly capable of openin' t'ings meself. Besides," I added, "it's dangerous, remember?"

"Oh, please," Jimmy scoffed, snatching the briefcase off my kitchen counter, only to fall to his knees immediately, gasping, sweat pouring out of him at such an accelerated rate that his shirt was instantly soaked and clung to him where it met his skin.

I leapt off my chair and kicked the briefcase out of his hand. Without the support, Jimmy slid to the floor, staring at nothing, gasping. I could practically feel the heat radiating off his body in waves. "Ye just couldn't leave it alone, could ye?!" I yelled, pissed that he hadn't listened to me. "Idgit!"

I took several deep breaths to calm down; screaming at Jimmy made me feel better, but it wouldn't save him. I quickly took stock of the situation, only to realize that—while I'd gotten used to braving what some might call hazardous or even life-threatening situations—I knew jack shit when it came to saving people.

In fact, at this point I'd proven immune to so many things that should have killed me that I didn't even have a First Aid Kit in my apartment. I cursed, feeling out of my depth for the first time in a long time. I had a grown ass man twitching on my kitchen floor, and my aunt was being held captive God knows where, and I didn't have my gun.

I seriously hoped this wasn't the universe trying to send me a sign, because "Fuck Quinn MacKenna" wasn't all that catchy.

My cellphone suddenly rang across the room. I knew I didn't have time to answer it, but I couldn't risk letting it go to voicemail when it could be the man who held my aunt hostage on the other end. I rushed to the phone and answered it, breathlessly.

"Hello," a woman's voice purred through my phone's speakers, her accent eerily similar to Christoff's, though much more refined.

Definitely not the Englishman, I decided. Which meant I was wasting time. "Listen," I said, "I can't talk right now—"

"Yes, I'm sure you're busy. Trying to save someone's life, am I right?"

I froze, my finger hovering over the End Call button. "Wait, how d'ye know that?" I asked, finally.

"Someone," she replied, "and I suspect it's not you or you wouldn't be answering this phone, tried to open the briefcase. Correct?"

I hesitated.

"I thought so," she said. "Who do you work for? Tell me, and I'll tell you how to save your friend."

"I don't work for anyone," I growled, too proud to let her insinuate otherwise. I'd worked too hard to get where I was to let anyone else take the credit, even if that meant admitting to a crime.

"Ah, a freelancer. You must be very good. I didn't think anyone would be able to survive the ward, not to mention unshackle Serge and make off with the briefcase."

"Wait, are ye sayin' ye were the one who attached the briefcase to that t'ing?" I asked.

"It's the only way to keep his kind in line, trust me."

"Well, it didn't work. He tried to kill me in a park, full of kids."

"Well, yes, once you let him off his leash. But I'll admit that is…unfortunate. I would have heard, though, if a werewolf had gone on a killing spree?" she left the question open-ended, as if giving me an opportunity to elaborate on what had happened.

I crossed over to Jimmy and felt for his pulse. It was harried, but he seemed to have stopped sweating. I wasn't sure if that was good or bad. "That t'ing wasn't a werewolf," I said, choosing to keep her in the dark; if she didn't know what happened to her pet skinwalker, I wasn't about to fill her in.

"No, it wasn't," the woman admitted, sounding surprised that I could distinguish one from the other. "Moonwalkers, skinwalkers…there's a difference, but not much of one in Serge's case. Anyway, if you won't tell me what happened at the park, you can at least tell me if the sweating has stopped."

"I swear I'm goin' to—"

"Please, threats aren't necessary. Your friend needs to get warm and hydrate, that's all. The ward was never designed to kill. Think of it more as a deterrent against theft. Like an alarm retailers attach to clothes, only with a little extra juice. You're a businesswoman, right? An independent contractor? Name your price. I'm sure we can afford to match whatever you were promised."

I pinned the phone to my shoulder, hooked my arms under Jimmy's armpits from behind, and half-slid, half-dragged him towards the bathroom. I twisted the bathtub's handle, cupped water in my hand, and poured it liberally down Jimmy's throat while I waited for it to get warm.

"So, how much?" the woman asked, clearly impatient.

"Listen," I said, too exhausted to lie, although part of me was curious how big a number I could throw out there, "I didn't want to steal your damn briefcase. To be honest, I don't even know who ye are or who this briefcase belongs to."

"Check the case," she said.

"What?"

"When the ward was activated, our name should have appeared on the side. That way, if we did not find you, you'd find us."

Jimmy groaned, sounding absolutely pitiful.

"I'll call ye back," I snapped, then hung up. "I'll be right back, Jimmy."

Hold on." I scrambled to my feet, almost slipping on the bathroom tiles as I ran back into the living room. The briefcase lay inexplicably upright against the wall where I'd kicked it, a series of letters emblazoned in thick, bold, black letters on the side.

GrimmTech.

What the fuck kind of name was GrimmTech?

CHAPTER 25

J'd gotten Jimmy in the shower, fully-clothed, and was gingerly feeding him water when my phone rang again. "Hello?" I answered. After hoisting Jimmy's body into the tub, it hurt to even hold up the phone; the muscles in my arms were a tight, knotted mess. Less cardio, more weights, I decided.

Starting next week.

"You were supposed to call me back," the woman said, sarcastically.

"I've been busy," I snapped.

"Oh, I know. I've been monitoring your online activity. So, you know who we are, now, and you know we can afford to negotiate. How much? And, do me a favor, don't up the price needlessly just because I'm asking politely. I won't waste my time negotiating."

"How do ye know I looked ye up?" I asked, baffled.

It was true, I had Googled the company almost as soon as I'd seen the name emblazoned on briefcase, scouring the internet for any and all information regarding GrimmTech. I found out it was a German-based company owned by a former CEO of a Fortune 500 company, though it had taken me a while to discover even that much; while the company was publicly traded, nothing about what they made, or what service they provided, was readily available. Of course, it didn't help that most the articles I'd found were in German, which I definitely couldn't read.

"I know what you searched the same way I know your phone number, Quinn MacKenna," the woman responded, sounding amused.

Damn, she knew my name, after all. I'd figured as much when she called, but held on to the momentary hope that it had something to do with the magic briefcase, and not caller ID. Still, that didn't change things. "I can't give ye the briefcase back," I confessed. "I'm sorry."

"What?" she asked, no longer sounding remotely amused. Part of me felt compelled to lie and tell her what she wanted to hear, to negotiate a deal that would get her off my back long enough to save Dez. But something about how she'd handled things thus far—telling me how to help Jimmy, offering to buy the case back, seeming genuinely startled by the idea that children might have been hurt at the park—made me want to trust her.

That, or I was simply desperate.

"The man who sent me to steal the briefcase has someone I care about. It's not about money," I explained, opting for the truth.

"I...see." The woman paused, and I could hear her clacking away at a keyboard, probably verifying that I even had an aunt to begin with. "Well, this is complicated."

"That's an understatement."

"Indeed. Tell you what, I'll send someone," she said.

"Send someone?"

"To retrieve the briefcase. To help." She paused and then rattled off my address. I paled considerably. "You should expect him tomorrow," she added.

"What if whoever ye send comes too late?" I asked, trying to keep my voice steady. "I can't afford to wait."

"Then you'll have to explain to him what happened, and hope he doesn't think you're to blame."

Oh, sure, because that sounded like a fair trial waiting to happen. I monitored Jimmy's forehead, glad to see some of his color had returned. "Why aren't ye comin', yourself?" I asked.

"I'm busy, or I would."

"Busy with what?"

"Getting ordained. Sort of."

Naturally. I cursed and checked my own forehead to be sure I wasn't sick, too. This could all be a delirious fever dream, after all. Maybe I was really having a stroke in a parking lot somewhere and this was all part of my twisted imagination?

I sighed.

If only.

"Can ye at least tell me what's in the case?" I asked. "How do I open it?"

"You don't. What's inside is dangerous, that's all you need to know. Don't mess with it. I'll be in touch."

"And who are ye?"

"Call me Othello."

"Really? As in Shakespeare?" I asked, wondering if she knew how unfortunate it was that she went by that name; Othello and Desdemona's story didn't exactly work out for anyone involved.

Spoiler alert.

Othello chuckled. "Something like that."

Then she hung up.

CHAPTER 26

*J*immy tried to speak, but ended up coughing instead. I offered him a cup of water, which he guzzled down before falling back into the mound of pillows I'd piled against the headboard. He looked better, at least, although it had been touch-and-go there for a little while.

"Quinn..." Jimmy croaked, his voice hoarse.

"Ye scared me half to death, ye know," I said.

"Glad I wasn't the only one dying," Jimmy joked, eyes closed.

I socked him in the arm.

"What the hell?!" Jimmy exclaimed, his eyes shooting open in surprise.

"The next time I tell ye not to touch somethin', what are ye goin' to do?"

He grunted. "Do you want me to be honest?"

I pulled back to sock him again.

"Kidding, kidding!" he yelled, holding his hands up in surrender. "Next time I'll listen, I promise." Jimmy's shoulders fell, and his hands drooped to his lap. "I wanted to help, that's all. I don't know what it is, but whenever I end up around you I feel so useless, and I hate it." He closed his eyes. "Feels like I left one war and walked right into another, sometimes. Except no one but you sees it. How is that possible?"

"How do Regulars not notice what's happenin' around 'em, ye mean?" I asked.

Jimmy nodded.

"They notice," I declared, after a moment's hesitation. "They aren't blind. But what else can they do? Once ye admit the monsters are real, what then?"

"So we just keep on pretending like nothing's happening, is that it?" Jimmy asked.

"The world is an imperfect place, Jimmy Collins," I said. "If this is the first your hearin' about it, ye should probably be in a different line of work."

Jimmy grunted. "You should work on your bedside manner."

"Oh, is that right?" I asked, leaning forward suggestively. "Would ye rather I kissed it and made it better?" I joked.

Jimmy cocked an eyebrow, then seemed to take stock of where he was for the first time. "Say, Quinn…"

"You're wonderin' how I got ye into bed?" I asked, anticipating his next question. "It wasn't easy, I can tell ye that. You're a right heavy fucker, Jimmy. Good t'ing I'm so strong, or you'd still be moanin' on the floor for ye ma."

The truth, of course, was that every muscle in my body was screaming, soundlessly, after carrying him from the bathroom to my bedroom; I'd made an appointment with a massage therapist for next week while he slept. I called the Englishman, too, leaving a voicemail confirming that I'd gotten ahold of his merchandise and was ready to make a trade.

It wasn't that I didn't trust Othello or want her help, but I wasn't about to let Dez stay a captive any longer than I had to. I was playing a dangerous game, and I knew it. But—between Othello's creepy access to all things Quinn MacKenna and the kidnapper's easy access to my aunt's unprotected throat—I didn't have the leverage I needed to do much else.

"Actually," Jimmy said, bringing me back to the moment at hand, "I was wondering why I'm naked."

Oh, right. That.

"Well," I said as I studied the ceiling, my cheeks burning, "ye started shiverin' after I got ye out of the shower, so I thought it best to get your clothes off and put 'em in the dryer. That, and I didn't want ye getting' me bed wet."

"Ah," Jimmy said, sitting up a little, the blankets I'd pinned beneath his armpits sliding down to rest in a pool around his hips.

Not that I noticed, of course, because I was still admiring the ceiling.

The plain, white, boring ceiling.

Jimmy took my hand and held it against his chest, which I realized was lightly coated in tight, curling hair. "You saved my life."

"Ye wouldn't have needed savin' if I hadn't called ye in the first place," I replied. I hated to admit it, but the truth was he'd probably be safe and sound in bed right now if it weren't for me. What's worse was the fact that a very selfish part of me was damn glad he wasn't, even if it had nearly cost him his life.

"Still, you saved me…".

I shrugged, deciding not to argue.

"And all so you could see me naked, huh?" Jimmy teased.

I tried to punch him again, except this time he dodged, laughing, the blankets falling away altogether as he rolled off the bed.

I forgot all about the ceiling.

"Well," I said, "it looks like you're feelin' better."

Jimmy glanced down at himself. "Could probably use a test drive, just to be sure."

"Oh, so you're a car, then?"

Jimmy shrugged and chuckled, the sound deep, masculine…and not too different from the purr of an engine. Did I mention how I felt about driving a well-muscled vehicle?

Yeah, that.

CHAPTER 27

*N*either of us bothered with the lights. The streetlamps cast a warm, honey glow over the room and over Jimmy, whose skin was usually a shade shy of obsidian. I hadn't quite realized how in shape he was until I'd had to undress him and tuck him into bed; Jimmy was one of those men who, because of their broad shoulders and sweeping thighs, loomed large in a suit, but who actually had a small, trim waistline. Part of me wished he'd been a little less fit; I didn't know how to stop from staring.

Fortunately, Jimmy had a solution.

He slid his hands up the slope of my neck, his thumbs just below my jaw, and pulled me in for a kiss. I let him. It felt good, being drawn upwards for once, my hands resting on the muscles of his chest and shoulder.

Jimmy's hands wandered, working their way up at first, fingers massaging little circles into my back, then back down, hands cupping my ass and raising me up into a deeper, fiercer kiss. It suddenly became very obvious that I was clothed, and he wasn't.

Turned out he had a solution for that, too.

My blouse came off first, then my bra. Jimmy laid both reverently down on the bed, never taking his eyes off mine, not even as he pried loose the button of my jeans. I felt a smooth palm glide down my abdomen and his fingers massage as he explored. I moaned, breathily.

It registered, faintly, that it had been a while since I'd been with anyone;

meeting the right guy was hard, especially since most of the men I knew weren't even human. Besides, I was picky and, after my last abusive relationship, hesitant to let anyone get too close to me—it's hard finding a man who can put you up against a wall the *right* way, after all.

It didn't help that I'd always been attracted to the rough, hyper-masculine types, and that, consequently, for a long time I'd confused violence with foreplay. These days I knew better; I wanted a man who understood that being an alpha male meant shutting up the other mutts, not barking loudest.

Thank God our tastes change.

After all, I hadn't always been attracted to Jimmy. Back in high school, he'd been a quiet kid, a looming, gangly giant roaming the halls on his way to and from classes neither of us cared much about. The only reason we got to know each other at all was because I got in so many fights that Dez had insisted I be escorted to and from school. She'd arranged it so, Jimmy—our neighbor from two blocks down—basically became my shadow. Now, even so many years later, I could admit that being around him still made me feel indescribably safe.

I reached out, squeezing my nails into his flesh. The muscles of his forearm were so firm I could feel them rolling beneath my palm as his fingers flexed and contracted.

"Not fair," I said.

In answer, he turned my head with his free hand and ground his mouth against my throat, licking and nibbling inches above my quickening pulse in time to the play of his fingers. Through the haze, I saw that I had a chance to turn the tables. I ground my body against his and felt his back arch, immediately distracted.

Men were so easy.

I ran my nails, ever so lightly, over his skin. He took a deep breath and then, without warning, dropped to his knees, taking my jeans with him. He tried to peel them all the way off, but couldn't seem to get them off my ankles. I laughed and obliged, lifting one leg and then the other. He grinned, staring up at me, but then his expression changed.

His eyes slowly tracked the scars I'd accumulated over the years: the surgical scar on the knee I'd shattered, the calcifications on my thighs from years of practice kicks, the stab wound on my stomach from the bastard I'd had no business dating, and the small mound of scar tissue above my left hip that I never talked about. He took stock of these and more, and then rose, the front of his body trailing against mine, and drew me to the bed as he swept the pillows from the headboard.

I thought about protesting on their behalf, but it turned out we wouldn't need them for quite a while, anyway.

I lay in the dark, weighing my options. Jimmy was fast asleep beside me, smothered in blankets, kicking off heat like a radiator. I hadn't been able to do the same, too busy replaying the events of the last few days, trying and failing to make sense of it all.

Mike and his band had reached out to me via e-mail a few days back, which came as a bit of a surprise; vampires weren't notoriously tech-savvy —still reeling from the idea of horseless carriages, I guess. They claimed they'd gotten the ring from a Turkish peddler they met on tour, and had heard about frozen blood crystals from a nightclub owner in London who insisted they try it.

Of course, I knew now that they'd planned to skip town without paying. I could only assume they'd had the same idea when they promised to make a deal with the Englishman. That's how it went in my world, though; Freaks got cocky.

Thing is, there's always a bigger Kraken.

Still, knowing all that wasn't getting me anywhere. Nothing about the way things stood made sense. What did the kidnapper want with a briefcase that belonged to a billion-dollar company based out of Germany? What was in the case that was so valuable, and so dangerous, that it needed to be protected with magic and strapped to a nightmarish shapeshifter?

I drifted, tossing and turning every few minutes, unable to get comfortable knowing my aunt was out there, right at that moment, being held against her will. Eventually, exhausted and frustrated, I sidled up next to Jimmy, burrowed my head in the slow curve of his neck, and went to sleep.

CHAPTER 28

*S*neaking out the following morning proved easier than I'd expected; Jimmy was a heavy sleeper, and a bit of a snorer. Although—given the fact that he'd recently survived a magical curse, not to mention how much energy we'd exerted the night before—maybe he was simply too exhausted to rouse himself. Whichever the reason, I was glad for it.

I didn't want him getting involved.

No matter how good his intentions were, Jimmy was still a Regular. What he'd done the day before—grabbing the briefcase because he didn't believe me—was a prime example of that. At first, I'd seriously considered letting him help; Jimmy was trained, strong, and solid backup...if I were going after your average, everyday criminal. But I honestly had no idea who or what I was up against, and the fact that Jimmy was a Regular who could throw down with the best of them only made things worse; in a dangerous situation, he'd do what he'd been trained to do: fight. Except he wouldn't be taking on meth heads or drug dealers, he'd be up against nightmarish creatures, or worse—men and women who looked normal, but could kill you in ways only nightmares could account for.

I'd seen it happen before.

During the Lollipop case, I'd seen a beat cop—a bald, bulky veteran—put six rounds into his target, center mass. It should have been enough to stop practically anyone, but it hadn't. The woman, a zombie so recently deceased that her make-up gave her cheeks a rosy sheen, had kept right on walking. The cop's screams still woke me up some nights.

In the end, I left Jimmy sleeping in my bed because I knew I'd end up babysitting him—whether he wanted me to, or not—and I didn't have that kind of time. Or patience.

A pissed-off Jimmy I could handle.

A dead and dismembered Jimmy, not so much.

I stood outside Christoff's pop-up bar forty-five minutes later, dancing in place a little to stave off the cold. Ryan had called the night before and left me a voicemail telling me to come see him as soon as I could, making it sound urgent. Fortunately, I'd planned to do that anyway, now that I had the briefcase; I couldn't get it open, but maybe Ryan could.

Hank—the grouchy bouncer from before—answered the door, the handle of a mop slung over one shoulder. He'd shaved, which made him look younger, but also less homeless. I eyed him, warily, wondering if he was going to give me any trouble.

"You could have just told me, you know," he said, holding the door open.

"Told ye what?" I asked, passing by him.

"That you were dating Ryan. I wouldn't have been such a jerk if I'd known. I thought you were one of those girls who think they can get whatever they want because they're pretty." He blushed. "I mean, well, you know what I mean."

"I—" I began.

"Quinn!" Christoff yelled from the top of the stairs, his upper body halfway out the doorway to the office. "You have to convince Ryan to stay. I do not know how I can replace him. And so soon! He will listen to you."

"What—"

"That's enough, Christoff," Ryan said, entering from the back with a case of beer. He gestured Hank over, who simply shrugged at me and took the case from him. Ryan brushed dust off his slacks and waved at me to follow. "Come on back. We'll talk."

Hank flashed us a knowing smile. "Have fun, you two."

Yeah, I *so* wasn't about to let that rumor circulate.

"You," I barked, pointing at Hank, "I am not datin' Ryan, and wipe that smirk off your face before I deck ye." Hank's eyes widened, but at least he wasn't smiling anymore. I whirled, glaring first at Christoff, then at Ryan. "Ye see, this is the first I'm hearin' about Ryan goin' anywhere. Which is why he and I are goin' to have a private conversation where no one can hear me yell at him. Isn't that right, Ryan?"

Ryan coughed and shifted his attention to Christoff. "If I don't make it back, it's because Quinn MacKenna murdered me. Make sure I get justice."

"Of course," Christoff said, sagely. "You will have nice funeral, and no one will ever find body."

Ryan blinked. Christoff smiled, held out his hands, and shrugged as if to say, "What else can I do?" I winked at the old man as I followed Ryan out back. He mimed catching it and putting it in the pocket of his vest.

And they say chivalry is dead.

CHAPTER 29

*T*he warehouse door creaked open, and Dobby poked his enormous head out, blinking away the morning light. He saw us approaching and started to perform some motion with his arm, but Ryan ushered him inside before he could finish.

"Ryan?" I asked.

"What?"

"Why is Dobby salutin' like a Nazi?"

Ryan sighed. "Hitler documentary. Christoff insisted. I've tried to explain it to him, but the more I talk about why it's offensive, the more he does it. It's like trying to reason with a child."

"Dobby," I called out, "when ye greet people, I want ye to wave like this from now on, alright?" I asked, waving my hand like a beauty pageant contestant.

"Yes, my lady," Dobby replied, mimicking my gesture as he hopped up on the lip of a liquor cabinet.

Ryan glared at me.

"What can I say? It's me maternal instinct kickin' in," I said, struggling to keep a straight face.

"Her sisters are looking for you," Dobby sung, kicking his legs back and forth, staring off into nothing.

Ryan waved away my baffled expression. "He does that. Listen, Quinn, we need to talk."

"You're leavin', is that it?" I asked, trying not to sound too disappointed. It wasn't like Ryan and I were particularly close, but he'd proven himself dependable more than once, and I'd miss having him around for the occasional brunch—even if it meant dodging dirty looks. That, and as one of the very few members of the Chancery I had any contact with, he was still the best shot I had at getting into Fae, no matter how reticent he'd been in the past.

"I don't have a choice," he replied, finally.

"And why not?"

Ryan wouldn't meet my eyes. "It's not important."

I scowled at him. "What d'ye mean it's not important? Ye tell me right now, Ryan O'Rye, or I'll knock ye senseless right here and ye won't be goin' anywhere," I threatened.

"Quinn, I want you to listen to me." Ryan put his hand on my shoulder, knowing how I felt about my personal space, which meant he was willing to risk losing his hand to say whatever it was he had to say. "Save Dez. Do what you have to do. But then get out of this city and find a different gig. A *Regular* job."

"And why's that, then?" I asked.

"There's a lot I can't risk telling you, but you should know that things are changing here in Boston. The Chancery isn't what it once was. Between that, and a friend I trust telling me that the Chancery has been keeping tabs on you lately…" he drifted off, shaking his head.

"What would they be wantin' from me?" I asked, perplexed.

Ryan gave me the look you normally reserve for a child, like I was being exceptionally obtuse. "With what you do? Why wouldn't they be interested in you?"

I frowned, my brows kitting together. "But why? Isn't the Chancery powerful enough without me help?"

"In theory, sure. But that's assuming everyone in the Chancery has the same agenda, which they don't. In their minds, whichever side claims you will have an advantage. And you don't want to get pulled in more than one direction, Quinn, trust me." Ryan dropped his hand from my shoulder.

"Ryan, ye know how me business works," I said, folding my arms over my chest. "I don't choose sides. Although, if I'm bein' honest, I'd make a killin' off a turf war." I would, too; whenever two groups got pissed off at each other to the point that they needed arming, business boomed.

No pun intended.

"I'm not telling you what to do, Quinn. This is simply friendly advice. If they come after you, looking to recruit, you need to be prepared. I won't be here to warn you. I've been...called back."

"Wait, ye mean you're goin' home?" I asked, taken aback.

Ryan nodded, seeming tired, deflated somehow. "In a manner of speaking."

"Alright, now you're bein' vague on purpose," I admonished.

That earned me a small smile. "I wish I could say more, but if I tell you anything else you could end up being targeted by the Chancery, which is exactly what I'm hoping to avoid."

"Why? What do they have to do with it?"

"They don't know I'm being called back. It's rare for one of us to go home, especially one of the exiled. They'll want to know how I did it, and why. And, if they don't like the answer, they might react...poorly."

I'd always known to avoid the Chancery, even without Ryan's advice, but I had to admit his take on their politics and reactions didn't bode well. If anything, they sounded like some horrific bureaucracy, concerned more about what its members were up to than protecting them from the outside world.

Like church, without the promise of an afterlife.

"Fine, then," I replied, finally. "But can ye at least tell me why ye don't seem glad to be goin' home?" I asked, voicing the question which had really been bothering me from the start. I mean, Ryan was always careful not to romanticize the Fae world around me, considering how badly I already wanted go, but that didn't stop him from talking about it with a wistful gleam in his eye. "Aren't ye glad to be seein' your pa, at least?"

"My father's dead," Ryan snarled.

I was too stunned to speak, both by what he'd said and how he'd said it; Ryan had never snapped at me before.

He took a deep, calming breath. "There was a...battle. Or something. I don't know all the details, yet. All I know is there were a lot of casualties. My father got caught in the crossfire."

"So are ye goin' home for his funeral, then?" I asked, gently.

Ryan's jaw clenched. "No, I'm going to take his place." Ryan studied his hands before speaking again. "We all have to put in our time, remember? I still owe."

"How long?"

"Thirty-four years."

Thirty-four years...meaning I'd be an old woman by the time he returned, assuming he did. Of course, with the time differences between the mortal and Fae realm, who knew how long that could end up being? Which meant Ryan wasn't saying goodbye for now...he was saying goodbye forever.

During the ensuing silence, Dobby slid to the ground, ambled over to Ryan, and took his hand. Ryan squeezed, then withdrew from the spriggan's grasp. "My ride should be coming for me any time now. Promise me you'll keep an eye out, Quinn? There are so many believers in this city...the walls here are thinner than they should be, and the cracks are wider."

I cracked a smile and ruffled his hair. "I promise I won't fall through any cracks, if ye promise me ye won't go and get yourself in trouble again."

Ryan flashed me a wry smile, which I mimicked.

Because saying goodbye through a fake smile is easier, I think.

CHAPTER 30

$\mathcal{R}$yan escorted me back to the door, but before we got there, I realized we still had to deal with the elephant in the room. Or the spriggan, as it were. "Wait, what about Dobby? Is he comin' with ye, or stayin' here?"

Dobby had disappeared behind a crate a moment ago, although that didn't necessarily mean he wasn't nearby, listening in. I was going to have to put a bell on him if he planned to stay. Probably something with his name and address on it, too, just in case he wandered off.

Like a collar.

"Oh, right," Ryan groaned, as if he'd flat out forgotten. "Look, I asked if he wanted to come with me, but he turned me down. Said he had unfinished business here, not that he would tell me what that even meant. But would it be possible for you to keep an eye on him?"

I sighed. The selfish part of me that refused to get a pet no matter how empty my apartment seemed sometimes was extremely against the idea. I preferred not to have to answer to or take care of anyone, if I could help it. But one look at Ryan's face told me he'd needed the reassurance. In a messed-up way, he was asking me to look after the stray he'd found wandering the street.

"Fine," I replied. "But he isn't movin' in with me."

"Oh, no. Christoff promised he could stay here as long as he didn't cause any trouble. He even promised to lock the warehouse up at night. But I didn't want to ask too much of him. He'll have a hard enough time finding another bar manager on such short notice."

"Maybe," I said, "but at least he'll finally end up with someone who knows how to make a decent drink."

Ryan's mouth puckered.

"*B*efore ye go," I said, remembering why I'd come here in the first place, "can ye take a look at this and tell me what ye t'ink?" I'd slid the briefcase out of the satchel I'd been carrying it in, filling him in on what happened to Jimmy when he'd touched it.

Ryan had the good sense not to do the same.

"So a Russian woman who works for a company called GrimmTech called you and told you someone would be coming to help rescue your aunt? And you believe her?" Ryan asked dubiously, after I was finished.

"She didn't give me much choice," I admitted. "I mean, she knows where I live, and I'm not about to move. If she wanted to come after me directly, she could. Besides, I trust her, though I can't tell ye why, exactly."

Ryan shrugged. "Well, I'll admit I hate that you have to do this alone. But at least it's a wizard you'll be up against, which shouldn't be too tough, for you."

"A wizard?" I asked, baffled. "How d'ye figure that?"

Ryan double-checked to make sure I was serious. "It's like I told you at the park, remember? Only a wizard could take off that manacle without getting hit with the curse on it," Ryan gauged my expression and rubbed the bridge of his nose. "You weren't listening."

"I was a little busy," I argued, defensively.

"Alright, the way I see it, whoever this guy is, he figured he could get the briefcase off the skinwalker and make his escape. Only wizards are that cocky." Ryan held up a finger. "But, since his magic won't work on you, you'll have the advantage."

Ryan was probably right, although I didn't have a whole lot of evidence to support that theory; my experience with wizards was pretty much limited to the one I'd met on the Lollipop case. Fortunately, he'd been the scholarly type, eager to answer any of my questions.

I'll admit, I'd been very disappointed to learn that wizards didn't use wands or cast spells—they had a school, but it didn't sound nearly as cool as the death trap that was Hogwarts. Apparently, being a wizard in real life meant having the ability to control things, like the elements or physics or whatever. Which basically made them God-damned Airbenders. Airbenders who didn't even age like the rest of us.

Vampires. Wizards.

Cockroaches, the lot of them.

"Well," I said, finally, "I hate to admit it, but I'm twice as sorry to see ye go, now."

"Huh? Why?"

"I didn't realize ye had a brain in that head of yours. Ye took so long to say anythin' worth listenin' to that I assumed ye had nothin' but that pretty face to offer," I teased.

"The body isn't half bad either," he added, snidely. "Come on, I'll walk you out."

"Will it be dangerous?" I asked, trailing behind. "Back home, I mean?"

"Maybe," Ryan replied. "It all boils down to power, in Fae. Who can you control? What can you take? Anything you can't control or take, you kill. Or you serve. I'm not exactly a powerhouse, so I'll be serving. But my master is one of the most powerful in Fae, which means I'll be safer than most. Of course, my father probably thought the same thing…"

"I'm sorry, Ryan," I said, realizing I'd yet to express my condolences, doing my best to sound like I meant it.

Still, it was hard to empathize; I'd never had a father, after all—I didn't even know his name. Dez swore up and down that my mother had kept his identity a secret, even from her, which I found hard to believe even as a child. During my bratty teens, I convinced myself that my mother had probably slept around, and Dez had lied to me to keep me from thinking badly of her.

Later, however, Dez confessed that my mother's secret had caused genuine friction in their friendship; she'd considered walking away altogether, maybe even returning home, but then my mother died giving birth to me, and she'd never looked back.

It had been tough growing up, knowing that my father might be out there somewhere, and that I might have known him if only my mother had confided in her closest friend. But then, in some ways, it felt better to think my father was alive somewhere, and that he hadn't abandoned me—that maybe he'd never known about me in the first place.

Or at least that's what I told myself.

Deep down, I could admit that I desperately wanted to find him, alive or dead. Which is where my fascination in the Fae realm had started, and—ultimately—what had led me to Ryan and his kind. I never told Ryan this, but I had a sneaking suspicion I was, in fact, part-Fae.

I couldn't explain why, except to point out the fact that I'd been born with this inexplicable ability to nullify all kinds of magic. Freaks like me cropped up from time to time, sure—people born with abilities out of the blue—but how many of them lived in Boston, home to the Chancery and its people? How many of them had a mysterious parent they'd never met? It all seemed like a coincidence I couldn't ignore.

"I appreciate it," Ryan said. "Anyway, I should get back inside before Christoff thinks you killed me—" Ryan began.

A peal of thunder interrupted him, so close we ducked for cover instinctually. Winds whipped, the chilly air becoming even more frigid, the clouds above us roiling, the sky tinted green—as if a tornado were moments from touching down. A wail, like the piteous scream of some dying creature, tore through the air.

"Damn," Ryan said. "My ride's here."

And that's when the headless horseman showed up.

CHAPTER 31

*T*he sound of hoofbeats on stone brought us both around and, in a burst of lightning, a headless rider appeared, tearing down the alleyway on horseback, skidding to a stop only several yards away. "Oh. How touching," the rider called out.

I realized Ryan and I had clutched at each other instinctively after the blast of thunder and released him, stepping away, moments from saying something snippety when I noticed the rider had a woman's head cradled in the nook of the creature's arm, right beside a rather unmistakable pair of breasts.

Horsewoman. Headless horsewoman.

Yay, equality.

"Damn, I was hoping I'd have more time," Ryan said, under his breath. "Play along, be polite, and keep quiet."

"Have ye met me?" I asked, my voice a hushed whisper. "Who is she, anyway?"

"She's one of the Dullahan. A headless rider."

"A Chancery member, then?"

Ryan scoffed. "Not even close. The Chancery would never let one of the Dullahan put down roots in Boston—too powerful, and too unpredictable. Anyway, try not to draw her attention. She's by far the most mild-mannered of her kind I've ever met, but that doesn't mean it's safe. Oh, and whatever you do, don't give her your number."

"Why would I—"

"Cassandra," Ryan interrupted, speaking over me. "It's been a while."

"And you, Riann O'Rye."

"They say it Ryan, these days."

"Psh, who can keep up with the way Manlings talk?" Cassandra scoffed. "Everything they have to say is nonsense, anyway."

"Cassandra here is in charge of media relations," Ryan remarked, bringing me into the conversation. "She keeps track of traffic—how often we're mentioned, what is said about us, that sort of thing."

A media specialist? I had no idea the Fae cared what we said about them, much less kept track of it. I could only imagine the headache involved in weeding through social media posts day after day. "That sounds... exhaustin'," I admitted.

"Ah! An Irish girl, that explains it," Cassandra said, leaning forward onto the pommel of her horse's saddle. "I wondered why Riann was dallying with a human, even one as gorgeous as you are. Are you two together? Like, officially?" Cassandra winked at me, squeezing her head against her chest in a way that might have been suggestive it wasn't so completely off-putting.

That said, I had to admit she was attractive, in a headless sort of way, with bright blue eyes and hair the same inky shade of black as her horse—a massive stallion which neighed in greeting before pawing at the pavement with one of its hooves, sending sparks flying.

"She's a friend," Ryan said. "That's all."

"Oh, well then...good to know. But yes, to your point, my job can be exceedingly dull," Cassandra confirmed. "I thought it was going to be a cushy gig, at first, back when all you Manlings had was word of mouth—you had nothing interesting to talk about back then, either, but at least you weren't so pretentious about it. Then along came the printing press and Shakespeare—the most annoying brat I ever met in my life—and now you have the internet and you use it to watch live video feeds of grass growing and Loch Ness in hopes of seeing Nessie—as if she would ever set flippers back in that lake after what you all put her through with your cameras and your tourism."

I gaped at the horsewoman; she hadn't taken a single breath during that whole tirade. In fact, she'd said it all so fast that I'd missed part of it.

"Don't let Cassandra fool you," Ryan said, turning to me, "she really does love her job, or she wouldn't keep doing it. They've tried to bring in other people—"

"They've tried to fire me! As if anyone else could do what I do. Do you know what most Fae think when they hear the word 'Manling'?" Cassandra asked me.

I shook my head.

"The same thing you think when I say 'monster,'" she explained. "But at least you lot have a basic understanding of the do's and don't's. See a faerie? Be careful what you wish for. Turn your clothes inside out. Iron, lots of iron."

"Gold," Ryan added.

Cassandra shot Ryan a glare. "Hush, Riann. The women are talking," Cassandra said. "Anyway, as I was saying, at least you all get things right from time to time, even if you don't always believe. But our lot? Most are convinced you're all sadists and slavers, metal-worshippers with all your skyscrapers and flying machines and such."

"It's true," Ryan interjected, ignoring Cassandra's withering stare. "When I first got here, I was terrified. We're told so many horror stories about Manlings when we grow up that few ever cross over."

"Well, that was the case," Cassandra added, "until several months ago. Now we have invaders and war on our hands and Fae jumping ship left and right. It's gotten so bad we've had to call some of our people back. Like Riann, here. Although, to be honest, I never thought they'd send me to collect him—when King Oberon banishes you, it rarely comes with an expiration date."

"Ye were banished by a king? For what?" I asked, immediately intrigued.

"It's a long story," Ryan said, this time glaring at Cassandra, who had turned her head around in her hands to look away.

It wasn't exactly subtle.

"Anyway—" Ryan began.

"It's really not that long, if you tell it right," Cassandra interrupted. "And I've had a day. I could use a laugh."

"A laugh?" Ryan asked, arching an eyebrow.

"Yes. It's a funny story," Cassandra said.

"The story where I get exiled from my home, and never get to see my family again?"

"Well, I didn't say it was a funny story for you to tell..." Cassandra admitted.

Ryan sighed. "Fine." And then he told us a fairy tale, "Once upon a time..."

CHAPTER 32

*O*nce upon a time…in another plane of existence, where time is measured not in minutes or hours, but in seasons…there was a child born into a prestigious noble family which had loyally served the Summer Court since before the Old Gods stepped away from the world of Man to build their own realms.

The boy was bright, beautiful, and fair. He had an infectious laugh, and everyone—even the Unseelie, who tend to destroy cute things on principle —loved him. This, more than anything, made the boy the perfect candidate to become a changeling—a child sent out into the world of Man to replace a Manling of similar appearance and age.

The principle behind the changeling raids, as they would later be known, was to raise the stolen Manling child among the Fae. Once it was old enough, the Manling would be sent back with stories to tell—fantastical, unbelievable stories. Some of these men and women you have heard of, I'm sure. The stories they told have become legends, steeped in fiction, but containing very real truths. Tales like those of King Arthur and his Round Table, Alice in a Wonderland through a Looking Glass, Peter Pan and his Lost Boys.

In a way, the raids were a bridge, allowing Manlings and Fae to glimpse each other's worlds without wanting to conquer them. The two races viewed each other with both fear and fascination. But, over time, things began to change. The Manlings closed themselves off, embracing their fear and rejecting wonderment. The raids slowed, and soon only the bravest, or stupidest, Fae were tasked with switching out a child.

But, with a boy like this one, even an inexperienced raider could perform the swap. With a Fae child like him, you could take any baby in the world from its mother and she'd never even bat an eye—she might even thank you.

Enter Riann O'Rye, the black sheep of the O'Rye family and house servant of Oberon, King of the Faeries.

Like many spoiled youths, Riann was tired of being treated like a child, and felt he was meant for bigger and better things. So, when he heard about this child, he came up with a plan—a way to improve his stock. Well, not a plan, per se. More like an idea.

A monumentally stupid idea.

Riann bribed the raider responsible for taking the child into the Manling realm, then did just that. Of course, having never been there before, Riann found plenty to distract him from his original mission.

Riann witnessed many wonders on their journey: Roman roads and Byzantine cathedrals and Italian bathhouses. He saw other things, too, of course: cruelty and savagery and sorrow. But, with the growing, precocious child as his companion, he found plenty to keep him happy.

In fact, over time, Riann realized that the child had become precious to him. That he didn't want to part with him, even though it was the duty he'd signed up for. So, in the end, he took the boy aside, not far from their intended destination.

Riann confessed his plan, and his reasons, to the boy. He asked that he be forgiven and insisted they return home. But the child, having also experienced the wonders of the Manling's strange world, refused to return.

"Are you sure?" Riann asked. "If the Manlings ever discover what you are, you could be killed. And do not forget that they are cruel, even to their own."

The boy merely smiled. "I know. But still, I pity them. Their lives are so short, and they burn through them so quickly...and yet so many live in darkness. So many die cold and alone."

"Then why stay?" Riann asked.

"I will become their sun," he replied.

Riann followed through with his plan after that, though his heart was not in it; he used his illusions to steal away the Manling child, leaving the boy he'd grown to love behind. When he finally returned to Fae, he did so with a heavy-heart and a dim-witted Manling child in tow.

The child would grow old in Fae, unbeknownst to Riann—far older than most who were taken during the raids. And this because the Fae child Riann loosed upon the world refused to return and fulfill his side of the covenant.

By the time the Manling finally was reunited with his own kind, decades had passed, and he was in ill-health. Despite that, he died a rich and powerful man, surrounded by material comforts and strangers who called him many names, although one was repeated more frequently than any other.

Charlemagne.

I raised a hand to interrupt Ryan's story, scouring my memory for who Charlemagne was. The name rung a bell, but history was never my strong point; that's what libraries were for.

Unless they made a movie.

I watched a lot of movies.

"Charlemagne," Ryan explained, exasperated, "was a Frankish king and general during the Middle Ages who pretty much single-handedly unified western and central Europe."

"Oh, right," I said, as if I'd known that all along. "Anyway, ye were sayin'…"

Ryan shook his head. "Anyway, many years before…"

Many years before the man known as Charlemagne passed away, Riann returned home. Riann's exploits became legendary as word spread that he'd managed to steal a royal child from the Manling realm. Some, of course, were angry. King Oberon, who felt slighted for not being informed of Riann's plan from the beginning, was one. But, given Riann's popularity, he had no choice but to promote the young Fae to the honorable palace guard alongside his father - to serve the traditional hundred-year term.

Eventually, decades passed, and the whole affair was gradually forgotten about. The Manling was shipped off to be paraded about in the Summer

Court, and no one but Riann thought about the Fae child he'd left behind. But, gradually, the nature of the Fae realm took over and Riann forgot all about his adventures in the Manling world.

Until King Oberon sent for him on his sixty-sixth year of service as a member of the palace guard.

"You have failed us," Oberon said, from atop his gilded throne.

"How have I failed you, my king?" Riann asked.

"You took one of our people to be raised among the Manlings."

"I did, my king," Riann replied, remembering the Fae child's bright laugh for the first time in what seemed like forever.

"And now we hear that the child you took will never return. That he doesn't wish to. That among them he is called King, even Emperor, by some."

In Riann's heart there leapt something proud and full of joy—the child had become the sun, after all. But King Oberon saw Riann's expression and leapt up from his throne, mistaking one emotion for another. "Betrayal! You sent him to do this!" King Oberon decried.

"No, my king!"

But King Oberon wouldn't listen. Instead, Riann was punished, forced to indefinitely guard the halls containing King Oberon's greatest treasures, suspending his honored position in the royal halls.

Centuries passed, and—away from the distractions of the Court—Riann thought often of his young charge, wondering what the boy was doing. But —after several decades—Riann resigned himself to his duty, which mostly consisted of guarding empty hallways - a far cry from his days among Oberon's Court.

Thus Riann, the wayward son of a palace guard, became the lone sentinel tasked with guarding the treasures of the Faerie King. It was dull. Very dull. None would dare steal from King Oberon, after all.

That was, until the day—after over a thousand years spent more or less diligently guarding the treasures of the Faerie King—Riann O'Rye fell asleep.

On this particular day, Riann fell asleep without warning, still standing, leaning on his halberd. In fact, that's how the King and his newest mistress found him: snoring on his feet. He woke to King Oberon's scream of outrage.

Riann never did find out what had been taken; he'd never been allowed to see the treasures themselves, of course. But, before King Oberon's Court, he was forced to confess to his negligence. Riann, convinced he would be executed, offered no excuse—what could he say that would make a difference? And yet, when whatever had been taken was never retrieved—not even by the King's most dedicated hunters, it proved someone or something very powerful had likely been responsible. Therefore, Riann was not sentenced to a gruesome, painful death, as he'd originally expected, but instead banished to the world of Man. For eternity, barring unforeseen circumstances...

"Like an attack on the Wild Hunt by a host of malicious sprites that wiped out a good portion of King Oberon's army," Cassandra piped up, before Ryan could finish.

"They what?!" Ryan yelled, whirling.

I guess he hadn't heard that part.

CHAPTER 33

*C*assandra arced an eyebrow. "Didn't they tell you what happened?" she asked.

"No," Ryan growled.

"Oh," Cassandra replied. "Well, yes, that's what happened. Your father was with the Hunt that day…" she drifted off.

"He always hated being part of the Hunt," Ryan muttered.

"You should also know the changeling raids were renewed, many seasons back," Cassandra added. "You never heard about them, I imagine, with that silly little club you all have here keeping things hush hush."

"They brought them back? Why?"

Cassandra shrugged her shoulders, her head rising and falling with an abruptness that seemed to disorient her. She glared up at her body, then returned her attention to Ryan. "No idea. The Queens have been busy lately. They're working together, which I haven't seen in centuries. But you know what they do with the Manlings they take…it's possible they wanted something to play with."

Ryan grimaced. "Sometimes I worry I've become too human to go home. Part of me looks at our kind and see children pulling off butterfly wings for fun."

Cassandra shrugged again, although much slower this time. "It'll come back to you. You know how it is. This world fades."

"So that's it, then?" I asked. "You're going back? To work for Oberon?"

"King Oberon!" Cassandra snapped. She seemed to be checking the alleyway, lifting her head high and spinning it like the beacon of a lighthouse. "You never know who's listening, Manling. Best be careful with your words."

I started to roll my eyes, but Ryan was also looking around cautiously, so I shrugged. "King Oberon, then."

"To answer your question, yes," Ryan said. "It seems he needs cannon fodder."

"Well, that, and he found out you weren't lying about the whole not falling asleep on duty thing," Cassandra added, absent-mindedly.

Ryan's eyebrows shot up. "He what?"

"Oh, right. You've been gone," Cassandra said. "The artifact that was stolen has been found. Not retrieved, but found. I heard about it from one of my girlfriend's people." Cassandra lowered her head until it was only a foot away from my own and whispered sultrily into my ear, "She and I like to spice things up every once in a while, if you're interested. Neither of us are the jealous type, obviously. We're very good at sharing. And she's a Banshee...which means she's a scream—"

"That's enough, Cassandra," Ryan hissed. "What do you mean they found what was stolen? Did they get it back?"

Cassandra mouthed the words "think about it" at me before answering. "No, they didn't. In fact, the Queens went after it with an army and came away reeling. It's all anyone's talking about back home."

Ryan shoved his hands into his pockets. "Why now? After all this time?"

"Oh, come now. Surely you've noticed?" Cassandra waved her free hand around in the air. "Something's happening. Feels like it did before."

"Before?" I asked. Until now, I'd done my best to follow along, rolling with the various punches—Fae treasures stolen, the changeling raids reinstated, the Wild Hunt attacked—but it was all becoming a bit much. Everything the two talked about seemed too unbelievable to be remotely true.

"Well, I think your kind called it The Flood," Cassandra replied, putting extra emphasis on the last two words.

"Wait, ye mean like *the* flood? Like Noah and his Ark and all that?"

"The day the Old Gods left to build their own worlds," Cassandra explained, as if I were a small child. "Weren't you listening to Riann's story?"

"She means," Ryan said, "it feels like the Apocalypse is coming."

Oh, so the Apocalypse was nigh.

Awesome.

CHAPTER 34

*C*assandra's horse shuffled uneasily. "Right," Cassandra said, "someone will be coming out here in a few minutes, according to Black Beauty. We better get going."

"Ye named your horse after a children's book?" I asked, incredulous, still reeling from the Cassandra's proclamation of impending doom.

"Of course not," she replied. "Anna named her book after my horse. She was a sickly young woman when I met her, but what she could do with her...well, you wouldn't believe me if I told you."

Ryan, who looked like he'd been hit by a metaphorical bus, didn't so much as crack a smile. I realized the circumstances of his exile had gotten significantly more complicated, and that—if he hadn't seemed eager to return before—he appeared even less enthused now. I wished I could throw him a lifeline, even a few words of encouragement, but after everything I'd heard, I couldn't think of anything uplifting.

"Alright," he said, finally, "let's go."

Cassandra thrust with her hips, and Black Beauty took a few plodding steps forward until both horse and rider were silhouetted by a brick wall. Cassandra drew out a piece of chalk and began drawing sigils on the wall with one hand—the other held her head and tracked the writing. "I hate this part," she muttered.

"Because it's hard to see what you're writing?" I asked, curious.

"Because I'm dyslexic," she droned.

"Oh."

Ryan turned to me. "Don't let what Cassandra said worry you. It's felt like this before, and turned out to be nothing. Well, nothing compared to the Apocalypse. But remember to keep your head down, alright?"

"That's what she said," Cassandra quipped, still scribbling.

"And who's gonna watch your back?" I asked. "Her?"

Cassandra scoffed. "Please, I'm just the gatekeeper. Once he crosses to the other side, he's on his own."

"Cassandra will follow me through, then we'll go our own way," Ryan admitted. "But don't worry, I'll be meeting someone on the other side. At least I hope so."

"And who's that?" I asked.

"Time to go, Riann!" Cassandra called. The sigils on the wall formed a series of lines that folded in on themselves, over and over again in eerily familiar patterns, sending shivers up my spine. Light began to pore along their seams, emerging golden and fierce, like the sun moments before it dips behind the horizon. I covered my eyes.

"Goodbye, Quinn," Ryan said, before following Cassandra, who marched through the portal she'd created with little fanfare. I could see the silhouette of a man on the other side of the gateway Cassandra had created, waving as Ryan approached. Ryan turned back and smiled, then disappeared in a surge of light.

I fought with myself as the portal began shrinking, seriously considering taking my chances and bolting through the gateway. But thoughts of Dez— of how I'd never forgive myself for leaving her behind—kept me rooted in place.

A moment later, the portal snapped shut, taking the light and my answers with it.

CHAPTER 35

A hand I couldn't see clasped my own.

"He found me wandering and gave me a place to stay," Dobby said, the silken purr of his voice so soft and deep I almost couldn't make it out. "I'd been lost for a long time."

"I'll miss him, too," I said. I squeezed Dobby's hand and had begun escorting him back to the warehouse when Hank came outside with two full trash bags in his hands. He saw me, froze in surprise, then ambled by to toss them in the nearby dumpster.

Dobby was nowhere to be seen.

"Where's Ryan?" Hank asked.

"Oh, shit!" I cursed.

"What?" Hank's eyes went wide.

"Christoff is definitely goin' to t'ink I killed him." I groaned.

"Wait," Hank said, realization dawning on his face, "Ryan left already?"

"Aye," I said, nodding.

"When did he leave? Why?" Hank sputtered. He balled up his fists. "What did you say to him?"

"Goodbye, mostly."

"Don't give me that shit. Ryan was supposed to be watching the door tonight."

"Of course, you're right," I said, realizing that—no matter how crazy

Ryan's departure had been—the real world still demanded attention. "I should go tell Christoff. He'll have to call someone in."

"He'll call me in!" Hank exclaimed. "He'll want me to cover, since I'm here, and I won't have a choice because I'm the new guy. I can't believe this shit!" Hank kicked the dumpster in frustration, "I was supposed to have a date tonight, damnit!" A vein in his neck pulsed.

"I told ye, I didn't—"

"I don't want to hear it, you—"

Fortunately for Hank, whatever he'd been about to say was abruptly cut off when an invisible something plucked him off the ground by his leg and dangled him upside down in mid-air. He started to scream, but then another invisible something clamped over his mouth, flattening the skin of Hank's face a bit, though his eyes kept right on bulging out of his skull.

So, that's where Dobby went.

"Dobby," I said, adopting the calm tone Ryan had used on the giant shadow monster, "Ye need to put him down. Gently," I added, hurriedly.

"He was angry with you, my lady," Dobby replied, his voice coming from at least twenty feet above my head. "I will not allow anyone to hurt you."

I winced as I saw the black trousers Hank wore get a little blacker. Yellow liquid dribbled down his shirt to the pavement. "Well, I'm pretty sure he won't do it again, Dobby. Now please, put him down, nice and easy."

Hank floated towards the ground and settled on his back. Whatever part of Dobby's body had pinned his mouth shut had disappeared, but Hank didn't seem inclined to scream anymore; he was likely beyond that point.

"Um, Hank," I said, stepping forward.

"Yeah?" Hank croaked.

"Do ye mind if I help ye up?"

"I think I'll just lay here a minute, if that's alright."

"Sure," I said, just as the lights in the alley turned themselves on for the night. Dobby's tiny hand took my own again, although he remained invisible. I led him to the warehouse door and gently urged him through it, patting the spot where I thought his back should have been.

"My lady," Dobby said, as I turned to leave.

"What is it, Dobby?"

"Can you shut the door? It's hard for me to turn the handle."

"Um, sure," I said, feeling a little ridiculous about having to do anything for the spriggan who'd held a man ten feet off the ground not a couple minutes before. But hey, this was what I'd signed up for, right?

"Night, my lady," Dobby called.

"Night, Dobby," I replied, shutting the door.

Then I helped Hank up, and together we walked inside.

CHAPTER 36

*C*hristoff headed us off and herded us towards the kitchen. A few chefs had already arrived, but they were too busy prepping their stations to take note of us. "What happened?" he asked, looking Hank up and down.

"Ryan's gone," I told him.

"I meant what happened to Hank—wait, Ryan has gone?"

I nodded.

Christoff gave me a long, considering look.

"And no, I didn't kill him."

"I did not say anything," Christoff insisted, though he looked visibly relieved.

I rolled my eyes. "Anyway, Ryan left, and Hank here slipped and fell in some homeless guy's mess while he was outside. He was helping me put something away in the warehouse," I lied.

"Oh? That explains smell."

"I t'ink ye should give Hank the night off. He hit his head pretty hard when he fell," I said, signaling Christoff with my eyes.

"I see," Christoff said. He tapped his chin thoughtfully. "I will call friend of family. He runs liquor store across town. He will send someone over to help, and I will watch door. Hank, you can go. Get some rest. I will get new schedule out tomorrow."

Hank, who hadn't said a word since we'd left the alley, nodded and shot a look of guarded surprise my way, as if waiting for the other shoe to drop —or for an invisible hand to come out of the sky and carry him off.

I gave him a nudge. "Ye heard the man. Go get cleaned up."

"Thanks," Hank said. He started to turn towards the back exit, but then thought better of it. "My car's out front," he muttered, as if he needed an excuse to avoid the alley.

I waited until he was out of earshot to fill Christoff in on what had really happened. I left out a few details, like Ryan's story and the lesbian overtures of the headless horsewoman; if Ryan wanted Christoff to know about his past he'd have already told him, and I still wasn't sure how I felt about being hit on by a woman with detachable parts. I finished by describing what Dobby had done to Hank.

"He grabbed him? Held him upside down?" Christoff mimed the motion with his hands, as if suddenly unsure if his grasp of English was as firm as he'd thought.

"Aye. But don't ye worry, Dobby's back in the warehouse, and he knows to keep out of sight. He was protectin' me, that's all."

"Protecting you from Hank?" he asked. Christoff's stare held more weight than I was used to—a subtle reminder that this was a man with two kids.

Christoff gave a mean dad look.

"He wasn't goin' to hurt me," I explained. "I'd have broken him in two if he'd tried. He was upset Ryan left without sayin' anythin', which is under-standable, and he lashed out—that's all. Dobby overreacted."

"And Hank? How did he handle it?"

I hesitated. What Christoff was really asking—whether or not he could trust his newest employee to keep his mouth shut—was a tougher question to answer. I wasn't the best judge of character; I disliked most people on principle and tolerated the rest.

"Well," I said, opting for the truth, "the truth is he could have freaked out back there, but he didn't." I shrugged. "It's hard to know for sure. He might be able to handle it. Not all Regulars are morons, after all." I didn't bother mentioning the odds of that happening; Christoff knew better them better than most.

Christoff smiled, his fangs glinting, catching the light from the kitchen, the feral gleam of his werebear form peeking out from beneath his chocolate brown eyes. "No," he agreed, his voice a low rumble, "Not all."

CHAPTER 37

$\mathcal{M}$y phone rang on my way out. I recognized the number and hurried up the stairs to Christoff's office, ducking inside and slamming the door closed before answering; I didn't want any of Christoff's staff overhearing this conversation.

"What the bloody hell do you think you were doing letting that thing go free?" The Englishman yelled, the moment I picked up.

"What are ye on about?" I asked, completely taken aback.

"The skinwalker!"

I frowned. Apparently, the kidnapper had his own source of information —I hadn't mentioned anything about the showdown in the park in the voicemail I'd left. "I'm sorry," I replied, tersely, "d'ye mean the shapeshifter ye conveniently forgot to mention when ye told me where to go and who to follow?"

"Shapeshifter? Skinwalkers aren't shapeshifters, you git. They're closer to demons—witches who sacrificed their familiars for power."

"Serge was a witch?" I asked, baffled. Not to be sexist, but until now I wasn't even sure men *could* be witches.

"He must've been. A witch, probably several hundred years old. I can't believe they stuck a leash on one of those things," he said, talking more to himself now than me. "Skinwalkers haven't been seen in over a century. There were rumors about a Siberian prison set up by Rasputin in a plot to overthrow the Tsar a couple centuries back...but no proof..." he drifted off, probably realizing he was babbling.

At least now I knew how Othello had come by a skinwalker as her bagman; she must have recruited him, quite possibly from that Siberian prison—yet another reason not to get on her bad side. Still, it was hard to wrap my mind around the idea that the pathetic, mild-mannered Serge might have been a witch.

But, the longer I thought about it, the more sense it made. I'd assumed the cool, dispassionate way he'd held me at gunpoint outside the alley when he'd perceived me as a threat was a front he'd put on, hoping to scare me. But what if it wasn't? What if that was the real Serge, not the hand-wringing foreigner who'd practically begged me for help?

I cursed, inwardly.

The Serbian bastard had played me.

"So what are ye goin' to do about him?" I asked, secretly hoping the two would go after each other, write a suicide pact, and burn in Hell for all eternity.

But of course I wasn't that lucky.

"We?" The Englishman scoffed. "You're taking the piss. I'm not going anywhere near that thing. It's their problem, now."

"They?"

"Yeah, they. The Justices. From the Academy. Them wizards steer clear of your city for the most part, what with the Fae infestation, but this one's too big to ignore. It'll look bad if they let it get out of hand."

"Who are the Justices?" I asked. I'd heard of the Academy—that was the name of the school that wizards attended—but not the Justices. Although, if I was being honest, they sounded a bit pretentious.

"Are you drunk? The Justices. Wizard police. You telling me you've never heard of the Academy Justices? What do you people do when some monster gets loose and runs around killing people? Or when a wizard goes rogue?"

I wasn't sure what he was talking about. Freaks living in Boston avoided causing mayhem, as a rule. Turf wars had been a thing in the 1800s—both the fire in 1872 and the blizzard 16 years later could be attributed to Freak activity—but these days it paid to stay off the radar. Thanks to Ryan, I knew the Chancery had a direct hand in the suppression, but even without their involvement—incidents were rare.

In fact, that was primarily how I made my living; even Freaks can appreciate deterrents, and nothing says, "get off my lawn" like a flaming sword that sings a haunting acapella rendition of "Light My Fire" by the Doors as you wield it.

"We wait," I said, finally.

"What?" he replied, incredulously.

"If someone makes a splash in this town, they don't last long. There's always a bigger, meaner fish waitin' around the bend," I replied, hoping the bastard would read between the lines and realize what a huge pile of shit he'd stepped in by coming here.

"You Yanks and your wild west bullshit," the kidnapper said, clearly exasperated. "No wonder no one comes out here. Anyway, nevermind that bollocks. Listen, ain't nothing changed between you and me. All your little stunt did was guarantee that time is no longer on your side. I want my briefcase, and I want it tonight."

I cringed. I'd hoped to have a little more time to wait for Othello's reinforcements, but it looked like I wasn't going to have that luxury. "Well, I want to know Dez is alright," I replied. "Let me talk to her, or ye won't be gettin' anythin' from me."

The kidnapper grunted, barked something away from the phone, and I heard a fierce series of curses I recognized. If I weren't already angry, my blood pounding in my ears, they'd definitely be burning from the choice things Dez had to say about Englishmen.

But at least she was alive and, apparently, in high spirits.

"There you are," the kidnapper said, "alive and well. Now, bring me the briefcase. I'll text you the address. Come alone, or she dies. If the briefcase isn't genuine, or you try anything funny, she dies. If you're even a minute late, she dies."

"If ye touch her—"

"I had hoped we were past that, love," the Englishman interjected, then hung up before I could respond.

"Motherfucker," I hissed, resisting the urge to chuck my phone at the wall; I couldn't risk breaking it before I knew where our handoff was going down. Christoff poked his head in a moment later, finding me curled up on his couch, clutching a pillow for comfort.

"I'm fine," I said, even though I didn't feel it.

"You look like you could use drink," Christoff offered.

"Aye. Somethin' strong," I said, rousing myself.

One drink.

Then I'd start calling in favors.

CHAPTER 38

$\mathcal{T}$he address was in Mission Hill, a few blocks from Roxbury Crossing. I decided to take the orange line rather than calling a car; most Uber drivers avoided that neighborhood at night, and I wanted plenty of witnesses to see me on the train without the briefcase—if everything went according to plan, I could use that as an alibi, later.

As if things ever went according to plan.

Still, I'd done my level best to anticipate the Englishman's next move and plan accordingly. Of course, it didn't take a genius to surmise he'd try to kill me the second he got the case. Dez, too. He'd let way too much slip, for one thing—like the fact that he didn't want to go toe to toe with a skinwalker, or face the Academy's Justices. No one with that many enemies could risk someone selling him out.

And sell him out I would, in an instant.

Unfortunately, it wouldn't be to Othello; I'd tried calling her to check on the status of her reinforcements, but all I got was that irritating modem sound a fax machine makes. Christoff had probed a little after I hung up, my frustration clear, but I'd declined his help. Having a monstrous Kamchatka werebear to watch my back would definitely improve my odds of making it out alive, but would probably hurt Dez's.

I'd executed too many handoffs to ignore the "come alone" directive—no matter how the movies made it look. In real life, showing up with a posse when you were explicitly told otherwise was a great way to get yourself killed.

Real criminals are all about shooting first and asking questions later.

So that was that. I was going in, without backup, to trade a briefcase owned by a billion-dollar company for my aunt, hoping we made it out alive long enough for me to tell her how sorry I was that what I did for a living had gotten her held against her will for days.

And praying she didn't murder me on the spot.

I stepped off the train and headed for the escalators. The chill from earlier had only gotten worse, and I could see my breath in front of my face. Fortunately, with fewer people out and about, the likelihood of running into any shady characters—something you had to be prepared for in this part of town—was slim. That didn't mean I was safe, but—compared to the shit I'd put up with over the last few days—I almost welcomed a mugger.

I wouldn't mind letting off some steam.

I left the station and located the street the address was on before I felt a tug at my jacket. I started, my heart in my throat. "Jesus Christ, Dobby," I said, my hand pinned to my chest, "don't scare me like that." I held out my other hand, felt the weight of the briefcase settle as he slid the handle over my palm, and watched as the case magically appeared the moment Dobby— still invisible—stepped away.

"Sorry, my lady," Dobby said, voice hovering a couple feet away.

"It's alright," I said, feeling silly for freaking out considering I was the one who asked him to accompany me with the briefcase in the first place. "Not your fault. Are ye sure ye know the way back?"

"I'm sure."

"Good. No detours, d'ye hear me? I don't need ye gettin' into trouble tonight. I've got enough on me plate already."

"Yes, my lady. Are you certain you don't want my help?"

I had to admit, the offer was tempting. I had no idea what the Englishman had in store for me, but having an invisible shadow monster on my side couldn't hurt. Sadly, I didn't know enough about how magic worked to risk it; what if the Englishman could sense I'd brought a friend along? Dobby was invisible, not undetectable. I sighed. "I'm sure. I'll see ye back at the warehouse tomorrow, alright?"

"Yes, my lady."

And with that, he was gone, streetlights flickering conspicuously as he went, like a scene from a horror movie. I shuddered and—not for the first time—thanked God he was on my side.

Because the night is dark and full of terrors.

CHAPTER 39

The house stood between an empty lot and an apartment building with no windows on that side, completely isolated from the neighborhood itself. To be honest, I was shocked we were meeting at an actual house. Typically these sorts of deals went down in more appropriate locales: alleyways, abandoned warehouses, strip clubs. The last one was my go-to, if you're wondering; I preferred places with decent security, a strict no-cameras policy, and plenty of distractions.

I approached from the other side of the street, unsure whether I should knock or ring the doorbell. Luckily, the door opened as soon as I reached the welcome mat. My eyes widened in recognition as Jacob—the stalker from the Kenpo class—stepped out onto the porch. He'd gotten a haircut since I'd seen him last, the sides so short all I could see was skin. He was easily more imposing in street clothes—between the tight black t-shirt and the fuck-with-me-and-I'll-cut-you expression, he would have made an excellent bouncer.

"Evening, Sensei," Jacob said, his tone cool, seemingly unfazed to see me. "Mr. Gladstone, she's here!"

"Well invite her in," the kidnapper, Mr. Gladstone apparently, replied from somewhere inside the house, his accent even more pronounced in person. "Wait, does she have the briefcase?"

I held it up for Jacob to see, too surprised to do anything else but stare.

SHAYNE SILVERS & CAMERON O'CONNELL

Then, realizing it really didn't matter one way or the other, I turned it over and held it out for him to touch. "See for yourself," I said.

Jacob scowled at me and ignored my offer. "Yeah, she's got it!"

"Is it a fake?" Gladstone asked.

"I don't think so," he called, "she tried to get me to touch it!"

"Alright," Gladstone replied. "Then, invite her in. I'll be there in a jiff."

Jacob cracked open a screen door with jagged holes in it, waving me through. I considered taking a swing with the briefcase; if it worked anything like how it had with Jimmy, Gladstone's errand boy would be down for the count in a matter of seconds. But, since I still didn't know where Dez was, it didn't seem worth the risk. Besides, I had questions for the bastard.

Questions I couldn't ask if he was unconscious.

"That's quite the security system ye got there," I mentioned, jerking my chin towards the battered screen door.

Jacob shut both the screen and main door as I slid past, leaving both unlocked. "I am the security system."

He escorted me to the living room, which was larger than I'd expected, given the size of the house. Of course, most living rooms were cluttered with furniture, whereas this one had been completely gutted; there were two folding chairs on either wall and nothing but hardwood floor between them.

"Cozy," I said.

Jacob indicated I should take a seat on one of the folding chairs, then crossed to the other side of the room and leaned against the wall. Mr. Gladstone seemed to be in one of the back bedrooms; I could hear him shuffling about, muttering to himself.

"So," I began, "care to tell me what the fuck you're doin' here?" I asked, refusing to sit.

Jacob flicked his eyes at me. "You didn't think we'd come after you without doing a little reconnaissance, did you?"

I frowned. "Ye were followin' me?"

Jacob nodded. "All day. Caught your little brunch date. Spied on you at the dojo, asked that girl a few probing questions. And, then, of course, I tracked you back to your aunt's place."

"You bastard!" I hissed, finally realizing how they'd found her, and cursing myself for being such an idiot.

I'd led them right to her.

"Well, that's done, innit!" Gladstone called from the other room. I heard his footsteps as he came down the corridor, my eyes still locked on Jacob, desperately wishing looks could kill. When Gladstone finally sauntered into the room, it took everything I had to turn away, my trigger finger itching.

Not for the first time, I offered up a silent prayer that Maria Machado would fall down a flight of stairs.

Gun withdrawals are a thing, people.

Gladstone—it turned out—was a short, squat man with several features too large for his bulldoggish face: a blockish nose, drooping ears, and a wide, cavernous mouth. He also seemed to be liberally coated in flecks of blood.

"You'll have to forgive me, dearie. Doing a bit of housecleaning in the back, nuffin to worry about." He rubbed his hands clean on a moist towel that was becoming pinker by the second. "Just a little lamb's blood. So, you have the briefcase, then?"

"I want to see my aunt," I said, eyeing his towel in disgust.

"Quite right you are. But first I need to see the briefcase. Now, I know we could do this dance all day, so I'll make it easy on us both, alright? I swear on my power that your aunt is safe and sound." Gladstone paused for effect. "See how easy that was? Now let us see that case."

I started to raise the case.

"Oh no, none of that. Just set it down and give it a good kick. My man here will take it from there."

I did what he asked, kicking the briefcase towards Jacob as hard as I could manage. Jacob started to reach for it, but Gladstone clucked his tongue as a reminder not to touch it—which sucked, because I was really hoping to see someone I *didn't* like get cursed for once.

Instead, Jacob kicked the briefcase like a soccer ball, sliding it across the floor a little at a time until it was in Gladstone's vicinity. The wizard bent down and began probing the case with his hand, testing the magic the way you might test to see if your air vent is putting off heat.

That's when my phone rang.

It was Wagner's "Ride of the Valkyries."

Dez.

CHAPTER 40

J stared at the caller ID for a moment before swiping to accept the
call, holding up my finger. "Sorry, I have to take this."

"Is she fucking serious?" Gladstone asked, turning to Jacob, who
shrugged.

Dez started speaking the moment I answered, her voice winded and
pained, but defiant. I fiddled with the volume so Gladstone and Jacob
wouldn't be able to hear her. "Quinn is that ye?" Dez asked. "Quinn, I
escaped. Where are ye?! I'm not too far from home, thank the Lord. It's cold
as Judas' miserable heart outside," she cursed, and I could hear her teeth
chattering. "Almost makes me want to double back to that warehouse they
were holdin' me in."

See. There was always a warehouse.

"This is she," I said, calmly, glancing at Gladstone and his companion,
doing my best to keep my expression neutral. So long as they were here, it
meant Dez stood a chance of making it home safe. I couldn't risk exposing
the fact that she'd gotten out on her own.

"She?" Dez sputtered. "Did ye not hear me?"

"Aye, that sounds good."

"Oh, Quinn, are ye with 'em now?" Dez asked, mournfully.

"I am, aye."

"Where are ye? I'm comin' right now."

"No, I don't t'ink that's for the best."

"Well at least—"

"Aye, I really t'ink ye should give Jimmy Collins a call, instead," I said. "He'll know what's best. Alright? Bye now." I hung up and turned my phone on silent. My guess is I'd have thirty or so missed calls from Dez by the time I checked it again, but that was alright; if she took my advice and called Jimmy, he'd make sure she was safe.

And that meant Gladstone had lost his leverage.

"Sorry about that," I said. "Lawyer. Tryin' to keep me out of prison. Says I need to start a twelve-step program, make it look good for the judge. Problem is, I don't even drink that much, except on weekends and the occasional weekday and whenever I get home and before I go to bed, so what am I goin' to talk about? I can't stand up and say, 'Hi, me name's Quinn MacKenna and there's not a damn t'ing wrong with me,' can I?"

"She's stalling," Jacob said. "The old Irish broad with the foul mouth escaped."

"She what?" Gladstone whirled to face Jacob.

"That was her on the phone," Jacob said, tapping his ear. "She must have gotten loose after we left. I told you she was more resourceful than she let on."

"I bound her with a spell!" Gladstone insisted.

Jacob shrugged.

Gladstone cursed. "We'll just have to tie that loose end up later. Take this one and get her ready. I'll get the briefcase open."

"Why don't you bind *her* with a spell?" Jacob asked, sardonically.

"Because I'm busy. Do your job."

Jacob shrugged, removed his jacket, and slid it over the back of the chair on his side of the room. "I'm sorry about this."

"Sorry about what, ye bastard?" I asked as I slid out of my own coat, still wondering how Jacob had heard my conversation with Dez from across the room. I shook my head, deciding it wasn't worth thinking about. A fight was coming, and I had no intention of losing because I was distracted.

Jacob began shadowboxing, throwing out jabs and crosses, loosening up his shoulders while Gladstone fiddled with the briefcase. The wizard glanced up, appraising me for a moment. "Make sure you don't kill her. I need her alive," he said, then headed for the back room with the suitcase in hand, muttering under his breath.

Jacob rolled his neck. "Whatever you say."

CHAPTER 41

*J*acob adopted a familiar stance as he stalked towards me.
Objectively, he had me at a disadvantage. He had a longer reach, which meant it would be harder for me to keep my distance, but he was also stronger—striated muscle like his came from hard labor, not from hours in the gym—which meant I'd have trouble going inside on him. If he grappled well, that difference in strength could cause problems. On the other hand, I had two things I could use to my advantage: the first was that I'd seen Jacob fight before, and the second was that he'd never seen me.

I dropped back into Kenpo's standard, staggered stance, guard up. Ordinarily I'd have maneuvered back and forth the way Jenny had until I got a good feel for my opponent, but I knew better than to play the positioning game with Jacob. He'd obviously studied several different styles of martial arts, which meant he could strike from multiple places using a variety of techniques. If I let him adapt on the fly—the way he had by charging Jenny —I would have a harder time anticipating what his next move was.

Instead, I waited for him to come to me.

Jacob didn't seem to mind. He closed the distance quickly and feinted a kick with his left leg. I ignored it, then slapped away the punch that followed.

He was testing me, gauging my response times.

I let him.

His next kick was real, a solid blow to the thigh that would have left bruises on an ordinary person. I barely felt it. See, what Jacob didn't know was that I'd trained in Muay Thai myself, and had spent many a warm-up session building up calcifications on my thighs and shins from rounds and rounds of kicking and being kicked. Which is why, when his kick landed, he found me smiling, his eyes wide in surprise.

Admittedly, the right cross I landed might have had something to do with that, too; I'd thrown all my power behind it, swiveling my hips, delivering the blow with my back and not my arm the way I'd been trained. Jacob winced and took a step back, rubbing his ribs where I'd caught him.

"That wasn't Kenpo," Jacob accused.

"No, it wasn't."

I went on the offensive, firing off front kicks to push Jacob back towards the middle of the room. I wasn't expecting any of them to land, but I didn't like the idea of getting caught with my back against a wall against someone his size.

Jacob skittered back without much effort. "What happened to your 'don't put your hands on me' philosophy?" he asked, derisively.

I shrugged, refusing to be baited. The truth was, while Kenpo was great in situations that required decisive action against an assailant or assailants, it had its limitations when going up against someone who knew what they were doing. You can practice reacting to a haymaker all day, but if a heavy-weight boxer ever tried to knock you out, you'd be hard pressed to stop him by simply redirecting his punches. Kung Fu movies made it look easy, but if you think about it, even Bruce Lee's famous one-inch punch would only knock someone down for a few seconds.

And I needed Jacob down for good.

Which is why, when he went in for a clinch—his hands locking behind my head, making it easier for him to thrust his knees into my side—I didn't dodge it. Instead, I clutched his shoulder with one hand, his forearm with another, and threw myself in the air, scissoring my hips until I had both legs wound around his shoulder. I let my momentum and the weight of our bodies drag us both down.

The move, commonly referred to as a flying armbar, isn't easy to execute. Remember *Dirty Dancing*? When Jennifer Grey goes leaping into

Patrick Swayze's arms at the very end? It's like that, but a lot less sexy. You have to commit, or you'll just fall flat on your ass.

Well, technically you'll fall on your ass either way, but in this case, I ended up with Jacob's arm trapped between my legs. Jacob tried to yank his arm out of my grip with sheer force, but my two hands were stronger than his one, and I'd locked him in tight. In a sanctioned fight, this would be the point where you'd apply a little pressure—a little thrust of the hips to bend his elbow backwards—and wait for the tap-out. But this asshole had kidnapped my aunt.

I wasn't going for the submission.

I jerked my hips upwards and listened with satisfaction as Jacob's elbow popped. He screamed in agony. I released him, rolled away, and rose. Jacob clutched at his arm, but did the same, his breath coming in short gasps.

Gladstone called from the back, "Keep it down out there!"

"I'm going to kill you," Jacob threatened.

"I thought ye were supposed to keep me alive?" I taunted. "Ye could leave now, ye know. There's a hospital not too far from here. I won't stop ye," I lied. The truth was, the minute he turned his back, I planned to pick up a chair and break it across his back.

Because no one fucks with me and mine.

Jacob hissed between his teeth and let his wounded arm fall. He straightened and took a few calming breaths. "No, you're right. Gladstone wants you alive. I'll just have to try not to rip out your throat and hope for the best."

I glanced down pointedly at his injured arm.

"Oh, this," Jacob said, "it definitely hurt. I really had planned on taking you down straight up. I might have, too, if I hadn't gotten careless."

"It happens," I noted, still glaring at him.

"How long have you been taking martial arts?"

"Since I was six," I replied. "I got picked on for me red hair when I was a wee thing, and me aunt—the woman ye attacked and took hostage? She decided I should learn how to take care of meself."

Jacob nodded to himself. "Sounds about right. I'd say...Kenpo, obviously. Boxing. Muay Thai. And...Judo?"

"Brazilian Jui Jitsu."

"Quite the variety."

"I get bored easy."

I suppose I could have told Jacob the real reason—that I'd never had many friends and eventually found it easier to fight people than talk to them. That even before I found out I was a Freak, I'd felt like one. Tall, with bright red-hair and an Irish accent I couldn't get rid of no matter how hard I'd tried to drop my R's like everyone else in school. That the only type of guy I went for was one who knew how to throw a punch, and that—more often than I cared to admit—learning how to throw one back had become a priority.

But something told me he wouldn't give a shit.

"Well, then what comes next should make you happy," Jacob replied. He went back to his chair and fetched a vial out of his jacket. The liquid inside was a deep burgundy. I tensed, expecting him to throw it.

But instead he drank it.

And that's when the real fight started.

CHAPTER 42

*J*acob fell to his knees immediately after swallowing the liquid from the vial. In moments, his flesh began to writhe. Between his small gasps of pain, he looked up at me, his face—the face Jenny must have seen before he'd taken her to the mat—contorted into something ugly and hateful as the skin tightened over his skull. Lines, like wrinkles but deeper, were carved into it, and his lips had peeled back so far that nothing remained besides gums and teeth.

His limbs began to spasm, twitching at odd angles. I noticed his injured limb had recovered. Either that or Jacob no longer cared how much it hurt to move it. He stilled, and then his eyes—so distended I thought they might pop out at any moment—settled on me.

When he finally rose, I was glad to see that he hadn't sprouted horns or wings or anything, but somehow the end result seemed worse, if only because it looked so wrong; his tongue flapped loose in his mouth like a dog's after a long walk in the summer, teeth exposed like a desiccated corpse. He rolled his shoulders, and that's when I noticed that his chest and shoulders had gotten broader, his arms significantly thicker. Veins pulsed beneath his skin, coursing down his arms like rivers after a heavy rain.

"Well that's a new one," I said. "What are ye supposed to be?"

"It's still me," Jacob replied, although his speech had an eerie, garbled quality to it, since he had a hard time using his lips to articulate. "Same body, same engine, better oil."

Sure, because that explained things.

"And what is that supposed to mean, ye ugly bastard?"

But Jacob didn't feel like talking.

Instead, he rushed forward, going for my legs the same way he had with Jenny's, only this time he was faster. A lot faster. And stronger; I hit the ground hard and the wind got knocked out of me before I could so much as blink. Jacob was mounted over my hips a moment later, one hand on my throat. My eyes fluttered as I tried, desperately, to think. To react. But he was so strong. Inhumanly strong.

Which made no sense.

In the past, whenever any magical creature—vampire, werewolf, skin-walker, whatever—had gotten this close, they'd lost control of their abilities. Their magic fled, and, in an instant, a claw became a hand, a deadly fang little more than your basic incisor, and so on.

That's why Serge had been unable to keep his form when I took hold of his tail, and why vampires like Mike and his band had found themselves outmatched by a girl with a water gun; I wasn't invincible, but I did have an advantage. An advantage I routinely used to exploit that moment of confusion, of indecision, and turn the tables on beings that were inarguably stronger and deadlier than I was. And yet, here I was, pinned and being strangled by a grip as strong as any Freak I'd come up against.

And yet, I could tell he wasn't using magic.

But still, I refused to panic. Panicking would get me killed that much faster. Instead, I tried to break his hold by slamming my balled fist into his wounded elbow. His grip only tightened. I dug my nails into the flesh of his forearm. I kicked and squirmed. Nothing worked.

I was going to die.

Then, without warning, Jacob let go.

The edges of the room dimmed as tunnel vision settled in, but I could hear Jacob scrambling away, crying out in pain. I curled into the fetal position, coughing and dry heaving. Every breath was agony, but I managed.

"I told you," Gladstone said, "I need her alive. Now get her up and bring her on back. I got the briefcase open."

I sensed Jacob edging towards me, but I didn't want to waste the energy to turn my head. I felt him work his arms beneath me, cradling my head and legs as if planning to carry me over the threshold. If I'd been a man, he'd probably have slid me across the floor by my arm. But I was a woman, and I was hurt, and so he picked me up, instead.

Idiot.

I took the knife I'd fetched from my back pocket during my coughing fit and stabbed him in the throat.

CHAPTER 43

I missed Jacob's jugular, clipping his clavicle with enough force to draw a deep gouge in his skin, but it was mostly superficial damage; I hadn't been strong or precise enough to do more than that. He dropped me, and I landed hard.

Fortunately, adrenaline kicked in at the last second, and I scrambled away just as Jacob's foot slammed into the hardwood where I'd fallen. Gladstone was cursing in the background, telling Jacob to back off so he could bind me and be done with it. But Jacob wasn't in the listening mood. A kick to my side sent me sliding across the floor.

I watched him stalk towards me, too broken to crawl away.

Jacob had bled through his mangled shirt, which I'd torn open when I stabbed him. I stared at the red stain as it spread; it's easy to forget how much damage a knife can do, how messy a wound it can cause. So much blood.

I blinked a few times. Shock. I was in shock. I cursed myself and tried to move, but between being strangled, dropped, and having my liver obliterated by Jacob's boot, I didn't have much fight left in me. I had one shot, if I was lucky. I rolled onto my back and brought my legs up, prepared to kick him once he got close enough.

Jacob grunted, but came at me anyway. He dodged my first half-hearted kick, then caught my second. If he'd been in his right mind, he'd probably have put me in a leg lock, or pushed past and grappled with me. Instead, he lashed out, trying to end it all with one solid haymaker to my head. I contracted my abs, using Jacob's hold on my leg as an anchor, and rose to meet him, ducking the punch. This time my knife sank, hilt deep, in his gut.

He fell on top of me, but I shrugged him off with the last of my energy, hoping to avoid getting stabbed myself. Sharp objects were unpredictable in a fight like this, and I wanted distance.

Besides, blood was a real bitch to wash out.

I wobbled as I got to my feet. Gladstone stood in the hallway, looking remarkably put out. Jacob lay on the floor groaning—his face had returned to normal. Well, sort of. He was beyond pale, and not just from pain and blood loss; his pitifully thin veins were visible all over his body—blue and sprawling, swarming his face, neck, and arms like the roots of a tree.

"Serves you right, you tosser," Gladstone remarked. "I told you there was a limit to how much your body could take." He sighed. "Good help is hard to find these days. I don't suppose you want a job?"

It took me a second to realize he was talking to me. I grunted, then groaned a little. My throat still hurt. A lot. "Not unless you're plannin' to pay me to kill ye," I rasped.

His lips pursed, then he flung out a hand, sending a wave of flames at me in an arc. I shielded my eyes and watched as they collided with an invisible wall, puttered, and died. Gladstone frowned and pointed directly at me. This time a tiny cone of jet blue fire, like the tip of a blowtorch, leapt from his finger like a bullet. It fizzled with a puff of smoke a mere foot from me.

"I'll take that as a no," I said, "but don't ye worry, I was plannin' on doin' that pro bono, anyway."

"Well that's a right neat trick, love. How're you doing that?" Gladstone asked, though his interest seemed mostly academic, like he'd just seen a monkey paint a mural. "You know what? Nevermind. Things to do and people to see." Gladstone waved a hand and Jacob soared through the air, squealing in pain, until he lay at Gladstone's feet. "One life is as good as another, ain't that right?"

Gladstone walked back down the hallway, Jacob trailing behind him, still screaming, the knife inside him digging and tearing. I'd love to say I relished in his pain, but—no matter how close the bastard had been to killing me or what he'd done to my aunt—the tortured sounds he was making made me feel a little queasy.

147

That, or I was still nauseous from the beating I'd taken.

Probably the latter, I decided.

"Hey!" I called. "I'm not done with ye!" I followed, fully intending to fetch my knife from Jacob's stomach and use it to slice the wizard from groin to gullet. But, by the time I stumbled down the hallway and made it to the back room, I found that Gladstone had already retrieved my knife...and used it to cut his partner's throat.

CHAPTER 44

A wet gurgle was all Jacob managed before his blood—what remained of it anyway—splashed into a bowl Gladstone held. The open briefcase lay against a wall painted liberally from baseboards to ceiling in shades of red. I didn't recognize the markings, but simply looking at them made my skin crawl. They were neat, uniform—running from one wall to the next with painstaking precision. It must have taken Gladstone hours…maybe even days.

"I wouldn't come much further if I was you," Gladstone remarked. He held Jacob's head back by pulling back on the dead man's forehead, catching as much blood in the worn wooden bowl as possible. Then, apparently finished, he tossed Jacob's body aside with as much force as he could muster. Jacob's eyes were still open, staring at nothing. In the dim florescence, he looked ghoulish and inhuman. I fought back another wave of nausea.

"Why?" I asked, finally.

"Because then you'll get caught up in the Gateway," Gladstone explained. He held up a metal sphere, like a marble, only larger. The outside swirled in Milky-Way patterns. "That briefcase took a bit of doing, but isn't she beautiful?" He let the ball roll around in his palm.

"No, I meant why d'ye kill him?"

"Oh, that moron? Who cares? Now step back." Gladstone set the sphere on the ground and crushed it beneath his heel, then hurriedly stepped away. I felt a tug at my back as the air in the room ended up sucked into a single point. Then, with a brutal tearing sound and a flash of light, a portal opened —a rift between this room and somewhere else. Darkness poured out of it like night was trying to invade.

Gladstone stepped nimbly over Jacob's body and through, unfazed by the sounds of insects or the darkness on the other side. I could only watch as he disappeared; even without his magic, Gladstone seemed fit. If I was fresh, I could probably take him without breaking a sweat, but at this rate he might be able to overpower me. I probed my throat and winced. I'd have some classy domestic violence bruises before long.

As I wavered between whether or not to go after him, I studied the portal, which stood a little taller than me and twice as wide. I couldn't believe I'd been carrying around something like this the whole time. What had Othello planned to do with something like this? I sighed, realizing I might never find out.

Because I'd decided to go after Gladstone, after all.

In case you were wondering, you should know I wasn't the heroic type; I sold scary, dangerous shit to scary, dangerous people, and I avoided asking stupid questions, questions like "what are you going to do with this?" or "where did you get that from?"

The truth was, I wasn't going after Gladstone because he needed to be stopped, or because he was the type of guy who could slit his partner's throat without blinking—people die every day, and Jacob hadn't exactly been a saint. No, I was going after him because Gladstone didn't play by the rules. My rules. Rules that involved paying for services owed. Rules that involved not targeting innocent people. And that's why, without trying to think too hard about the physics of what was about to happen, I stepped through the portal.

Directly into a trap.

CHAPTER 45

I felt the rope before I saw it, binding my arms to my sides and jerking me sideways. In the murky gloom, I could barely make out Gladstone on the other end, tying it around a pillar with his magic, weaving his arms in the air. I tried to pull away, but he secured the knot with a flick of his wrist, then stepped well out of reach.

"Took you long enough," Gladstone said. "Felt like I was standing there for ages waiting for you to follow me through."

"Seriously?" I asked, tugging with my whole body. "Where did ye even get the rope?"

Gladstone grunted and waved his hand around. I realized we were surrounded by ropes. And stone. The light was dim, but the longer I looked, the more I could make out: massive stone pillars reaching high into the air only to be swallowed up by a canopy of foliage. Lichen dangled from the ropes, which ran from one pillar to the next, haphazardly. I couldn't see any walls, but I sensed we weren't outside. The whole place felt contained, somehow. The lack of wind, maybe?

"Where the fuck are we?" I muttered.

Gladstone ignored me and walked towards a slab of stone some twenty feet away, untouched by the plant life that had strangled everything else. He set the bowl of blood he'd collected on the slab, which reminded me of something I'd seen often in my life: an altar.

"Is this some sort of temple?" I asked.

Gladstone flinched, repositioned the bowl, and then strolled back to sidle up against a pillar. "Now we wait."

Deciding it was better not to know what we were waiting for, I struggled to free myself from the rope once more. Unfortunately, I was still exhausted, and the rope was uncommonly thick; it might as well have been a boa constrictor, wound so tight it made it hard to breath. "So," I said, drawing closer to the pillar where Gladstone had tied the knot, hoping the slack would provide some relief, "ye won't tell me where we are. How about ye tell me what Jacob took? What was in that vial?"

He ignored me.

I grunted. "Unless ye plan on comin' over here to kill me, ye may as well answer me questions. I promise ye I can annoy ye to death, if ye let me."

Gladstone sighed. "Alchemy."

Oh, sure. Alchemy.

"Wait, what?" I asked.

Gladstone used one of the pillars as a support and lowered himself to the ground. His eyes never wavered from the altar. "Alchemy. It's like chemistry, but without the limitations. Never really caught on in a big way. Regulars lacked the imagination to make sense of it. But some of us wizards thought it might be worth checking out. Mind you, they're all dead now. But I'm still here, and I know a trick or two. Like how to redirect blood flow."

"So you're what, some kind of pharmacist?" I taunted.

Gladstone turned his attention to me and raised an eyebrow. "You know, you really are a mouthy broad. I don't know if it's a charm or an enchantment or what, but just because my magic don't work on you doesn't mean you're safe from what's coming."

"And what's that?" I asked, leaning against the pillar. In truth, it was the only thing holding me up; but Gladstone didn't need to know that. So long as he thought I was a threat, he'd stay on his side of the temple. Maybe long enough to let me catch my breath, if I was lucky.

Or at least I hoped so.

Gladstone rolled his eyes and returned his attention to the altar. "Don't worry your pretty little head about it, love. When I'm done here, the Academy will be thanking me."

"I thought ye said the Academy were like the police? Ye sounded scared of 'em."

"I wasn't scared," Gladstone snarled. "I didn't want them sticking their noses in where they didn't belong, that's all. The Academy used to be a proper bunch, back when I was a member. We sorted out the riffraff and all that. Punished the buggers who went off on their own to cause mayhem. There were loads of perks. It was a right fun job, it was."

Gladstone froze, his head cocked. I whirled toward the altar, but saw nothing. The wizard shrugged and continued, "These days, though, things ain't what they used to be. Turns out most of my friends in the Academy were spies, working for a different group. But then they went and died before I could find out why or who they was working for. Got ourselves in a right mess after that, a bloody war. Rest of my friends died, then. A couple of us old folks are still mucking about, of course, and remember the good ol' days, but ain't a one I could get a proper drink with."

Gladstone fetched a flask from his pocket. "I'd offer you some, love, but I know better than to get too close after what you did to my man." He took a swig. "Anyway, as I was saying, it's just me now, and the Academy ain't nuffin like it was. Letting an outsider tell us what to do, push us around. So, I gets to thinking, 'how come?' How come we's got to put up with that?"

The sound of a tree branch snapping brought us both around. I couldn't make out where it had come from. Gladstone seemed pleased.

"Where are we?" I asked, again, fighting off a heavy sense of dread.

"I'm getting to that part, dearie, be patient," Gladstone insisted. "So, as I said, I ask myself that question and I do a little research and, come to find out, there's a whole black market out there for entrepreneurs like me. Like you, too, am I right?" He tipped his flask and took another swig.

"But then I catch wind of something real special," he went on, "a piece of merchandise that'll take you places ain't nobody supposed to go. Places that ain't supposed to exist. And don't it just make sense that it belongs to the tosser who started everyfin—the shakeup and the war and everyfin else."

I thought I heard something from the portal behind me, like the slamming of a door, but Gladstone didn't seem to notice anything. I frowned. "Ye still haven't told me where we are," I said.

"You're right. But see, I'm still trying to figure that out, love. Let me ask you sumfin, have you ever met a god?"

"A god?"

"See, I think that portal there is special. Tell me, if you was to talk to a god, how would you do it?"

My thoughts reeled as I tried to keep track of Gladstone's ravings. "I don't know. Pray?" I suggested.

Gladstone snapped his fingers and mimed shooting a gun at me. "But say you wanted to have a proper chat, right? Sit down as equals over a cup of tea. And say you didn't want to wait for someone to come round and open the door...You ever heard of Mount Olympus? Camelot? Valhalla?" Gladstone held his hands out wide. "I've been thinking about it," Gladstone admitted. "and I'd say we're somewhere between our world and one of those places. Judging by that altar and all the hanzi, I'd guess somewhere near Diyu."

"Diyu?" I asked, the name completely unfamiliar.

"Chinese hell," Gladstone clarified.

"Seriously?" I asked. Not only was that hard to believe, but it challenged most of what I knew about the laws of time and space. I'd always thought of Heaven and Hell as abstract concepts—states of being like euphoria and agony. The idea that Hell could be ethnocentric, not to mention real, seemed ridiculously farfetched.

"Well," a new voice said, "close, but not exactly."

CHAPTER 46

*G*ladstone propped himself using the pillar and faced the newcomer —a monstrously tall woman lounging on the altar, her legs drawn neatly to the side, swirling the blood in the bowl with her index finger. She was a study in contrasts: porcelain skin beneath a white shift, her hair and eyes darker than the gloom that surrounded us. She was beautiful, but hauntingly so, like a dense, smothering fog.

"Did you think you could tempt one of us with this?" she asked, dubiously studying the bowl and its contents.

Gladstone shrugged. "I hoped it would get your attention."

"Oh? And what am I, mortal?"

Gladstone shrugged again.

"You hope to lure my kind? With rancid bait such as this? You are very stupid. And so very far from home. Leave this bowl, and leave this place, and I will not kill you."

"Oy, lady, does that deal extend to me, too?" I called out. I didn't necessarily want to draw attention to myself, but I liked the idea of being left behind to die in an alternate dimension even less.

The woman's eyes flicked towards me, then widened. "You have bound this woman?"

"She's my second offering," Gladstone clarified. "The blood of a dead man and the life of a maiden. Probably not a virgin, though. You ain't a virgin, is you, love?"

"Go fuck yourself," I spat.

"Right. Not a virgin, but still, she's prized goods."

The woman unfolded and rose, towering above us both. I hadn't realized how alien she was—her proportions were ideal, but distorted somehow, like an image that had been stretched vertically. She approached me, sniffing. Something—and not only the fact that I'm sure I smelled awful after my bloody fight with Jacob—made me cringe and shy away. That's when I noticed her pale shift was torn; tendrils of it fluttered out behind her...except there was no wind. She stopped only a few feet away and settled back on her haunches. "She is not pure enough," she said, finally.

"Well, right, not a virgin, as I said—"

"That is not what I mean. She would not satisfy me. She is not a believer. She has no faith in anything but herself."

I winced, but didn't deny it. I'd been raised Catholic, of course, but that hardly meant anything these days. I enjoyed Mass—the cultish pageantry of it had always entertained me—but I'd balked long before my Confirmation, opting to enroll in public school and attend services only at my aunt's request. It wasn't so much that I didn't believe in God...

I simply believed in myself more.

Gladstone studied the woman. "That would make you a demon then, eh?"

The woman leaned forward until she was on all fours. Her claws pierced the dirt as white fur erupted up her arms. The drifting tendrils of her dress became tails, bushy and white.

Nine of them, by my count.

She began to stalk Gladstone. "I am a fox spirit. A man-eater. In fact, the more you talk, you odious little man, the more appetizing you become."

"I don't know about that. I summoned me a demon, not too long ago. A proper one, with horns and everyfin. We had us a chat, and you know what he told me? He says that demons, they like causing mischief, but they can only do so much, right? Somefin about balance. Can't rock the boat or it'll all go to shit. But I don't give a shit about the boat. So, I come looking for trouble, and now I've found you, Foxy."

The nine-tailed fox demon, or Foxy according to Gladstone, lunged at the wizard, but Gladstone danced backwards out of reach and held up his hands. "Hold on now. I've got a little proposition for you that you may want to hear, first. See, I want someone dead, and I think you and I can make us a deal."

"You know nothing, mortal," Foxy growled.

"I know you prefer the flesh of holy men. Unless the scholars got that wrong. Wouldn't be the first time."

Foxy hesitated.

"Ah. So they didn't it wrong. Well then, let me ask you a question," Gladstone continued, a gleam in his eye, "Do you know how many churches there are in Boston?"

"What's a church?" she asked, finally.

As you can imagine, the conversation didn't go well from there.

CHAPTER 47

I stopped listening soon after Gladstone began describing the world we'd left behind—specifically the abundance of religious people in it. Fortunately, in that span of time I'd had a chance to recover and felt like I could make a break for it, especially if I could get this damn rope off me. Once I managed that, I'd figure out how to close the portal before Gladstone released a fox spirit on Boston's unsuspecting religious population.

Something flickered at the edge of my vision as I studied the knot Gladstone had tied, trying to figure out how to unravel it. I glanced up to see a rope swaying above my head. The wind, maybe? Except I'd already figured out there wasn't any wind. Meanwhile, Gladstone and Foxy were too engrossed in their conversation to notice.

Another rope twitched, high above us. Something was up there. A moment later, I saw it: a brown huddled mass so dark it was almost indistinguishable from the backdrop of foliage and branches. It moved gracefully, swinging among the ropes above our heads without making a sound. The creature paused, hanging from one of these, upside down, and stared at me with large, owlish eyes that glinted in the dark.

What's up?

The voice spoke inside my mind.

The voice spoke. Inside. My. Mind.

You get used to it.

A quick glance confirmed that Gladstone and his companion were still busy talking, so they obviously hadn't heard anything. Which meant the thing hanging above us was able to communicate with me directly.

Thing, huh? Well that's rude.

I ground my teeth. I was tied up in an alternate dimension listening to a throat-slitting wizard describe my fellow Bostonians like a waiter at a fine dining restaurant—absolutely scrumptious, plenty of fat despite strides to resolve the obesity epidemic, lightly scented according to the composition of various bath bombs—to a woman who could dunk without jumping and pop a basketball with her razor-sharp claws, and this thing was worried about semantics.

Really?

The creature drew closer, dangling thirty feet above our heads until I could make out the fur-covered features of its face. It bared its teeth in a garish smile, pink tongue lolling about in its mouth, eyes twinkling in a visage that was almost human. He—and there was no mistaking his gender now that I could see his densely muscular upper body, visible even beneath a coarse brown coat of hair—was the missing link. Somewhere between homo sapien and monkey, he'd have looked perfect smack dab in the middle of one of those shirts detailing the Evolution of Man.

Except he wore pants and had a staff strapped to his back.

Call me the Monkey King. Or Sun Wukong. Whichever works.

Whichever works? What the hell was that supposed to mean? And what the hell kind of name was the Monkey King?

It means you don't speak Chinese, and your brain is filling in the gaps. And it's a god's name.

I blinked. A what?

A god. Little g.

So, to recap, I was chatting with a telepathic monkey hanging out in an alternate dimension...who claimed he was a god. Little g. I wasn't sure how to respond to that. I mean, I'd met some crazy powerful, otherworldly creatures over the years, but never anything as daunting or implausible as a god. Shouldn't my retinas be burning, or my mind melting?

Please. Quit being so dramatic.

A flood of questions came to mind, but I didn't have time to voice any of them; while I'd been busy chatting with the Monkey King, Gladstone and

Foxy had reached a consensus. The wizard held her hand in his as though he were about to propose, which was almost comical given how much taller she was than him.

"Very well. I will join you in your world and feast on the righteous," Foxy was saying, "but what is it you wish in return?"

"There's a bloke I want you to kill," Gladstone replied, matter-of-factly. "Problem is, he's protected. People like me can't get near him; he's got too many friends and he's too cautious, besides. I've asked around, tried to make a few deals, but—even though plenty of people want to see him dead —ain't none of 'em willing to risk it." The wizard shrugged and splayed his hands.

"Word is he's pissed off his own people recently, though. Which means he's vulnerable. And I heard he can't help himself when there's a pretty bird in trouble. Once you've got a full stomach, even he won't be able to stop you. You kill him, and we're square."

Well, that is a very dishonorable way to kill someone.

That was his issue with Gladstone's plan? I scowled up at the Monkey King. Unfortunately, I'd met guys like Gladstone before—men who sought revenge at any price. More often than not they turned out to be sad, impotent creatures, but Gladstone was a wizard with decades, maybe even centuries, of experience and power to fall back on.

Which meant he'd do whatever it took to see his plan succeed.

A wizard, huh? Excellent. I haven't fought a wizard in quite some time.

"Once I am satisfied," Foxy said, the sound of her voice overlapping the Monkey King's voice in my head, "I will do as you wish." She drew a nail down Gladstone's forearm in the blink of an eye and a razor-thin line of blood began to bubble up along the wound. Gladstone winced, but didn't move as Foxy hunched over and lapped at the blood.

Distract them.

I rolled my eyes, but did as he asked. Anything was better than waiting to find out which one of the two demented sociopaths would come after me, first. "So, is that how ye seal a contract around here?" I yelled, drawing their attention. "Because where I'm from, that's how ye get diseases."

Foxy didn't even bother looking at me. "No, I simply wanted to remember how his kind tastes. It has been centuries since I have swallowed a man whole."

"Oh, nice. D'ye hear that, Gladstone? You're an appetizer."

Gladstone yanked his arm back, clearly irritated to find out her sampling of his blood hadn't been some elaborate ritual like he'd thought. "We have a deal, then?" he asked, tersely.

Foxy grinned, her lips and teeth stained with his blood—because apparently having elongated canines wasn't creepy enough. "We have a deal, mortal."

That's when Sun Wukong, the Monkey King, struck.

And that scrappy bastard could *fight*.

CHAPTER 48

*T*he Monkey King leapt from the rafters and used Gladstone as a springboard to dropkick Foxy in the face. In a high-pitched wail that reminded me of the chimp exhibit in the Franklin Park Zoo, he screamed something in Chinese which seamlessly translated in my mind.

Get out of my temple!

Suddenly, the ropes made a lot more sense.

Gladstone lay stunned, groaning. Foxy, on the other hand, took the strike gracefully—well, as gracefully as anyone can after getting dropkicked in the face—and came up swinging.

She fought ruthlessly.

Each strike was meant to maim or kill, without hesitation or remorse. Wanting to hurt someone that badly usually made you sloppy, but Foxy's combat style reminded me of those special forces training videos you see floating around the internet—the ultra-violent ones that make regular people cringe.

And yet, Sun was completely unfazed. The Monkey King barely moved at all by comparison; he dipped and ducked and dodged, clouting Foxy again and again with either edge of his staff. She couldn't get anywhere near him, no matter how fast she struck or from which direction. And, with every blow he landed on her arms and legs, I could see her frustration grow.

White fur spread across her arms and shoulders as she lashed out in anger, her stunningly smooth, mask-like face sprouting whiskers. Her strikes inched closer, claws barely missing Sun's eyes as she went for a gouge. Sun pulled back with a moment to spare, then hopped up and head-butted her right between the eyes.

Foxy stumbled back, clutching at her face. By the time she recovered, her gaze had become feral, almost feverish. She dove forward with a teeth-gnashing snarl, snatched Sun's staff, and tried to jerk it out of his hands. He let her. As soon as she'd taken it from him, he flipped over her, turned, and grabbed the staff from behind in a movement so smooth it looked choreo-graphed—like a scene from *Crouching Tiger, Hidden Dragon*...featuring a monkey.

Sun drew the staff tight against her throat.

Surrender.

I wasn't sure how she was supposed to respond while being choked from behind, but—judging by the expression on her face—she wasn't interested in throwing in the towel, anyway. She struggled to free herself, stomping at his feet while clawing at his face, but Sun simply leaned back and increased the pressure against her windpipe. After having been recently strangled myself, I found myself cringing; it was like watching someone get punched in the stomach, or poked in the eye. In fact, I almost felt bad for her.

Almost.

At least until Gladstone stepped in.

CHAPTER 49

$\mathcal{T}$he Monkey King released Foxy and dove for a nearby rope as Gladstone's fireball erupted in the space where he'd been standing, but—because my eyes had adjusted to the dark—the sudden burst of light seared my retinas, and I couldn't tell if Sun had gotten away clean. I blinked away tears.

More sounds of fighting echoed around me, and I could feel the heat of numerous fires burning nearby. By the time my eyes adjusted, I saw that Sun had chosen the high ground and was swinging between pillars while Gladstone sent blasts of flame toward the ceiling. Sparks drifted down as ropes and greenery caught. Fortunately, stone didn't burn, or the whole place might have gone up in smoke.

Of course, that didn't mean I was safe; as the ropes burned, the smoke rose, filling the air with an acrid stench. I hunkered down next to the pillar, hoping the air was clearer the closer I was to the ground. I kept an eye on the fighting, but also on the portal—did it have a time limit? I squirmed, giving myself rope burns in the process; I desperately wanted to be on the other side of that thing when it closed—dying of smoke inhalation in Hell, or wherever Sun's temple was located, didn't sound optimal to me.

"The wizard is powerful," Foxy remarked, startling me. I glanced up and saw her towering over me, her obscenely long claws hovering beside my face. "Soon, the Monkey King will tire. And then I will kill him. My father will be pleased."

I frowned, but said nothing. I wasn't sure what kind of triggers a fox spirit—or demon, or whatever she was—might have, and I sure as hell didn't want to get torn to shreds because I'd inadvertently insulted her ancestors. Frankly, I'd never met a demon of any kind before and felt a little out of my depth. As far as I knew, demons were Biblical reprobates who went around corrupting and defiling, opposed by archangels and exorcists.

Guess I needed to expand my horizons.

Foxy strode forward into the fray, content to let Gladstone continue hounding the Monkey King, waiting for her chance to strike, ignoring the drifting sparks which nestled in her hair like fireflies. I had to admit it was a solid strategy; divide and conquer. I only wished I could break free and help, somehow. Or, you know, dive back through the portal, close it, and pretend like this had never happened.

The three combatants disappeared behind the pillars on the far side of the temple, though I was able to track them through the occasional flashes of light.

"Well," a voice said, "this place isn't creepy. Nope, not one bit."

Jimmy stepped through the Gateway. He was easy to make out now that Gladstone had lit most of the temple on fire. Everything about him read off-duty cop: black leather jacket over a grey hoodie, dark denim jeans, a dark t-shirt, and boots. His badge hung on a chain around his neck.

Of course, none of that explained what he was doing here. I eyed the distant fighting and, confident they wouldn't overhear, called out to him. "Jimmy!" I hissed.

"Jesus," Jimmy said, spotting me tied up to a pillar like some virgin sacrifice. He rushed over, leaning in close so I could hear him over the din of Gladstone's shouts and Sun's fierce battle cries. "Where the hell are we?" Jimmy asked.

"How about ye start with what the fuck you're doin' here?" I asked. "Why aren't ye with Dez?"

"Dez is fine," he replied, tersely. "She called me like you asked, but I was already here, so I told her to go home and I'd send an officer her way."

I could tell he was pissed; his jaw was bunched, and he wouldn't meet my eyes. Of course, that could have been for any number of reasons. The fact that I'd skipped out on him the morning after, the fact that I'd taken the briefcase, the fact that he'd had to step through a portal to an alternate dimension to rescue me…take your pick.

"It's a temple," I explained. "Now get these ropes off me so we can get out of here."

"A temple?" Jimmy replied, eyebrow raised, scouring the area.

"Aye. There's also a fox spirit who eats holy people, a monkey god, and a fuckin' wizard over there. Now get me out of here."

Jimmy stared at me with an anesthetized look in his eyes. I didn't blame him; it was a lot to process. Of course, this was *exactly* why I hadn't brought him along in the first place—I couldn't afford to hold his hand in times like these. I shoved him with my shoulder. "Jimmy! Ropes!"

Jimmy grunted and began fumbling with the rope wrapped around me as an errant fireball slammed against a nearby pillar, spewing flames in all directions. Jimmy flinched, but I could see his head was at least in it, now.

Over Jimmy's shoulder, I saw the fighters reemerge as the Monkey King nimbly dodged yet another blast, hopping and swinging from one rope to another. But then, with a brutal snap, Sun landed on a rope that had been too ravaged by fire to support his weight. It gave out, and sent him tumbling to the floor.

Sun groaned, but rose. I could see patches of fur that had been singed. He glanced over at us, and I felt Jimmy jerk upright, his grip on my shoulder tightening.

"What is it?" I asked.

"Um, I'm pretty sure that thing just spoke. Except—"

"Ye heard him in your mind, aye," I said. "Ye aren't imaginin' t'ings. What'd he say?"

Jimmy frowned and shook his head as if to clear his thoughts. "Nothing important. Come on, let's get you out of here." He began working on the rope once more, trying to pry it up and off me. Sun's gaze lingered on us for a moment longer, but then quickly shifted to his two opponents as they materialized out of the smoke.

It seemed the Monkey King had nowhere to run.

CHAPTER 50

*G*ladstone prepared another blast of flame as Foxy leapt at her opponent, still struggling to pair off against Sun's staff, which licked out at her faster than my eyes could track. Somehow the Monkey King managed to angle his attacks to keep Foxy between himself and Gladstone, which was the only thing preventing the wizard from blasting away. It was working, but I knew it couldn't last forever; eventually Gladstone would find an opening.

"How's that rope comin'?" I asked.

"There's no give," he growled, yanking at the rope in frustration. "What's this thing even made out of?"

"The hair of a thousand virgins," I quipped.

Jimmy's eyebrows shot up, and his hands stopped working. "Really?"

"No! Idgit."

Jimmy scowled, then rose to study the knot around the pillar, much like I had thought to do before realizing that—with my hands locked to my sides —there was little I could do but gnaw at it with my teeth.

Which, admittedly, I had considered.

I glanced over at the fighting and noticed Gladstone was pointing at Sun, no longer trying to blast him, but instead ominously tracking the monkey god's movements with his index finger—though, with Sun doing backflips off pillars and pole-vaulting around the temple itself, even that was proving difficult.

"Did ye bring a knife?" I asked, nudging Jimmy.

He grunted. "I'm carrying two guns and enough ammo to reload twice. I figured if I needed a knife, I was pretty much dead anyway."

"Some boy scout ye are," I admonished.

"Well, where's your knife, then?" he fired back.

"The wizard has it. Used it to cut that man's throat. The one on the other side of the portal."

"Yeah, I saw that." He sounded a little relieved.

"What? D'ye t'ink I had somethin' to do with it?"

Jimmy didn't answer.

"Seriously? Ye should know me better than that."

"I thought I knew you pretty well, until I woke up alone this morning," he muttered through clenched teeth.

I had nothing to say to that. If Jimmy wanted an apology, he knew me even less well than he claimed. I wasn't sorry I'd left him behind—I stood by that decision. I was only sorry that I needed his help; being the damsel in distress didn't sit well with me.

At all.

I felt the rope shudder; he'd done something to loosen its hold on the pillar, although it was still tight around me. "Besides," Jimmy continued. "what if he was threatening you? If it was between you and him?"

I hesitated.

"Exactly," he said. "I didn't ask because I didn't want to know. I'm glad it wasn't you. But, for the record, it wouldn't have mattered, as long as you were safe."

"Jimmy…" I trailed off, then sighed. "I'm glad ye came," I admitted.

He nodded. "Me, too. Sorry I wasn't here sooner. But after you ditched me," Jimmy said, then held up a hand before I could defend myself, "it took me a while before I could track you down and follow you out here."

"Ye were followin' me?" I asked. I shook my head, realizing how oblivious I'd been over the past few days. First Jacob, and now Jimmy. Between tailing Serge and being tailed by two rather conspicuous men, I was zero for three in the sleuthing category.

I had homework to do, if we survived this.

"At a distance," Jimmy admitted. "But when you didn't come out of the house right away, I got suspicious, so I broke in."

"Broke in? Jimmy, the door was unlocked," I said.

Jimmy's tugging stopped for moment, then resumed.

"Ye kicked that poor door open, didn't ye?"

"Who doesn't leave their door locked?"

"The dead guy, that's who."

Jimmy grunted, then fell to his knees as a flash blinded us both. I lost my balance and fell back into him. By the time I was able to sit back up, the air around us was singed and heavy with the stench of burnt hair. Gladstone chuckled in the eerie silence that followed. "Got you, you bloody bastard."

"What was that?" Jimmy whispered.

"Pretty sure he shot lightnin' out of his finger," I replied, praying the spots behind my eyes would one day go away, and that I wouldn't be blind for eternity.

"Seriously?" Jimmy asked, eyes wide.

"Welcome to me world."

"Quinn!" Jimmy hissed.

"What?"

"I think the monkey god is glowing."

"He's probably on fire," I replied.

I pinned my eyes shut until something other than residual light registered, then opened them and squinted. Gladstone seemed exhausted, shoulders slumped, his clothes covered in both blood and mud at this point, smoke rising from his right hand. Foxy was on all fours, growling, patches of bloody skin and welts visible beneath her fur from the series of blows Sun had landed —apparently her plan to let the wizard tire Sun out hadn't worked out so well.

I scoured the area until I spotted Sun some twenty feet away. A black stain marred his chest from where Gladstone's lightning bolt had struck, a stain which became more and more visible as the glow around his body expanded. A golden aura licked at his limbs, sending his hair straight up and causing it to clump together in spikes as though pinched together by static electricity. The temple rumbled, and the pillars, already damaged from the fighting, creaked and groaned as dust poured down sporadically above us, sending sparks flying whenever it hit a patch of untended flame.

Sun began to howl, his voice full of rage. His hair flickered between a dark brown and a solid shade of gold, back and forth between blinks. Waves of searing wind pulsed out from where he stood, the ground beneath his feet cracking as stones defied gravity, spinning laconically in midair.

Turns out The Monkey King wasn't on fire, after all.

He was simply going Super Saiyan.

CHAPTER 51

*T*he final seconds of the Monkey King's transformation shook the temple's foundations and sent all of us flying backwards. I landed on Jimmy, the rope around my torso pulling taut, abrading my arms yet again. At this point, I didn't want to think about how many parts of me were going to be bruised or torn if and when we survived this—not that I didn't already have plenty of scars already.

Thank God for health insurance.

Looking around, I realized the temple was in a worse state than I was; flames licked here and there along blackened ropes, and smoke drifted like fog among the canopy. A few pillars were cracked, and their shadows flickered in response to the flames and the Monkey King's aura, which emitted its own pure, golden light.

Jimmy shrugged me off, and I rolled onto my knees in time to see Gladstone sit up. He raised his uninjured hand and desperately shot another bout of flames at Sun, but this time the Monkey King didn't even bother dodging; he strode into them, oblivious to the heat.

Gladstone scrambled backwards, but refused to let up on the flames as he scanned the temple. I could tell he was searching for Foxy, but the blast from Sun's metamorphosis had thrown her out of sight. Sun waved at the flames in front of his face as if they were little more than insects obscuring his vision.

Suddenly, I felt Jimmy's solid weight at my back disappear. I fell backwards, which gave me a perfectly horrific view of Jimmy in the fox spirit's grasp.

Foxy had pinned Jimmy's mouth closed with one clawed hand, the other draped delicately over his exposed throat. The threat was clear enough that, when Sun emerged from Gladstone's inferno, he froze immediately. I tried to get to my feet, but the angle was wrong, and I ended up falling onto my side and cracking my shoulder against the pillar.

"Let him go!" I screamed.

"Hush," Foxy said, "this does not concern you." The fox spirit slid her nails along Jimmy's throat as if brushing the strings of a guitar. "I think we should settle this a different way," Foxy said, meeting Sun's intense stare.

"Maybe you should have thought of that before you entered my temple without an invitation," Sun replied, speaking in Chinese, but translated in real time in my mind. "Very rude."

"I was...enticed. By the mortal."

"Right." Sun sniffed and turned to Gladstone, who had given up on the pyrotechnics in favor of rising to his feet. "And what is your excuse?"

"Huh?" Gladstone seemed to be struggling with the whole dubbed, telepathy thing.

"For entering my temple, uninvited. For placing the blood of a killer on my altar."

"Well, I—"

"Actually, don't speak. It's not important. I'm feeling generous today. You fought well, and I do love a worthy opponent. If you all leave my temple, now, all will be forgiven."

Foxy took a breath as if preparing to accept, but nothing came out. Instead she sniffed, gingerly, at the nape of Jimmy's neck. Jimmy struggled, but she barely had to exert any energy to keep him from breaking free. With strength like that, I realized she could snap his neck in an instant.

"Did you know," Foxy said, her voice riddled with a raspy vibrato, "that righteous men come in all shapes and sizes? It's not their faith that makes them so tasty," she purred. "It's their willingness to sacrifice themselves for others. To take on other people's burdens." She lifted Jimmy's badge and turned it over in her hand, then looked me directly in the eye, the placidity of her face settling into something cold and cruel.

"No! Don't!" I yelled.

But it was too late.

Because she'd already torn out Jimmy's throat with her teeth.

CHAPTER 52

immy landed beside me, his face mercifully turned away. If I thought my throat ached before, it was nothing compared to what I was experiencing now; I screamed his name, telling him to get up, but he didn't so much as twitch. I fought against the rope so hard I could feel my skin tear. Foxy, meanwhile, strolled casually around Jimmy's body, avoiding the pool of blood spreading beneath him, which was odd considering how much had spilled down her chin and throat.

The Monkey King hadn't moved, but he was no longer bathed in golden light, and he seemed smaller, frailer even. I could see the distress and anger on his face, but something else too—resignation? I wasn't sure what that meant, but at this point I didn't care; I needed to get to Jimmy.

Foxy began licking her fingers clean, lapping at them with a tiny, darting tongue. Aside from the blood dribbling down her front, she appeared more or less as I'd first seen her—horrifically tall and freakishly pale; her wounds had healed completely and she no longer sported claws or whiskers.

"Grab the woman!" Gladstone insisted. "We can trade her to get—"

"That's enough," Foxy said, flinging her hand in his direction. Gladstone fell to his knees, a shallow wound appearing across his chest, as if someone had slashed at him with a knife. "I have everything I need to defeat the *great* Sun Wukong. His temple has been desecrated, and I have eaten. You know... I'd forgotten how invigorating it was to consume a man." Foxy turned her attention to Gladstone. "When I am done here, I will come to your world. I will hunt down your people. And, when I am fully satisfied, I will come for you and use your bones as toothpicks for presuming to make a deal with me."

Gladstone blanched.

"You should get out of here while you can," Sun said, his voice oddly calm. "Free the woman and flee together. This is no place for mortals."

Sun faced off against the much taller adversary, and I could read the eagerness in him, as if everything up until this moment had been some sort of elaborate preamble to the fight that was about to take place. I hated him in that instant—hated him for not killing Gladstone, for letting Foxy take Jimmy, for being excited by the prospect of fighting her now that she was strong enough to give him a real challenge.

Sun bristled a little.

I'd forgotten he could hear me. This time, I thought at him directly, louder. I screamed at him and called him a coward. I demanded he let me go so I could take Jimmy and get out of there.

Your friend is already dead. I knew she might use him, and so I told him to flee, but he refused. I'm sorry, but you should go.

With that, Sun took off towards Foxy, spinning his staff in one hand, howling as he went. He no longer seemed eager to fight, which was a small victory, I guess. Foxy grinned and lowered herself into a squat, anticipating his charge.

Gladstone, meanwhile, grimaced, shuffled until he was well out of Foxy's reach, and then bolted for the portal, pausing only to examine Jimmy's body. He nudged Jimmy's shoulder with his boot, causing the detective to flop over on his back.

Jimmy's eyes were mercifully closed, his jaw cocked away from the rest of his face. Except for the gaping wound at his throat, he could have been sleeping. I inched closer, trying to see if he was breathing, hoping to cover that awful, gruesome gash.

Gladstone caught a glimpse of the badge dangling from Jimmy's neck and sniffed. "Fucking coppers, always sticking their noses in where they ain't wanted."

Something inside me snapped.

I got my legs underneath me and lunged at the bastard, howling. I managed to tackle him, but, with my arms pinned, I couldn't do much more than ram into him. Gladstone fell with me on top of him. He froze in surprise, then—realizing I was still tied up—kicked me off and backed up until I was out of reach. He wiped at the grime that covered his shirt and trousers. "Stupid bitch, you'll get what's coming to you."

He scurried through the portal.

I spit in his general direction, then sluggishly began sawing at the rope with the knife I'd managed to retrieve from his pocket when we'd fallen. "Don't ye worry, Jimmy. I'm comin'. Hold on, I'll be there soon," I whispered.

CHAPTER 53

oxy smashed the Monkey King's face into a pillar, sending chips of stone flying to the ground. His face was a bloody, mangled mess of cuts. His staff, broken, lay several feet away. And yet, still, he fought. He somersaulted backwards, trying to create some distance, but Foxy pressed her advantage, kicking him in the side hard enough to send him flying.

"And to think, all those stories they tell about you...and look at you now," Foxy chided, stalking him.

Sun tried to rise, but the fox spirit swept his legs out from under him, then pressed the heel of her foot on his tail, pinning it to the dirt. Sun howled in pain, his eyes pinched shut. Foxy hunched over, the blood on her chin dry and flecked, her teeth stained pink. "But then, you almost always had help in one form or another, didn't you?"

"Ye really are a bitch, d'ye know that?" I asked, standing behind her, finally free.

Sun's eyes shot open.

Foxy spun to face me.

And I put a bullet through her teeth.

Then another. And another. I unloaded Jimmy's pistol, then pulled out his smaller handgun. I kept firing until Foxy's face looked like a plastic surgeon's worst nightmare...and then I fired some more. I reloaded while she stumbled around blindly, then aimed at her knees, taking out her kneecaps with a few well-aimed shots. She toppled, falling forward onto her hands. I moved on to her wrists.

Funny things, guns.

There were plenty of Freaks out there who could stare down the barrel of a firearm without the slightest twinge of fear—unless you had silver ammunition, a werewolf could heal a bullet wound in a matter of minutes; zombies were oblivious to damn near everything, including dismemberment; and, short of firing iron musket balls at them, the Fae were more irritated by the obnoxious noise guns made than being hit by a bullet. But, at point blank range, with plenty of ammunition and no one to stop me, I could do some serious cosmetic damage—enough to cripple any Freak for at least a little while.

And Foxy was no exception.

"Get up!" I screamed at Sun, who looked up at me in total shock, one eye swollen completely shut. He managed to stand, woozily, his body shaking from exhaustion.

By the time I turned back around, Foxy had managed to raise herself back up onto her knees, and her skin was already knitting. I watched an eyeball reform, its gaze malicious and promising pain. Once her tongue grew back, I knew she'd have plenty of stupid shit to say, but I wasn't interested in hearing any of it.

I only wanted her to hurt.

"How do we stop her?" I growled.

We don't. Get out of here, while you still can.

I shifted, swinging the barrel of Jimmy's gun until it rested against Sun's temple. He raised an eyebrow.

I'm a god, remember?

"Then act like one," I replied, which sounded cool, even though I had no idea what that actually meant; he was the first god I'd ever met, after all. I drew the gun back to my side—I was out of ammunition, anyway. I slid the handguns into the pockets of Jimmy's jacket where they hung, awkwardly, butts protruding, then I slipped out of the jacket itself.

I knew I'd run out of ammo eventually, so I'd brought along another option—a thick coil of rope that I'd cut free after I escaped. I swung it a few times to test out the balance. Sun sighed and retrieved his staff, twirling the broken ends in each hand.

As soon as she gets up, take her left.

"Fuck that," I said.

I took two steps forward and swung the rope as hard as I could. It collided with her face and sent her sprawling onto her side. I brought it down, over and over again, whipping her with it until her tongue finally grew back and I could hear her screams of outrage and pain.

This isn't a fight.

"No. It. Isn't." I brought the rope down on her with each word.

It isn't honorable.

"Eat shit, monkey," I said, through gritted teeth. In my head, all I could see was Jimmy's face. The feel of his still chest beneath my hands. I screamed wordlessly, lashing out with all my hate at the creature who'd killed someone I'd care about.

And it wasn't enough.

Enough.

Suddenly, everything went white.

CHAPTER 54

$\mathcal{T}$he first thing I heard was the ocean.

I stood, panting, clutching a rope soaked in blood, completely alone on a black sand beach. I pivoted on my heel, scanning the horizon. Ocean waves frothed and crashed against the shore while storm clouds gathered in the distance. Behind me loomed tree-covered mountains.

Despite the gloomy weather, I had to look away from the glare of those vibrant green slopes, my eyes watering. That's when I noticed the man in the ocean, paddling hard towards the shore in a flimsy rowboat.

He is destined to drown.

The voice, the same one that had spoken in my head before I arrived here, did not belong to the Monkey King; it was harder, somehow, edged with authority. I scanned the beach, searching for the speaker, but saw no one. Which meant I was either going crazy—at this point a distinct possibility—or someone else had been hijacking my mind and body for a one-on-one. Part of me wondered whether telepaths had to tune in to other people's minds, like you would a radio, and whether there was a way to change frequencies.

Because I was over these little chats.

The man in the rowboat drew closer, although each wave threatened to capsize his tiny vessel. I found myself rooting for him, inexplicably, the way you so often do when you see someone taking on the elements. It's that defiant streak we all have, I think—that urge to stand in the pouring rain and listen to thunder pound so hard against the sky that you feel its vibrations in your bones.

A single wave, larger than the others, emerged. The man saw it, too, and angled the prow of his boat to cut through the wave. But he was too late, and the wave too big.

His boat snapped in half.

The man disappeared beneath the surface, and the rogue wave slammed against the shore a few minutes later, pitching the snapped handles of his oars onto the sand.

An elderly man I hadn't seen until now fetched one of the broken oars and studied it before tossing it back out to sea. He didn't seem to mind the biting chill of the wind, wearing a corduroy jacket and tattered slacks, his face deeply wrinkled, but cleanshaven. He prowled the sand until he found and did the same with the other oar, and soon both disappeared beneath the surf.

"Who are ye?" I asked.

The elderly man stared out at the ocean but said nothing.

"I asked ye a question. Who are ye?" I repeated. "And, where am I?"

"Do you think he regretted anything?"

"What?"

The elderly man pointed with his chin and tucked his hands into the pockets of his jacket. "That man who died out there. It was quick, you know. Hit his head and drowned. But I think about this a lot. Whether all mortals perish with some tiny regret in their hearts. Not those frivolous bucket lists with their skydiving and travel, but real regrets—people they wish they didn't have to leave behind, stories they never got to tell, versions of themselves they never got to be."

I frowned, considering his question. I felt more than a little crazy, standing on a beach in the middle of nowhere, bantering about philosophy after everything I'd been through; I ached, and the salty air burned where it licked my skin, but—beyond those sensations—I felt raw and exposed, emotionally drained. "What does that have to do with—" I started to ask.

"Would you like to know what James Collins' regret was, the moment he died?" The elderly man faced me, his eyes full of pity. "He regretted not being able to save everyone. And I do mean everyone. Can you imagine? The sheer ambition of that regret."

"Shut up," I whispered.

"Did you know he kept a list by his bedside table? A list of everyone he believed he failed. Friends, even enemies, in some cases. Some of the names weren't even names at all, only what he remembered. Brown Jacket. Kid with the Red Scarf. Some part of him was relieved, I think, to die. To let go."

"Shut up!" I screamed.

"I'm not saying this to hurt you. I'm saying this because you have a choice to make. The balance has been tampered with, and I wish to set things right."

What the hell did that even mean?

It means he can return.

The man smiled, gently, at my floored expression. "But," he said, out loud this time, "I cannot interfere directly. It must be your decision. You are his friend. You will have to take responsibility for bringing him back. You—"

"I'll do it," I said. "Tell me how."

The elderly man looked as though he wanted to say something else, but nodded, instead.

CHAPTER 55

I wrapped the rope around Foxy's throat and tied the best knot I could, which was less than stellar given how thick it was and how little function remained in my hands. But when I yanked, it held fast, allowing me to draw her towards Jimmy's body, which lay thirty feet away at least.

What are you doing?

Sun's voice cut through my head. I glanced back over my shoulder at the Monkey King. "I'm bringin' me friend back."

That is not—

"And you're goin' to help me," I said. "Grab her feet."

I do not think—

I dropped Foxy, whose hands were recovering enough to grip the rope and claw at it, and shoved my finger into the Monkey King's densely muscled chest. "Ye owe me," I said. "I know what ye told Jimmy when he got here. Ye didn't tell him to run, like ye claimed. Ye told him that, if he stayed, I would end up free, but he would end up dead."

Sun bowed his head but didn't deny it.

I snatched the rope and began dragging Foxy once more, speaking through gritted teeth. "As if that idgit would ever leave me to die in a place like this or pass up a chance to be the hero. But I don't care what that bastard wants, I'm not leavin' him here, either. Now, grab her fuckin' feet."

The Monkey King grabbed her fucking feet.

Together, the two of us managed to lay Foxy beside Jimmy's body. He was on his back where I'd left him after retrieving his jacket and pistols. Foxy—the lacerations from the rope closing much slower than her other wounds had—struggled to rise.

I kicked her in the face, sending her sprawling. "Tie up her legs," I instructed Sun. The Monkey King snatched a rope and tied a much more secure knot around her lower half, the rope looking almost dainty in his overlarge hands.

Now what?

"Now we follow directions," I said, peering over Sun's shoulder at the elderly man from the beach. He clucked his tongue. "She should have known better than to consume a holy man in your temple, Sun."

Sun whirled around, his uninjured eye wide, and immediately dropped to one knee, chattering in Chinese. My brain didn't pick up on any of it, this time.

I guess it was a private conversation.

The elderly man waved a hand. "It's not your fault. Neither is it hers. We all act according to our natures." He stepped forward and leveled a hand at Foxy, whose eyes—completely regrown—shone with hatred, then despair.

"What are ye goin' to do?" I asked.

The elderly man snorted. "Have you ever tried to balance on the edge of a sidewalk with someone pushing you from behind?"

I shook my head.

"Because it would be really hard to do, yes?"

I shrugged. "Sure."

"Well, quit pushing me and stand back. I have work to do."

CHAPTER 56

I hefted Jimmy, hooking his arm over my shoulder, and half-carried, half-dragged him through the portal. He was semi-conscious, able to shuffle his feet and little else, but his wounds were gone—the blood stains on his shirt crusted over. On the other side, I nearly slipped in a pool of liquid that turned out to be Jacob's pooling blood.

I cursed.

To be honest, I'd almost forgotten he was there; it felt like everything that had happened on this side of the portal had taken place a long time ago—like waking up from one of those long naps after which everything seems disjointed and unreal.

A wordless shriek echoed behind us and the portal snapped shut. Beneath the dim florescence I could make out Gladstone's bloody shoeprints, and decided to follow them, both relieved and upset to find he'd fled. As we were, Jimmy and I would prove easy targets, but Gladstone knew things—like where to find me and those I cared about. Maybe Ryan was right, and it was time to take an extended vacation; I didn't want to spend the rest of my life looking over my shoulder, after all.

Before I could decide either way, I noticed the tell-tale pulse of red and blue lights through the windows. "A little late," I muttered as I readjusted Jimmy's weight. The shoddy door lay in shambles—no doubt thanks to Jimmy's overzealous entrance. I gingerly stepped out onto the porch, only

185

to be greeted by a series of surprised shouts and a few very bright flashlights.

"Don't move!"

"Freeze!"

"Move and I'll shoot!"

A woman's voice I recognized interrupted the shouting officers, her authority shutting them all up at once, "Guns down, you morons! That's my partner!"

Detective Maria Machado rushed up the steps, gun in hand, but pointed at the ground, finger off the trigger. She looked frazzled; strands of hair poked out from her usually tidy, no-nonsense bun, and the small lines around her eyes seemed deeper, somehow. I wondered how we looked, Jimmy, covered in blood, and me, beaten half to death.

"Jimmy!" she cursed, under her breath.

"He's alright," I said. "Took a blow to the head, that's all."

"But ma'am," one of the uniformed officers behind Maria said, before she could respond, "we did a sweep of that house. There was no one in it! Where did they come from?"

I frowned. Come to think of it, how the hell had they missed the gaping portal in the middle of the back bedroom? And what about the dead man who lay inside? I searched Maria's face, but saw no ready answers there; she looked at us like we were ghosts—our existence both implausible and inescapable. I was about to reassure her that we were, in fact, real, when I saw one of the officers leaning against the side of police cruiser, smoking a cigarette. I narrowed my eyes, staring at his nondescript face. There was something there. A shimmer as he turned to look at us, standing out like a sore thumb compared to the seamless illusions I'd seen Ryan pull off.

Suddenly, I realized who and what I was looking at.

Gladstone, his face obscured by second-rate illusion magic.

"Maria," I said, "that officer over there—"

"It's Detective Machado, MacKenna, how many times do I have to tell you?" Maria snapped.

"Listen! This is important," I urged. "That man over there—no, don't look—have ye ever seen him before?"

Maria took a step forward as if peering into the house over my shoulder, but instead used her peripheral vision to look back towards the squad cars. She grunted. "He was here when we got here, but now that you mention it, no," she replied. "He could be a rookie? I don't know everyone in our precinct."

"He's not," I replied, then cursed. Maria was one of those Regulars who refused to believe in the unbelievable; I couldn't tell her there was a wizard impersonating a cop not thirty feet away.

"Listen," Maria said, taking a good long look at me for the first time since she'd approached, "you look like you may have taken a beating of your own. Why don't you let us get you to the hospital? You and James, both."

Too late, I realized Maria thought I was out of it, to the point where she wouldn't take me seriously no matter what I said. I didn't blame her, not for this, anyway; hell, I probably *was* in shock. But that didn't mean I was wrong. At this point, my only option was to force Maria to listen to me—to accuse Gladstone of something she'd have to investigate. Unfortunately, only one thing came to mind…

And it wasn't going to be pretty.

"He's got a bomb strapped to him," I insisted, my voice a low whisper. "That's the man who attacked us, and he has a bomb."

"A what?" Maria asked, too thrown by my accusation to freak out.

In hindsight, I knew how it sounded. But, as far as I could tell, it was the only way to get her attention *and* make sure she didn't do anything reckless. I'd seen Gladstone throw fireballs around all night long, which meant if the cops tried to corral and question him directly, he'd simply end up roasting them alive. This way, at least, they'd be on their toes.

"Listen, he stuck around, waitin' to finish the job. But he only wants me. If ye can get me close enough," I implored, "I can take him down."

"You can disarm a bomb?" Maria asked, her face incredulous.

"He showed me how it works," I lied. I didn't bother mentioning that my plan to disarm it was to get close enough to Gladstone that he'd be rendered powerless, including the illusion he still wore making him look like a cop. Once exposed, maybe I'd get a chance to put him down for good. But either way, I wanted to end this here and now.

"Alright, well we should call in backup. The bomb squad, in case—"

"There's no time!" I hissed. "If he t'inks you're waitin' for no reason, he'll get suspicious. Ye can't risk it."

"If you die," Maria said, finally, "I'll lose my badge."

"Aye," I said, "but then at least you'll be rid of me?"

Maria snorted. Her eyes lingered over the blood on Jimmy's shirt, visible beneath his jacket, and the bruises and scrapes that I'm sure covered every inch of my body. "What the hell happened in there, anyway?" she asked, shaking her head.

"I'll fill ye in later," I said. "Or, better yet, Jimmy will. For now, ye need to get him somewhere safe."

Maria looked skeptical but didn't have any reason to argue with at least that part of my plan. "Alright. Officer Hanson, come over here!"

Hanson approached, holstering his weapon. Maria leaned in as he approached. "Get him out of here. We have a 10-79. Follow procedure," she whispered.

Hanson gulped, but took Jimmy—who groaned a little as I transferred him to the smaller, but easily more muscular, officer—without another word. I fought the urge to rub my aching neck and shoulders. My lower back ached from the strain of holding Jimmy up, so I arched it a little. "Guess it's your lucky day, Maria," I said.

Maria glanced warily at me. "How so?"

"Ye finally get to put me in handcuffs."

She snorted.

Then she arrested me.

CHAPTER 57

*M*aria marched me down the porch steps toward the patrol car Gladstone leaned against as if taking me into custody. Jimmy was already in the back of Hanson's vehicle and on his way to the nearest hospital, which meant no matter how this played out, at least Jimmy would be safe.

Gladstone seemed surprised to see Jimmy in the back of a squad car instead of in a body bag, but clearly wasn't concerned about the detective's well-being, at least not enough to break the illusion. Meanwhile, I had to consciously remind myself not to glare in his direction.

Now that Maria knew he was there also, she'd be under the same strain, but I knew she could handle it; I'd seen her keep her cool in tougher situations than this. Still, I could sense she was worried for the other officers present. I couldn't blame her; if things went sideways, a lot of her people could get hurt, or killed.

If I was being honest with myself, however, I didn't care as much about that as I did making sure Gladstone died here and now. Sure, my priorities might have seemed a little mixed up, but if I wanted to keep my friends and family safe, it was a risk I had to take.

In the end, I'd rather play fast and loose with the lives of strangers than the lives of people I cared about.

Gladstone seemed content to wait for me; he finished his cigarette, drawing one last pull from it before flicking the burning cherry into the street. I wondered what his plan was, and why he hadn't simply run when he'd had the chance. Unfinished business, maybe? Maybe he'd stuck around to keep an eye on Foxy, assuming she'd try to follow through on her promise to kill him, or maybe he was the cautious type in general?

There was no way to be sure, but in the end, it didn't matter; it wasn't like I planned to give him the chance to explain himself. He'd have to be breathing for that to happen. Unfortunately, when we were about ten feet away, I caught a flicker out of the corner of my eye. I turned, just in time to see Gladstone's illusion fall away, revealing a blockish Englishman covered in burns and dried blood.

"Hey, who's that?" one of the officers behind us asked, pointing at Gladstone.

Fuck.

Gladstone's expression soured as he realized his disguise had failed. "Well, love, I'd hoped to do this quietly, but..." He raised both hands. "I wonder how the Regulars will explain this one? Gas leak, maybe? Spontaneous fire breaks out, killing several officers?" He shrugged, then grinned as flames danced over his palms.

Only to abruptly die out.

"Everyone get down!" Maria yelled, ducking behind a car and dragging me along for a ride. Several other officers followed suit, drawing and pointing their guns in Gladstone's direction, but holding their fire. Gladstone stared at his hands in wonder. He tried to ignite the air around his palms a few more times, but nothing happened.

It was almost as if his magic wasn't working...

It was me, I realized.

I don't know how I knew for sure, but I could sense I was the one interfering with his magic. It was there in the stifled air: my field—the shield that protected me and nullified magic—had expanded. I immediately shut my eyes and felt for it with my other senses, seeking out the edges that typically clung to me as tightly as a second skin. I found it, spherical, like a bubble, reaching all the way to Gladstone.

My field drew back an instant later, as if called. I wasn't sure how, but I knew I could perceive it now, if I concentrated. Once retracted, it felt almost like a layer of lotion resting on top of my skin—invisible but noticeable. With that came a host of questions, but none of which I had time to mull over, because—unfortunately—the second my field returned, so did Gladstone's magic.

And he wasn't inclined to waste any time.

Apparently, having decided his flames were no use, Gladstone had switched gears. Maria pulled me down further behind the patrol car as wind whipped about, so strong the cars themselves started to slide across the pavement. The other officers dropped out of sight below their cars, unable to see with so much wind hitting them in the face. Gladstone's laughter could only barely be heard outside the gale.

"What the hell is that?" Maria yelled over the din.

I ignored her, concentrating instead on the field around me, urging it to loosen its grip on me and swallow Gladstone once again. But it was no use. I wasn't sure what had made it expand, but I suspected it would take a while before I could control it at will, if ever. Which meant my only chance was to get closer, like I'd originally planned. I tried to stand, but the wind was too strong.

I dropped back down and glared at Maria. If only I had my gun, I could at least try shooting the son of a bitch. Though, on second thought, I'd probably never get off a clean shot. Besides, killing someone in front of a bunch of cops was basically asking for the death penalty, especially when my only defense was "he was trying to blow me away with gale-force winds."

On second thought, that could work.

Padded cells were probably pretty comfortable, right?

A sudden crash of thunder made a few of the officers around me cry out in surprise. Rain pelted down, careening left and right as the droplets got caught in the wind. I realized Gladstone was channeling a storm, using his control of the elements to whip the sky into a frenzy.

A flash of lightning forked, colliding with the ground nearby as well as one of the squad cars. Two officers fell to the ground, twitching. Maria screamed, clutching at her eyes; she must have looked directly into the light. I'd kept mine shut, which was the only reason I was able to glance over the hood of the car.

And see Gladstone get what he deserved.

CHAPTER 58

*T*he wind died abruptly. Gladstone stood, partially hidden behind an impossibly tall, shadowy figure that I recognized—Magnus, the vampire I'd met in the alleyway.

My backup.

I did a mental fist pump; it'd taken calling in more than a half dozen favors to track the fanger down—not to mention enduring a host of threats before I revealed it was Gladstone, and not I, who had strung up Mike and his band—but it was totally worth it to see Gladstone's face as he stared up at the vampire, his mouth pleading silently, his eyes wild with fear.

Magnus glanced back, met my eyes, and nodded. Then, in the blink of an eye, he and Gladstone practically vanished—little more than a dark blur speeding off into the night, a stray shadow, gone in an instant.

Maria poked her head up, her gun propped in both hands, elbows mounted on the hood of the squad car. She stayed that way, blinking, then let out a slow breath. "You've got to be fucking kidding me," she said, finally. "Where'd he go? What the hell just happened?"

I closed my eyes.

Now came the fun part.

*B*efore Maria could get too worked up over what had just happened, I urged her to check the house again. As tempting as it was to leave Jacob's body behind and avoid all the questions it would raise, I knew that he'd be found eventually, and I didn't want to risk getting dragged in for murder—my bloody shoeprints leading away from the body would make likely for some pretty compelling circumstantial evidence, after all.

I watched Law and Order; I knew how these things worked.

After finding the body, an irate Maria had put me in handcuffs for the second time. I let her. I knew I was going to the station, either way. Between the dead body, her partner wounded, blood everywhere, an alleged bomber that got away, and inexplicable weather disturbances, I'm sure she had plenty of questions...

Of course, that didn't mean I had the answers she was looking for.

"So," Maria said, her grip tight on the steering wheel, "you gonna tell me what happened back there, or what?"

"Shouldn't I have me lawyer present?" I teased.

"Can the shit," Maria hissed. "Look, my partner's career is on the line. Maybe mine, too. If you don't tell me the truth, I can't promise any of us will walk away from this. I've got a detective and two officers down, not to mention a body, and a bomb threat to explain. Walk me through it."

"Off the record?" I asked.

"Yeah."

I sighed. "Ye won't believe me," I said.

"Try me."

So I told her. I told her all of it—everything that had happened since I first got Dez's phone call in Christoff's office. I talked until my raw throat couldn't take it anymore, and then I talked some more. The only part I left out was Jimmy's death and resurrection—even I would have a hell of a time believing that shit was possible.

When I was finished, Maria ran a hand over the loose strands of her hair, pinning them against her scalp. She took out her cellphone and sent out a text message, her expression, lit by the pale blue glow, oddly soft. When she faced me, her angry, contemptuous face held nothing of that softness. "You're right. I don't believe you. And neither will they. So...this is what happened."

CHAPTER 59

A uniformed officer dropped me off at Dez's house several hours later. I hadn't been charged with anything, but giving my statement had taken a while, even though it mostly consisted of saying things like, "I'm not sure" and "you'd have to ask Detective Machado."

I'd stuck as narrowly as I could to her version of events: that Jimmy—who'd received the same tip as the department had while driving me home after asking a few follow-up questions regarding the park incident from the day before—had gone to take a look since he was in the neighborhood. There, he'd found Jacob's body, and tried to subdue the assailant, but had been knocked out. When Jimmy hadn't returned, I'd followed, and had also been attacked. The assailant had then hidden us in a backroom and fled the scene, only to return and confront Detective Machado and I before fleeing again.

The story was flimsy, at best, but—because protocol dictated that Jimmy not leave the briefcase out of his sight—at least it explained why it was found at the scene. It also meant that, at worst, Jimmy would have to explain why he left a civilian in his car while responding to a call—an error in judgment, sure, but not worth a formal reprimand.

The fact that the officers hadn't located the backroom during their initial sweep seemed to bother my interrogators, but considering a whole crew of cops had missed it, that couldn't be laid at any one individual's feet

—even if Maria was technically in charge. Her bomb threat claim would be criticized, but—given the damage to the area and the two hospitalized officers—I doubted anyone would entirely discount the idea.

Frankly, the only concern anyone had at this point was the fact that the guy got away; until they caught him, all they had were questions that no one but Jimmy—who was unconscious in the ICU—could answer. Fortunately, Maria had that angle covered; it was Jimmy she'd texted on our way to the precinct, telling him to keep his mouth shut until they could talk about what happened. I'll admit I was surprised to find out how devious Maria was—it was almost enough to make me like her.

Almost.

In the end, I'd left them to their manhunt; I had other places to be. I walked stiffly up to the door of my childhood home, doing my best to ignore the fact that I'd been up for over twenty-four hours, been beaten within an inch of my life, and had to replace a whole outfit—they'd taken mine as evidence and thrust me in a pair of Boston PD-issue sweats that fit me like a smock.

I knocked. "Dez? Dez, are ye home?" I called. I turned the knob and felt a flash of panic as it gave beneath my hand; there was no way she'd have left it unlocked on purpose. I tore through the living room. "Dez!" I realized the lights were on in the kitchen, so I booked it down the hall. "Dez!"

"I'm here, Quinn, stop yellin'! We're in here!" Dez called from the dining room. I heard Dez say something in a softer voice. I changed directions, trying to slow my racing heart.

"Who's we?" I asked.

"There's a detective here," she said.

I froze.

I'd totally forgotten that Jimmy had sent someone to check on her. Shit…if her statement got back to Boston PD, they'd have no choice but to question everything I'd told them. My aunt getting kidnapped the day before I survived an animal attack and two days before I witnessed a murder?

Yeah, *that* wouldn't be conspicuous, at all.

I slowed my walk to a crawl, debating on what I would say to convince the cop to keep his trap shut…I could play the dutiful daughter, pull the detective aside and confess that Dez was really a senile old bag trying to get attention, maybe play it up with a sob story about how I didn't want anyone bothering her, and that I would be sure to get her into a home, soon?

Of course, if that didn't work, I could always throw out a number.

Something like that would never work on a stand-up guy like Jimmy, but there were plenty of Boston cops out there willing to wade into grey areas if you could make it worth their time—and I could throw out some pretty large numbers.

I stepped into the dining room, prepared to do or say anything to make sure the detective left without anything to report. Dez turned to me, her smile soft, looking exhausted and pale. She must have changed and showered—her clothes were unsoiled, wrinkle-free and her hair was still wet.

"Quinn, please, I'd like ye to meet this nice detective," she said, clearly trying to tell me something with her eyes. "He says he's been waitin' to speak with ye about a briefcase?" She snuck a look at me, an eyebrow raised in curiosity. Then both shot up. "Quinn! What's the matter with ye?"

I didn't know what to say to that. I didn't know what to say at all. Seated across from my aunt, dressed in an impeccably tailored suit and tie, was a young, teenaged boy. The boy pushed himself out of his seat and stood, offering his hand.

"Hello, Miss MacKenna."

He stood there for a long moment before Dez reached out and swatted my hand, "Quinn, where are your manners? Say hello to the man."

The boy pulled his hand back and rubbed at his hair absent-mindedly, a thin-lipped smile on his face. "Please, Mrs. Jones, call me Hemingway. Everyone else does."

CHAPTER 60

"Mrs. Jones," Hemingway, the teenaged boy said, "I'm sorry, but would you excuse us for a moment?"

"Oh, it's Miss Jones, actually," Dez replied with a predatory smile that made me feel all sorts of icky. "But are ye sure you're alright, dear?" Dez asked, eyeing me up and down, her gaze raptorial now that she was turned away from the boy.

"I'm fine," I managed. "Go ahead, I'd like to talk to the…the detective, alone."

Dez squeezed my arm as she left and—in a voice too soft for Hemingway to hear—said, "We need to talk."

I sighed, but nodded. It was a shame…I'd lied to the police, helped kill a fox spirit bent on feasting on half of Boston, survived a wizard, fought an alchemically enhanced bodyguard, and chased away a skinwalker…only to die at the hands of the aunt I'd been trying to save all along.

"So," I said, once she was out of earshot, "d'ye want to tell me why a little boy is playin' detective? And how ye managed to fool me aunt?"

Hemingway blinked owlishly before glancing down at himself. "Well, that's new," he said, sounding surprised.

I raised an eyebrow.

Hemingway shrugged. "My appearance often depends on who's doing the looking. Of course, until now I've always appeared older than everyone

I've met. It's a comfort thing, I think. A side effect of the job..." His eyes narrowed as he studied me. He took a half-step forward, then shuddered. "Another first."

"What are ye on about?" I asked.

"I don't see your death."

"My what?"

He started to respond, but seemed to think better of it, waving my question away before taking a seat at the table. "It's nothing, nevermind. Forget I mentioned it," he insisted. Despite his assurances, however, I found his heavy-lidded stare extremely discomforting; he looked at me like he was a biologist who'd recently counted the tentacles of an octopus and gotten to twelve.

Mind you, *not* how a woman wants to be looked at, even by a child.

"Anyway," he continued, "I'm here about the case. You spoke to my... friend, correct?"

My mouth gaped open, realizing for the first time that this—this child— was the person Othello had sent to help. What had she expected him to do, kick Gladstone in the shins and run away? Had I been wrong to put my faith in her, after all?

I noticed the kid was kicking his legs, since they didn't quite reach the floor, waiting for my response. "It's the small things," he admitted, seeing my incredulous expression.

"What d'ye want?" I asked, finally.

"Well, I was hoping to take a certain briefcase off your hands. I didn't find you at home, however, so I tried this address instead. Interestingly, I was told that your aunt had been kidnapped...and yet, here I find her, safely tucked away at home." Hemingway's boyish grin transformed into something calculating and cold, his insinuation clear.

"Listen here, ye smug little bastard," I said, barely resisting the urge to hit a child, "if you'd have shown up when ye were supposed to, ye might have the right to question me. But, as it stands, ye *and* Othello can go fuck yourselves."

Hemingway's eyes flashed. "I was...preoccupied. Where's the briefcase?"

"Did ye know what was in it?" I asked, my voice a hushed whisper.

Hemingway grimaced. "I was only recently informed. I didn't think Othello would go so far to help our mutual friend. If I had known, I'd have told her it was a foolish plan."

I didn't know who their "mutual friend" was, but I didn't care. The fact that he knew what the briefcase held meant he was just as liable as Othello for leaving me to fend for myself. "So ye knew it would open a gateway to another dimension?" I asked, my temper flaring.

Hemingway's eyes widened. "You mean it worked? Where is the portal now? Where did it lead?" His little hands clutched the arms of his chair, already halfway to his feet.

"The portal is closed, no thanks to ye and yours! A god closed it." I knew that sounded ridiculous, but something about this kid—his jaded nonchalance, maybe—made me think he wouldn't bat an eye at the mention of a deity's involvement.

I was right.

"I can't believe she was successful," Hemingway said, settling back in his chair. "Did the gateway lead to Hell?" He waved that away before I could respond. "Nevermind. I don't want to know. The less I know the better."

"The less you know?" I hissed. "Me friend almost died tryin' to help me stop a madman from releasin' a man-eater on the city, and ye don't even want to know why?" Hemingway didn't so much as raise an eyebrow, which only pissed me off further. "And by almost died, I mean he died and had to be brought back! But that's alright, because you were *preoccupied!*"

Hemingway rocked back onto the hind legs of his chair, shocked by my outburst. But then I realized it wasn't my anger that had driven him back, but my anti-magic field; it pressed against him, repelling as surely as a two magnets driven apart by their similar polarities.

Hemingway's shock faded in increments. "I'm sorry," he admitted, finally. "You're right. I should have come sooner. Creating doorways to other worlds the way Othello planned is...frowned upon, although—thankfully—not easily managed. Opening yet another could have been catastrophic. I'm...grateful. Very grateful, that you stepped in."

"Next time lead with that," I chastised, my anger dissipating.

For the first time in a long time, I was too tired to fight.

"I will," Hemingway said. "And I want you to know that Othello's heart was in the right place. She had no idea what she was creating. She was trying to save a friend from making a horrible, foolish mistake." His expression had turned wry. "If I'm being honest, perhaps part of me hoped she'd find a way to save him from himself, after all..."

I sighed and fell into a chair, my field retreating, cozying up next to me once more. "I t'ink ye should let people make their own mistakes, don't ye?"

Hemingway grunted as the legs of his chair hit the ground. "You obviously haven't met the man. When he makes mistakes, we all tend to get caught up in it." He probed at the air in front of him until he was sure the field had dispersed, then readjusted his chair. "Your friend? Is he, she, alright?" Hemingway asked.

"He. And yeah, he's fine."

"Are you sure?"

I shot him a glare.

He ignored it. "This is purely speculation, but you should know that bringing someone back to life is not easily achieved. A god can do it, of course. A few mortals have even managed. But there is always a cost." The expression he wore didn't belong on a face that young and, for a moment, I thought I saw something ancient and...familiar, in it.

"Well, we'll cross that bridge when we come to it," I said, finally, though part of me dreaded the fact that he might be right.

Hemingway nodded as he fetched a card from his suit jacket. "If you have trouble, please, contact me." He set the card on the table. "I'll tell Othello what happened here. She may have questions of her own, though."

I cradled my chin in my hands, elbows on the table—Dez would definitely kill me if she caught me doing that, but I was too exhausted to care. "I have a few, meself," I admitted.

Hemingway steepled his fingers. "Yes. I expect you two have a lot in common."

"Tell me," I said, rising to study the sunlight pouring through the dining room window, my back turned. "The way ye reacted a minute ago, and that bit about my death...D'ye know what I am, then?"

I glanced back, but he was gone.

The motherfucker had Batman'd me.

CHAPTER 61

I marched up the stairs to Dez's room like a woman heading to the gallows.

Granted, I was being a bit melodramatic, but now that the adrenaline had worn off, I realized there was no way around what was about to happen —Dez would have to learn the truth. About me. About what I did for a living.

She met me at the door to her room, silhouetted in the doorway like some dark, spectral presence. I shivered and ducked my head the same way I had the day after coming home from that concert I wasn't supposed to go to. "I'm so sorry, Dez."

"D'ye know why your ma and I left Ireland?" Dez asked.

I glanced up, surprised by the question. "The Troubles?" I volunteered. The Troubles were a period of Irish history during which significant social upheaval—including religious persecution and acts of terrorism—had swept over much of Ireland. From what Dez had told me, she and my mother had been involved in a dangerous paramilitary organization known as the Irish Republican Army. Dez never really talked about what they'd done, but I knew she regretted it with every fiber of her being.

"Aye, but that wasn't the only reason," Dez admitted. "We left because your ma wanted a better life for the children she one day planned to have."

I hung my head. "And ye t'ink I've disgraced her memory...I swear, it wasn't like I planned to do this, to deal goods to Freaks. But I'm good at it," I argued, fiercely. I took a deep, calming breath. How could I explain to Dez that what I did wasn't just a job, but a way of life—that, without it, I wouldn't feel whole?

Dez snorted. "I don't care what ye do for a livin', Quinn MacKenna, short of sellin' yourself on the street."

I frowned. "What are ye sayin', then?"

"I'm sayin' ye need to be more careful," Dez said, the look in her eyes flinty. "And I don't mean for me sake, but for yours. If I show up at St. Peter's gates and have to explain why ye showed up before me, your ma will make Hell seem like Aruba."

I stared at my aunt for a moment, slack-jawed, and then laughed. I laughed so hard I worried I'd pop a rib. "Aruba…" I whispered, flicking a tear out of the corner of one eye.

"I'm glad I could amuse ye," Dez said, sarcastically.

I straightened and settled a hand on her shoulder. "Are ye sure you're alright?" I asked.

Dez shrugged. "I've been through worse," she admitted, her expression closed off.

"And since when d'ye own a gun?" I asked, remembering the shots I'd heard over the phone.

"Patricia suggested I buy one," Dez said. "For protection. I told her Southie is safer now than it used to be, but she insisted."

Well, looked like I owed Patricia an apology. Maybe I'd send her flowers. Or a basket full of Bibles to pass out to the needy.

Whatever worked.

"Well," Dez said, finally, "I need to have me a lie down. And ye look like ye should be in the hospital." She eyed my throat, where bruises were already beginning to form. "Ye remember what I said, ye hear?"

I nodded and bent down so Dez could kiss my cheek—something she'd been doing ever since I was a little girl. We said our goodbyes, and I shut her door with a sigh of relief. Honestly, it felt like a huge burden had been removed; I hadn't realized how hard it had been, keeping things from the only family I had in all the world.

But she was right.

If her kidnapping had taught me anything, it was to be more careful, for her sake as well as mine.

*B*y the time I left Dez's, the sun had completely risen in the sky. I decided to walk a little before calling an Uber while I tried to order my chaotic thoughts. Deep down, I wanted to believe that I could follow through on my promise to Dez, but I knew better than to think that would be an easy task. After the last several days, it had become more and more apparent to me that my city wasn't as safe a place as I once thought.

I'd always thought Boston was like any other city, and that I—its resident black magic arms dealer—was simply providing a much-needed service. But now I knew Boston was a hub for all sorts of irregular activity; that even the wizard police stayed far from it as a rule, and that, beyond the Chancery's reach, the world was going to shit—Gladstone had mentioned a war, Cassandra, the Apocalypse, and Hemingway, whoever he was, had implied that Hell was perpetually one Gateway away.

For the first time in a long time, I felt like I understood my clients and their desires to build an impregnable fortress, to carry the biggest stick; the world was a dangerous place, and it paid to be ready for it.

I halted, realizing I was being watched.

"You have finished?" Serge asked, standing on the sidewalk outside my aunt's house in a light jacket and jeans, a baseball cap tucked low to hide most of his face. He waved at the space in front of his nose with an exaggerated motion. "Smells like death here. Is he gone?"

I reached for the gun I kept holstered at the small of my back, then cursed, remembering that it remained in lockup; Maria had refused to return it when I'd asked, glaring at me so hard I figured I'd have better luck buying a new one than I would getting my old one back.

"Dumb bitch," I muttered.

Serge frowned and titled his head quizzically, like a dog. "Pardon me?"

CHAPTER 62

"*How*'d ye find me?" I asked, ignoring his question. At this point, I was in that state of delirious exhaustion where you sort of accept everything that's happening to you, regardless of whether or not it makes sense. As such, I don't think I was even surprised to see him.

Go to another dimension? Check.

Watch a man get brought back to life? Check.

Survive a magic-induced thunderstorm? Check.

Chat with a skinwalker outside my aunt's place? Sure, why not?

Serge cocked his head. "Find you? No. You are very busy girl, but not so busy I could not follow."

"You've been followin' me this whole time?" I asked, exasperated. How had I noticed none of these damn men following me? Was I that blind? Never again, I swore to myself.

Never. Again.

"Mostly, yes," Serge replied. "But, when I lose you, I follow policeman."

"Aye, well now what? There are people lookin' for ye, ye know," I said, trying to gauge Serge's intentions. He couldn't have picked a better time to ambush me; I'd been pushing the limits of my body for hours now, and I didn't think I could arm wrestle the portly, middle-aged man in front of me, let alone tangle with the mangy skinwalker he could become.

"The Academy, yes, I know this."

"Bit dangerous standin' out in the open where they can find ye, don't ye t'ink?" I asked.

"They can find me anywhere," Serge said, with a shrug. "Here, at least, I can talk to you."

"And what is it ye want to talk to me about?"

"I wish for protection."

"Come again?" I asked, arcing an eyebrow, certain I'd misheard him, or that something had gotten lost in translation; I didn't always understand him.

"I—"

With a resounding clash, two figures in dark robes appeared out of nowhere, huddled against each other, wearing silver masks with mirrored faces that would have fit in well in a Studio Ghibli film—one the face of a masculine sun, the other a feminine moon. I could tell from their voices that the masks were gender appropriate.

"By the spirits," the man exclaimed, turned away from us, "I'd heard the rumors, but I had no idea they'd actually be there!"

"Those Candy Skull masks!" The woman released her hold and took a step back, turning to her companion. "What do you think it means?"

"It means we may have to figure out a new method of transportation," he replied, with a sigh. "Shadow Walking may be too dangerous."

The woman's shoulders drooped. "I hope they don't try and bring the nimbus clouds back. I hated that trend..."

"You only say that because you kept falling off."

"You said it was like riding a horse!"

The man laughed. "I did, yeah."

The woman punched him in the arm. "Not funny, *niisan*."

I studied the man, who was hardly visible beneath his robes. He didn't exactly look like a Nissan. There wasn't anything particularly Altima or Maxima about him, either—if anything he seemed quite small and compact.

More like a Honda.

"You're right, *imuoto*. No more teasing, I promise."

I realized they were using pet names for each other and felt a brief flush of embarrassment. "Um," I said, coughing to cover my slight blush, "I hate to interrupt, but who are ye people?"

The masks whirled to face me. "Oh, damn, we ended up a little closer than I thought," the man said. "I was hoping to track the skinwalker to a less public area."

"Where there would be no risk to civilians," the woman added. "Our apologies." She bowed a little.

"They are Justices," Serge answered, on their behalf. "From the Academy. They are here to kill me." His eyes began to glow green. But, at that precise moment, the two Justices lifted their hands, a surge of gold and silver light flashing as twin bolts of lightning arced out towards the skinwalker, missing him by only a few feet as he dove to his right. Patricia's yard smoked, the grass scorched and littered with clods of dirt.

Maybe I'd buy her flowers.

CHAPTER 63

"What the fuck are ye doin'?" I hissed, trying not to wake the neighbors. "You're not goin' to fight here, d'ye hear me?"

"The woman is saying something, *niisan*."

"We'll wipe her memory later," the man insisted. "First, we need to capture the skinwalker. Doctor's orders."

Both figures spun to face Serge, who had torn off the ballcap and jacket and was even now tearing away swatches of his own skin to reveal the fur beneath. Despite having seen it before, I had to admit the process still weirded me out.

The Justices split up, edging in either direction to keep the skinwalker from making a run for it. Lightning crackled at their fingertips. Each seemed to have considerably more control over it than Gladstone had. I wondered if wizards had elemental preferences, sort of like how pitchers could throw knuckleballs and changeups—but leaned heavily on their fastballs in a pinch.

Sadly, I didn't get a chance to ask; the woman rushed Serge, who had fallen onto all fours, his transformation nearly complete. She lunged forward, a slender arm darting from beneath her robe to reveal an arc of lightning that trailed behind her like a comet's tail. The blast hit Serge directly in the face and sent him flying into Mr. Robertson's iron wrought gate. I winced.

Serge, in full skinwalker mode, rose shakily. He growled and whipped his head about the way a wet dog might. "That tickled," the skinwalker said in that weird, ventriloquist voice of his. "We do not like being tickled."

The woman turned to her companion. "Your turn."

He nodded, then proceeded to go full-on Emperor Palpatine on Serge's skinwalker ass; waves of golden, sizzling lightning spewed from his hands, lancing into Serge's body at voltages I couldn't pretend to gauge. The smell of burning hair permeated the street, and I wondered how much longer it would be before some innocent bystander, or one of my neighbors, wandered out into the middle of all this.

"What are ye doin'?" I asked over the sound of Serge's pitiful whimpers. "Are ye tryin' to kill it?"

"Actually," the woman responded, "quite the opposite. Skinwalkers are already dead, possessed by their sacrificed familiars, which means they can't be killed, or even really wounded. Technically, I think you'd call them zombies, only with animal characteristics and willpower, which is what makes them so dangerous. Fortunately, my brother and I are experts at resuscitation. Now please, stand back. We'll take care of this and be right with you."

With that, she strode forward, her silver lightning taking over for her brother's gold, which flickered and died a moment later. He waved his hands a little as if trying to improve blood flow.

The skinwalker, meanwhile, was no longer whimpering, but pleading. "It hurts," it groaned. "We can feel, and it hurts to feel. Stop. Make it stop."

I suddenly realized what the woman meant; the skinwalker was dead, which meant it had no pain receptors, no nerves firing to tell its brain that it was wounded. That's why my bullets hadn't even fazed it—I'd been shooting at a corpse.

Except now, with who knew how many volts of electricity spiking through it, the skinwalker could feel things—things like pain.

You know when your leg is asleep, and you get up to walk it off, and it feels like a thousand little needles are pricking you all over? Well, my guess was it felt like that times, like, a hundred. The skinwalker whipped back and forth, each wave causing it to shake and clench. The glow of its green eyes began to fade, and I could see Serge's brown eyes peeking from beneath, desperate and pleading.

Had someone told me several hours ago that I'd consider saving Serge from a pair of masked wizards, I'd have had them, and then me, committed. The Serbian was clearly dangerous, and he'd threatened me more than once before—but he was also powerful, and I wouldn't mind having someone like him owe me one. Besides, Othello had used him as her personal smuggler—maybe she'd be grateful to have him back under her thumb. Grateful enough to give me access to some of the other merchandise GrimmTech had in development.

Shiny balls that created Gateways to inaccessible places?

Yes, please.

"Goddamnit," I cursed, grinding my teeth. "Fine." I marched over to the Justices and tapped the brother on the shoulder. He spun to face me, although his mask hid any surprise he might have felt. I waved a little. "Oy, I'm sorry, but could ye please stop attackin' this creature in the middle of me street?"

"Please," the man said, bowing a little to me, "do not interfere."

"Why do ye want to capture him?" I asked.

"I am sorry," the man said, reaching for me. "But it would be best if you go to sleep, now." Little tendrils of electricity danced along his fingertips... until his hand settled on my shoulder.

He stared at his powerless fingers, dark brown eyes visibly wide beneath the holes of the mask. "No, I'm the one who's sorry," I said, before I socked him in the gut, as hard as I could. He dropped to his knees, huddled over. I leaned down, so he could hear me. "It would be best if you go to sleep now." I brought both hands down on the back of his neck, and he crumpled to the pavement.

"*Niisan!*" The woman yelled, turning her lightning on me. When nothing happened, she hurriedly backed away. "What are you?" she asked, her voice hushed.

I raised my hands. "Listen, I don't want to fight with ye. I t'ink ye and the rest of your people should leave, that's all. Boston can handle things without ye. I'll take it from—"

The skinwalker attacked, interrupting what I'd been about to say, launching itself at the woman, catching her arm between its teeth and gnawing.

"Oh, ye dumb mongrel!" I growled. I rushed forward and swung a swift, vicious kick at its side, hoping to distract the mangy fucker long enough to get the woman free. My kick connected, and the skinwalker yelped, kicking out at me at the last possible instant. I felt the kick connect with my stomach, driving the breath from my lungs. I dropped to my knees and heard one of them—my previously injured knee—pop.

Which was the last sound I heard before I blacked out.

CHAPTER 64

I dreamt.

An old man, his hands wrinkled and knobbed, weaves signs in the air which illuminate, briefly, like the strobe of a neon sign. A woman's body, draped in a white shawl like a burial shroud, hovers above the ground. A garbled prayer echoes behind me in a language I do not know. A mantra, repeated again and again by inhuman lips. A soul rises, pure white, like crystal wrapped in starlight.

But it isn't enough. The orb isn't completely full. There's an instant of hesitation. The old man weaves another sign, and a shadow fills the void, shoved into the corner where it won't make as much noise, where it might not even be noticed. The old man doesn't know I can see what he's doing, that I can guess where he found that shadow lurking. Still, I don't interrupt as he replaces the soul, shoving it deep within the stomach of a body lying still upon the ground.

Jimmy's eyes flare open, and the irises are pale blue, like the eyes of an arctic fox.

I dreamt.

The fire is so hot I shy away from it instinctively, inching away from the heat towards the back of the room. This time, I don't find the paperweight on his desk, shatter the window, and leap to safety. This time, I burn beside him, clutching his corpse, whispering, "I'm sorry, I didn't mean it," over and over again.

I dreamt.

I hold my mother's hand. I hold my daughter's hand. Generations of mothers and daughters hold tight in an unbroken procession in either direction. Our features change, sometimes drastically, sometimes incrementally—an identical nose followed by a softer chin, brown hair that gives way to red, a gap-toothed smile and a thin-lipped frown. I glance down the line, both ways, until the women are indistinguishable, like lines of traffic fading into the horizon. They look back at me, expectantly, as if waiting for someone, anyone, to let go and break the chain.

I dreamt.

A man and a woman, their features distinctly Japanese, stare down at me from either side. The woman's gaze is soft, the man's hard. They are a study in contrasts, although I can tell they once shared the same womb. That's the way it is with siblings, I think to myself; each a different note, but on the same scale.

In this dream, I am not an only child.

CHAPTER 65

I woke to the steady beep of an EKG machine.

My eyelids fluttered. The light was dim, but oddly harsh, and tinted neon orange. It cast a sinister glow over the tubes attached to my arms and the bag of saline that dangled overhead. I fought the urge to pry the tubes out as I struggled to make sense of where I was and how I'd gotten there.

I remembered the fight outside my aunt's house. Blacking out. Odd dreams, some little more than memories, others too surreal to be believed. Some had felt real. I stretched out my senses, gauging my body, flexing my fingers and toes—good, at least I wasn't paralyzed. I did feel odd, however. Medicated. Opiates, judging from the floating, euphoric sensation that swaddled me like a childhood blanket made out of rainbows and Christmas cheer.

I turned my head, slowly, so as not to draw attention. Figures darted here and there nearby, setting up tables and chairs as if preparing for a banquet of some sort. I was on a cot in what seemed like a very large bunker, but which was likely an underground tunnel that had either been abandoned or was still under construction. Either way, no one seemed concerned about me one way or the other, which was comforting. Maybe if I stayed very still, they'd leave me alone. I felt like I could very easily drift off again.

"So, you're finally conscious. Good."

Damnit.

A woman I hadn't noticed sat at a table several feet away, partially obscured by shadow. She leaned forward, studying a clipboard. She flipped a few pages. "I'm not exactly licensed, but for the record I would advise that you seek out legitimate medical attention once we're through here. Your injuries aren't life threatening, but from what I could tell after examining you, you may have some permanent damage to contend with. Your knee, especially."

I smiled. "I keep hopin' they'll give me a bionic replacement, but doctors are stingy."

The woman nodded as if that were perfectly logical, her face a mask of professionalism. She had blonde hair pulled back in a pony-tail that left two strands of hair dangling, tucked behind her ears on either side. Her glasses were red and thick-rimmed, her eyes a moody blue. She wore a white lab coat over a red cardigan and dark denim jeans. I couldn't see her shoes, but something told me they'd be expensive, multi-colored sneakers—functional, but stylish.

"Did you hear me?" she asked.

"Depends," I said, "were ye sayin' somethin' about bein' beautiful?"

She arced an eyebrow. "I was saying my name is Lisandra Novak. I'm with the Academy's medical branch."

"Wizards have medics?" I asked.

"Ah, so you know who we are." She snapped her finger and two of the figures stopped what they were doing and approached.

"I know ye," I said, waving with the arm not attached to an IV. "You're the twins."

The two figures looked at each other. They looked much better without their masks. The Japanese man had stunningly sharp features, his cheek-bones prominent, his skin smooth. His twin sister, by contrast, had a rounder, but more pleasant, face. She smiled at me; he scowled.

"It seems she knows about the Academy," Lisandra said.

"I told you!" The brother hissed.

"Wait," I interrupted, "Lizzie, do ye mind if I call ye Lizzie?" I continued before she could respond, "Why am I hooked up to this t'ing?" I asked, pointing a thumb at the EKG machine.

"While medical magic is practiced by many of us here, we've discovered the scientific apparatus employed by Regulars have remarkable utility," Lisandra explained, her tone clinical, at best. "Using magic to constantly monitor your heartrate would be exhausting. Plugging in the machine, on the other hand, costs us nothing. If you exclude the electricity bill, of course."

"That," the Japanese woman said, "and Lisandra and her people weren't able to heal you using magic. In fact, no one here wants to get near you. We had a few wizards meet us here, including Lisandra, once we realized we wouldn't be able to travel using our preferred method. One or two of our people happened to make incidental contact with you in the process. Do you know what happened then?"

I giggled, then frowned. I never giggled. How much morphine had they given me? I shook my head, trying to clear it. "Lost their magic, probably," I responded, finally.

Lisandra and the twins exchanged glances.

"Stop doin' that," I said.

"Doing what?" Lisandra asked.

"Readin' each other's minds. It's rude."

Lisandra blinked. "We weren't reading each other's minds. Telepathy is not a common practice, and hard to master."

"Hmph. Well, I've had two gods," I held up two fingers for emphasis and grinned, "in me head today who could do it. Wait…what's today?"

"She's insane," the Japanese man said.

"She's heavily medicated," Lisandra amended.

"It's only been a few hours," his sister replied, ignoring them both.

I nodded as if that made all the sense in the world.

"So," Lisandra asked, "do you know why they 'lost their magic?'"

I rolled my eyes. "Don't talk to me like I'm five." I gathered my thoughts. "Me guess is they encountered me anti-magic field. That's what I call it, anyway. I thought it was me, ye know, innate-like, but then I used it to fight a wizard and to scare a wee boy and now I know it's something else, like a…" I sought out the word. "A nullifier. A magical no-fly zone. A—"

"So that's how you managed to punch me, huh?" the man interrupted.

I snorted. "No. I punched you like this." I shoved my fist towards the ceiling.

"Why did you attack us?" his sister asked.

"Why did ye attack the mutt?" I asked.

She and her brother looked puzzled.

"Serge," I clarified. "The gamma-radiated pooch. The skinwalker."

"You were defending the skinwalker?" the man asked, outraged.

"Technically," I said, "I was defendin' his right to a fair trial. This is America, ye know. Electrocution by twin wizard executioners is cruel *and* unusual. Double-stuffed."

Lisandra fiddled with another bag hiding behind the saline. "I think that's enough morphine. It's hard to gauge tolerance. I've never had to use some of this equipment before."

"So why did you try to stop him from hurting me?" the Japanese woman asked, self-consciously rubbing her forearm, which looked surprisingly unblemished.

"I didn't want any of ye fightin'," I admitted. "Especially not on a public street in the wee hours of the mornin'." I didn't mention that they'd been duking it out outside my aunt's place minutes after I'd promised her to be more careful—the fewer who knew where she lived, the better, as far as I was concerned.

The three of them looked at each other once more, but I didn't feel like commenting on it. The euphoric sensation had begun to fade, incrementally, and I felt a familiar twinge in my knee that made sweat break out across my forehead. I glanced down at myself but couldn't see my condition beneath the BPD-issued sweats—at least they hadn't removed my clothes.

I was willing to bet it wouldn't look good, though. Feeling pain through morphine is scary as shit; it meant I was guaranteed to hurt. A lot. I almost asked Lisandra to dial it back up, but now that the mental fugue had lifted a bit, I realized I needed my wits about me; I was technically at the mercy of a group of wizards I'd never met—at least one of whom I had assaulted, and that's if you didn't count Gladstone, who I'd tried to kill more than once.

"This anti-magic field," Lisandra began, "how—"

"No, first I want to know how she knows the skinwalker," the Japanese man interrupted. He and Lisandra stared at each other. Eventually, she turned away with a dissatisfied grunt. Was he her superior, I wondered? For some reason, I didn't think so. I was willing to bet they were simply in different departments, one of which had priority over the other; Lisandra didn't seem like the type to take orders.

"I met him a couple days ago," I said. "We wrestled. He ran away. So it's honestly me fault ye had to come at all."

A woman poked her head through the wall, the physics of which were improbable at best. "Actually, that would be my fault."

The two Justices fell back with remarkable quickness, offsetting shades of metallic lightning surging from their fingertips, brightening the gloomy tunnel. Lisandra seemed unperturbed, busy as she was studying my charts, probably looking for some hints as to why I repelled magic. I don't know what she expected to find; I'd checked myself over for a lightning-shaped scar years ago. No dice.

"How did you get in here?" the Japanese woman asked.

The newcomer shrugged and smiled as she stepped into the tunnel through a portal very similar to the one I'd seen the night before. "Gateways are sort of our thing."

"Who are you? Tell me right now!" The Japanese man took a step forward, and the light from his magic illuminated an attractive woman, maybe a little older than I was, definitely shorter, dressed in various shades of black. She had a thickness to her that defied logic: a big chest, wide hips, but with a trim little waistline. The edges of her smile threatened to pop her bubbled cheeks.

"My name is Othello. And you have something that belongs to me," she said. "Oh, hello, Quinn." She waved.

I waved back, weakly, wishing I had some popcorn to munch on; whatever happened next was going to be entertaining, assuming we all survived.

"Hey, Lizzie," I craned my head a bit until I could meet the woman's eyes, "could ye turn the morphine back up? I want to enjoy this."

CHAPTER 66

*L*isandra reached for the morphine drip.

"Whoa!" I said. "I was only jokin'. For Christ's sake."

Lisandra shrugged and resumed perusing my charts.

"We don't have anything of yours," the Japanese man retorted, "but we can't allow you to wander unmolested into one of our bases without taking you into custody."

"*Niisan*," his sister said, her magic fading as she lowered her hands, "I think we should listen to her."

"But—"

His sister gave him one of those looks smart people give exceptionally obtuse people when they're being exceptionally obtuse. "She uses Gateways. Her name is Othello. Doesn't that sound familiar? She works for him."

"For who?"

"Him. Nate Temple."

Temple...wait, that asshole who commandeered my Uber?

"I don't work *for* him. If anything, he works for me," Othello said, smirking. "Though you should probably say we work *together*. That way he doesn't have to face the fact that he treats me like his own personal Alexa."

The way she said it make me think she didn't really mind, that she might even be proud of that role. My mind was still reeling from the revelation that she worked for...with, Nate Temple. Which meant the jerk who'd forced me to high-five him was also the owner of GrimmTech, the organization responsible for Gateways to other dimensions. That also meant Temple was the man Gladstone had hoped to kill...suddenly, I was a little sorry I hadn't let the fox spirit have her way.

One less pretentious billionaire playboy out there sounded like a win to me.

Okay, not really. But still.

I jerked back to the conversation at hand, realizing I'd been too busy filling in the blanks to follow the exchange Othello had been having with the two Justices. Apparently, there seemed to be plenty to disagree about despite Othello's credentials.

"I'm sorry," Othello was saying, "but I'm afraid the Academy doesn't have jurisdiction in this case."

"Skinwalkers are a threat to everyone," the Japanese man argued. "It's our job as Justices to ensure their safety."

Othello nodded reassuringly. "I appreciate your stance on the matter, but your information is outdated. Skinwalkers are a historically persecuted community of witches who turned to violence only after their shapeshifting counterparts ostracized them for what they saw as perverse practices. They became dangerous to society because they were no longer welcome, and only then because they were unable to support themselves. Eventually their legacy became less than reputable, as a result."

"Your skinwalker attacked me, and reports suggested he caused an incident at a local park that could have exposed us to the Regular community, which is what our office is primarily assigned to address," the Japanese woman said, though she seemed far less antagonistic than her brother. If anything, she seemed interested in debating Othello's assertions from an intellectual perspective. "You can't expect us to hand him over to you simply because he was victimized in the past."

"Oh, Serge is most certainly an evil, manipulative monster. I have no interest in absolving him of anything."

"Then what is your interest here?" the brother countered.

"Serge is an employee of GrimmTech. What he has done is a breach of contract. A contract which is both legally and magically binding."

The Japanese woman studied Othello, then smiled. "I see. You may have him."

Her brother whirled around. "What?"

"I'll explain it to you later."

"No, I—"

"Oh, shut up," I chimed in. "Don't ye get it? What Othello here plans to do to that bastard is probably ten times worse than anythin' ye can do to him, ye idgit."

Othello pretended like I hadn't said anything. "May I have a word with Quinn here, please? In private? I'll send someone to come and collect Serge shortly."

"But the preparations…" the Japanese man muttered under his breath.

"I'm sure the Grand Master will understand," his sister replied. "She's had her own run-ins with Temple, after all."

"I still have a few questions for Miss MacKenna," Lisandra piped up, ignoring the glares from the two Justices.

"Lizzie wants to dissect me," I whispered to Othello, although loud enough that everyone could hear.

Othello looked me up and down, frowning at the acronym plastered across my hoodie, and shrugged. "We all have our kinks."

I sighed.

"But, I don't think Quinn should be interrogated *or* dissected without her lawyer present," Othello said.

"Her…lawyer?" Lisandra frowned.

"It's how things work here in Boston, I'm afraid. I've only dealt with them a few times, but the Faerie Chancery is very particular about that sort of thing. It's in the name, after all. Chancery."

All three wizards took a half step back from where I lay.

The Japanese woman spoke first, her voice a hushed whisper, barely audible. "You're a member of the Chancery?"

"I mean, they don't exactly give ye a card," I said, "but I do business with 'em, every now and then."

Another exchange of looks.

Othello raised an eyebrow. "Oh, right. I'd forgotten. I believe the Academy gave up jurisdiction here years ago, so technically you're all trespassing right now, aren't you?"

I chuckled, and everyone's attention shifted to me. I held up a hand. "Sorry. I was only thinkin' that, if ye were all readin' each other's minds just now, I bet there was a whole lot of 'oh, we are so fucked' goin' on up there."

They didn't find it as funny as I did.

CHAPTER 67

*O*thello helped me onto my couch, which—considering our height differences—must have looked more than a little comical. I settled in, propping my injured leg up onto the coffee table, testing my knee's range of motion with a grimace. Despite Lisandra's advice, I'd opted out of seeing a doctor; I could put weight on it without passing out, which was good enough for me. On the way over, Othello had fed me a few pills from a bottle of Ibuprofen she kept in her purse, and the swelling had already gone down in the time it had taken her to escort me from the Academy's secret underground base to my apartment.

Once we'd arrived, she'd insisted on guiding me up the three flights of stairs to my door. I'd agreed without a second thought; the lingering effects of the morphine had left me giddy and surprisingly pliant. Somewhere along the way, I'd asked about Serge and what Othello intended to do, but she'd told me not to worry, that she'd have her people remove him from the Academy's custody and take him home.

"To the prison in Siberia?" I asked, half-jokingly.

"How did you know about that?" Othello had responded, leveling a suspicious gaze at me.

It was only then that I realized that, for this woman, knowledge was power—and I had just inadvertently flexed a little. I explained that I'd heard it from the kidnapper, a Londoner who'd worked for the Academy, with a major hard-on for her boss. Then I filled her in on a few other relevant details: how I'd tried to reach her after he'd called, the fallout from Gladstone's use of the Gateway, and the conversation I'd had with Hemingway only a few hours before.

"Yes," Othello said, her expression lightening considerably, "he filled me in on what you told him. In fact, that's why I came. I thought I would apologize in person, especially for not answering. Getting licensed to perform marriage ceremonies is a pain. So many forms..." Othello's eyes hollowed out, as if she were describing something much more horrific.

I snorted, drawing her back from the abyss.

"But yeah," she continued, "when I got there and saw the damage outside your aunt's apartment, I assumed something unfortunate had happened. It took a little digging to find out what, but by the time I discovered Serge and the Academy were involved, all I could do was track down the defunct bases the Academy had established in Boston before the formation of the Faerie Chancery in the mid-1800s and try to find out which one was currently in use."

"And exactly how did ye find all that out?" I asked, arcing an eyebrow. From our previous interaction, I knew enough to guess she was a hacker of some kind; she'd obtained information that could only be gleaned from unrestricted data access. But in this case, there had been no eye witnesses to speak of and no way to know who had been involved or why. Not to mention the inexplicable fact that she seemed eerily familiar with the Chancery's policies, as well as its history—neither of which could be accessed with a simple Google search.

Believe me, I'd tried.

"Traffic cameras, mostly," she'd explained, idly toying with a zipper on the pocket of her leather jacket. "If they'd been able to Shadow Walk, I may never have found you, but because their abilities didn't work in your presence—something Hemingway told me was likely—all I had to do was keep an eye out for a large, conspicuous car pulling into that neighborhood in the early morning. I had to guesstimate the time, but it didn't take long to find the footage I was looking for.

"They cloaked themselves, of course, but they didn't bother hiding the car once they had you. Rookie mistake, but then wizards aren't usually as concerned with technology as they should be. In fact, hacking the Academy's bank accounts to find out which car service they'd used was literally child's play—I broke tougher codes than that in secondary school," Othello mockingly brushed invisible dust off her shoulder and grinned.

"Anyway, after that, all I had to do was contact the driver and confirm that you'd been taken. He told me about Serge. Everything else I found out from reaching out to a friend in the Chancery, who had old records of Academy hideouts that had been abandoned. Only one remained in its original form—the Tremont tunnel."

"Who's your friend in the Chancery?" I asked, dubiously. As far as I knew, the Chancery rarely reached out to Freaks in town, much less Regulars—a status she'd confirmed shortly after we left the Academy hideout—from foreign countries. They preferred their anonymity, operating from the shadows, or through intermediaries—Faelings like Ryan, usually, who could pass for human most of the time.

"I'll introduce you, sometime," Othello said. "She's a fan of yours, actually."

"A fan?"

Othello grinned and shrugged. "We all have our kinks."

I wasn't sure what to say to that, but apparently Othello found my expression particularly amusing. She rose, still chuckling, and walked the length of my apartment.

"This is a nice place," she said, from my bedroom. I realized she was one of those people—the ones who didn't care about things like boundaries or privacy. Good quality in a hacker, I'm sure, bad quality in a human being. But then she had helped me up three flights of stairs...

"T'anks," I replied.

My apartment—a remodeled, upscale loft in Beacon Hill that overlooked both a picturesque neighborhood and a quaint cobblestone courtyard, depending which window you looked out from—had been my first adult purchase. The furniture fluctuated between antique and modern and had a vaguely masculine air to it. I had impulse buying issues, which accounted for the brass phonograph I never listened to resting on the fireplace mantle in my bedroom, the Indian motorcycle I'd never ridden propped in the corner of the dining room, and the impossibly large LED screen I never watched mounted on the living room wall. But I kept it clean and clutter free, despite visitors being few and far between.

I was proud of it, of what it said about me.

"Will you be alright?" Othello asked, sauntering back into the living room. She did that a lot, I realized—moved her hips like their default switch was set on swivel. Most women looked ridiculous doing it; I saw it most often in the strut of a plastered sorority type, her eyes locked on either a man or a meal. But Othello didn't seem to notice she was doing it. I found myself bizarrely glad I had the knee injury to contend with, or my mannish left-right-left approach would have been stark and unflattering by comparison.

"I'll be fine," I said. "As long as no one comes after me or mine here in the next few days, at any rate. That's how long I plan on sleepin'."

"I'll put one of my people on it," Othello said, whipping out a tablet from her purse that seemed bigger than she was.

"Oh, that's not what I meant," I said, stammering.

Othello continued playing with the tablet. "It'll make me feel better to know you're safe until you recover. You and your aunt. I owe you that, at least."

I didn't feel like arguing. Having someone keep an eye on Dez, at least while I was out of commission, seemed like a great idea. "Can ye tell me somethin'?" I asked. "Why did ye come yourself? T'wasn't your fault Gladstone got hold of the briefcase. And I stole from ye. I mean, I had no choice, but still."

"I've stolen things from people before," Othello said, after a brief silence. "I've taken their identities. Sometimes their livelihoods. I've taken their right to privacy. And every time I do, I wonder if I'm making the right decision. And then I think about the people I care about, and I realize I don't care." She took a seat across from me on the sofa. "If you had tried to come after someone I care about, I'd have ruined you. I'd have drained you dry and left you homeless, nameless, and wishing you'd never set foot outside your apartment door." She held my eyes with her own. "I think you understand why. Because I think, if I messed with the people you cared about, you'd find a way to make me pay. You and I are alike, in that way." Othello smiled. "Basically, I'm glad I didn't have to come after you."

I sighed and shifted, swinging my leg gingerly around until it settled on the arm of the couch. "Ok, one more question," I said, propping myself up with a pillow. "Did we just become best friends?"

Othello chuckled at my remarkably well-timed *Step Brothers* reference. "I'd say let's do karate in the garage, but I've seen your resume. No thanks." She rose as if to leave, but seemed to remember something, "I've still got questions. About the wizard who blackmailed you, and what happened when you went into the other dimension."

"I wouldn't worry about him," I said, confidently. "And trust me...you'd rather not know what the afterlife is like."

Othello blanched, started to say something, and then shook her head. "Yeah, once was enough," she admitted.

CHAPTER 68

I spent the next three weeks hobbling back and forth between my bed and the couch. Othello promised she'd give me a call once things had settled down on her end—apparently St. Louis had more going for it than what little I knew, including a growing were-animal community, a resident wizard overlord named Nate Temple, and a variety of demigods, heroes, legends, and even gods who called it home.

I wanted nothing to do with it.

The idea of running into mythical figures was appealing, sure, but I have more than enough on my plate stockpiling for the apocalyptic future to worry about taking a vacation. Judging from what Othello told me about the Midwest's trajectory over the last few years—the multiple wars and other narrowly avoided world-ending catastrophes—I have every reason to believe that Ryan and Cassandra's instincts were right on the money.

I still haven't heard anything from Ryan, not that I expected to. Christoff hired a new bar manager, but I haven't been by yet to see if he's any good. Something tells me I won't like him, on principle. Hank showed up for his next shift as if nothing happened, and Christoff has let that stand, for now. At some point, Christoff may reveal his secret to the new guy, but as a solitary werebear far from home, I doubted it.

We Freaks tend to hoard our secrets.

Speaking of which, Dobby the Big-as-a-House Elf seems to be acclimating to his role as warehouse poltergeist. A few members of Christoff's staff claim the warehouse is haunted, but so far there haven't been any incidents. I've let the little guy visit once or twice during the day. He insists on watching over me when I sleep—which I do often thanks to the pain meds I'm taking. It's creepy finding him staring at me from across the room, I'll admit, but somewhat reassuring at the same time.

All my contacts seem to be laying low at the moment, which makes sense considering the ruckus Serge, Gladstone, and the Academy caused in the span of a few days. In fact, the Chancery delivered a summons requesting I report to a hearing later next month; it appeared on my dining room table as if by magic. Frankly, I'm not sure I can refuse, or who I would call to refuse if I did. Was there a Faerie representative in charge of my district? Did Faerie representatives even have phones?

In other news, Jimmy seems to have lost his and hasn't bothered to get a new one. I'd planned to visit the man once I'd recovered enough to move on my own power, but then Maria called to let me know the park incident had been resolved, and that I could come collect my personal effects, including my gun. When I asked her how Jimmy was holding up, she'd seemed surprised. Apparently, Jimmy had checked out the next morning, given his statement, and gotten right back to work as if nothing had happened. The only thing he'd done that was out of character, in fact, was not reach out to me.

It hurt.

Part of me wondered if he still held a grudge for me running out on him after we'd slept together, or if he held me responsible for the fallout at his job over Gladstone and Jacob. Another part of me hoped that was all it was, and that what the old man said about Jimmy wanting to die had nothing to do with it. And then there was the matter of his shifting eyes—I still wasn't sure if I'd dreamt that or not.

Maria must have picked up on my frustration, because she'd insisted Jimmy had a good reason to avoid me—Gladstone was still at large and the whole department was intent on taking him down. She assured me she'd let Jimmy know we'd spoken. I wasn't sure what upset me more, that Jimmy had brushed me off, or that Maria felt enough pity for me to soften the blow of his rejection by blaming his job.

Of course, if that was the reason, Jimmy might never call me back; Gladstone wasn't going to be found anytime soon, if ever. I'd made sure of that.

Last I heard, Gladstone's corpse was on display at Magnus' house—a rustic mansion in upstate New York. I didn't want to think about the décor, but the concept gave me plenty of satisfaction.

Other than that, there's not much to report. Dez has completely recovered, though she had a few choice words regarding the state of her neighbors' yards—Patricia was convinced she'd been pranked by atheist teenagers on a drunken bender. I tried to explain that it wasn't my fault, but Dez didn't believe me. Fortunately, I looked pitiful enough when she visited that the lecture ended almost before it began. She and I have been watching a lot of old movies at my place, since it's easier for her to come to me at the moment, although part of me wonders if it's because she doesn't feel safe at her house any longer. I wish I could tell her that the men who'd taken her won't ever be coming back, but I know she wouldn't approve. Thou shalt not kill is a pretty firm rule in her book, pun intended. And—while I hadn't been the one who'd done the deed, technically—I had to admit I was partially responsible for their deaths. Not a great feeling.

But then sometimes I look over at Dez as she studies the tumultuous relationships of the silver screen, and a dark, inexplicable fear overshadows the guilt—the fear that one day I won't be able to protect her. Her, Dobby, Christoff...even Jimmy. A growing list of people I'd hate to lose.

Thou shalt not kill, huh...

Good thing I'm not Catholic anymore.

Turn the page to read a brief excerpt from **COSMOPOLITAN**, the second installment of the Phantom Queen Diaries, and get a taste of what's in store for the black magic arms dealer as she hits up the Big Apple.

Or get a DISCOUNT when you preorder HERE. It will be wirelessly delivered to your Kindle on June 19, 2018.

SAMPLE: COSMOPOLITAN (PHANTOM QUEEN #2)

*T*he blubbery lip of the brutish, hulking bridge troll in front of me quivered in frustration. He gnashed his teeth together, staring me down with jaundiced eyes. I wondered, idly, how many people he'd eaten. How many bones had he splintered and mangled over the centuries with those elephantine tusks? My opponent fidgeted, and I could sense he was about to make his move; it was there, in his tensed shoulders, half as wide as I was tall, and his twitching hands, each large enough to palm a beach ball. I waited, pinned to my chair by his beady-eyed gaze, holding my breath. Almost a month's preparation boiled down to what would happen in the next few minutes, and I couldn't afford a single distraction. The gargantuan, green-skinned monster slumped forward, snorting through his pierced snout—the rusty septum ring as large as a bracelet—and rested his elbows on the table until it creaked from the strain.

"Fold," he said, in a plodding, gravelly voice that would have done Andre the Giant justice.

I threw my hands up. "Ye can't fold, ye idgit. You're the big blind!"

Paul, the aforementioned bridge troll, studied the cards in his hand once more before nodding. "Fold." He flipped them over and slid them across the table towards the dealer. Christoff, the owner of the bar and host of this little get together, glanced at me before collecting Paul's cards and insisting everyone else return theirs. I rolled my eyes and tossed my hand on the table, face-up—pocket Aces. Paul didn't even seem to notice, but the other members of our impromptu bi-monthly poker night certainly did; Christoff shrugged at me apologetically, but the other two—our newcomers, Othello and Hemingway—barely managed to stifle their laughter.

Othello was a charming Russian hacker who'd rescued me from a debacle several weeks back that had nearly put me in the hospital. We'd been in touch regularly over that span, exchanging information and gossip in equal parts, and she was fast becoming one of my very few friends, despite the fact that she was rarely around; she and her cohort of friends spent the vast majority of their time in the Midwest, oscillating between St. Louis and Kansas City.

Both cities had experienced more than their fair share of supernatural snafus in the last several years, most of which could be classified as Biblical in proportion; some of her stories made rivers of blood and locust plagues seem dull and mild by comparison. At this rate, I wasn't interested in a Midwest layover, let alone a vacation.

I had enough drama in my life already.

Not that leaving Boston was on my agenda, anyway. Sure, Titletown came with its fair share of baggage, especially for those of us who'd grown up in some of the rougher neighborhoods. But there was something about it I loved—a brutal, vicious history which had bled into its foundations, many of which still stood. I could sense that same hard edge in myself, sometimes

—that urge to provoke, to hit and get hit. I don't know if that made me crazy, but it sure as hell made me a Boston native.

Thing is, you had to be a wee bit batshit to do what I did for a living; peddling magical artifacts sounds like an entertaining gig, I'm sure, but if you think selling drugs or guns on the black market is dangerous, you've never met a hungry Bandersnatch or pissed off a Jabberwock.

I've stared down creatures out of storybooks and squared off against nightmares, and I had the scars to prove it.

Which is why, as a black magic arms dealer, I knew it paid to have people you could rely on in a pinch; you never knew when you'd end up over your head or up to your neck and need to call in favors. Maybe that's why I'd invited Othello to tag along tonight; I figured she and Christoff would get along, plus we were a man down what with Ryan returning to Fae at the behest of the King of the Faeries.

That's right, I still believe in faeries. I do, I do.

On the other hand, I doubt I would have invited Hemingway if not for Othello's insistence. The guy creeped me out. He'd aged significantly since I first met him, although he still appeared younger than the rest of us by more than a couple years; I didn't have the gall to tease Othello about her jailbait boyfriend—I was pretty sure she'd retaliate by stealing my identity and leaving me penniless on the street. But at least he looked legal, now, as opposed to the prepubescent kid I'd met a few weeks before. Lately, Hemingway reminded me a lot of Matt Dillon in *The Outsiders*, both in appearance and temperament—he came off jaded, acting like nothing in the world could surprise him. What really bothered me about him were his eyes, though—it was like he was always staring at ghosts, until he looked right at you, and then he made you feel like *you* were the ghost.

I motioned for Christoff to deal again. The older man smiled and graciously followed through, expertly tossing cards before each of us. He and Othello chattered back and forth in Russian, flicking their eyes between me and the troll. Hemingway seemed to be following the conversation with little difficulty; he even sniggered at one point. I glowered at them all as I checked my cards. The Five of Spades and the Seven of Clubs. I sighed, inwardly, then put in the big blind—a blue chip that was supposed to represent money but, in this case, represented information. Othello, who sat to my right, put in the small blind after a moment's hesitation.

Turns out she'd played before, but not with chips.

I'll let you figure out what she'd used instead.

The troll peered at his cards and grinned, his pale purple gums on display. Not much of a poker face, but—as you probably noticed—Paul rarely set himself up to fail. Fortunately for me, the game was rigged so that no matter who won, I got what I wanted. Which is the only kind of game I would play, really. Paul matched my big blind with a blue chip of his own, and the others followed suit.

"Burn and turn," I told Christoff. Christoff turned the first card face down and set it aside, then turned the next three face-up: the Ace of Hearts, the Five of Clubs, and the Five of Diamonds. I stifled my smug expression and studied my opponents, but—other than Paul, whose broad smile had grown into something leering and grotesque—there was no telling what anyone had; Hemingway might as well have been a still-life, and Othello's cherubic grin could have meant anything, or nothing.

Ordinarily, we'd have taken turns betting, but Paul didn't seem inclined to wait. He swatted his pile of chips, spilling them forward into the center of the table, and bellowed, "All in!" Hemingway's eyebrows rose at the outburst, then he casually slid his cards over to Christoff.

Othello studied her own chips before mimicking her boyfriend's nonchalant expression. "I'll call."

Paul seemed to deflate somewhat, but his grin hadn't faded.

"Me too," I said, drawing his unwelcome attention.

The bridge troll grunted. Apparently, he hadn't expected us both to go in with him—and anything that confused Paul made him mad. I'd met plenty of men like him, but none who could yank trees out of the ground and use them as whiffle bats; the bastard still owed me for what he'd done to my poor car. Not that he had any money to speak of—Bridge Tolls in the modern era were strictly a federal form of extortion.

Paul's residence notwithstanding, he lived on the goodwill of the Faerie Chancery, a shadowy organization that represented the interests of the various Faelings who had settled in Boston over the last few centuries. I knew very little about them, although I suspected they were behind a great many of the deals I'd made in the past. Paul's relationship to the Chancery was, in fact, the primary reason I'd invited him to join us for poker night.

All part of the plan.

"Alright, Christoff, turn the rest," I insisted.

He did, burning the first, turning the second, and then repeating the process. I stared down at the cards as if they mattered, flicking my gaze from the Ace of Hearts to the Five of Clubs, Five of Diamonds, Four of Hearts, and Five of Hearts. But, really, I was biding my time before the big reveal; I'd lucked into a four-of-a-kind—the third-best hand in poker—early on. Paul, growing impatient, tossed his cards down on the table with a self-satisfied chortle.

He'd had pocket Aces.

I grinned and turned my cards for him to see. Christoff adjusted the cards he'd turned so three suits worth of Fives sat higher than the rest. "The Full House is trumped by Four-of-a-Kind," he declared. I could sense Paul's confusion; he never had been very good at counting past two. A moment later, I could make out the faint crunch of the wooden table splintering beneath his grubby, waffle-sized hands as he realized he'd lost. Christoff growled in warning, which seemed to register, somehow. Paul shot Christoff an apologetic look, released the table, and begun picking up the splintered wood, popping the slivers into his mouth like M&Ms. He chewed with his mouth open, snorted, and folded his arms over his extraordinarily wide chest.

"No fair," he grumbled.

"Ye can never be too sure what the cards have in store for ye, Paul, me friend," I chastised. "Ye should know that by now."

"She's right, you know," Othello quipped, holding a single card up for us to see, her grin wider than I had ever seen it.

"Oh, that's fuckin' garbage," I cursed, glaring at Christoff, who had the good grace to at least pretend he had nothing to do with the turning of the tables.

Othello slid the Two and Three of Hearts across the table.

"The Straight Flush wins," Christoff declared, coughing into his hand to hide his amusement. I stared down at Othello's cards in disbelief, knowing that she'd gone all-in with absolutely nothing; she'd had no reason to think she'd win. And yet, she had.

Fucking Russians…

~

Get a Discount by clicking HERE to Preorder COSMOPOLITAN. It will automatically appear on your Kindle on June 19th, 2018!

∾

*Turn the page to read a sample of **OBSIDIAN SON** - Nate Temple Book 1 - or **BUY ONLINE (FREE with Kindle Unlimited subscription)**. Nate Temple is a billionaire wizard from St. Louis. He rides a bloodthirsty unicorn and drinks with the Four Horsemen. He even cow-tipped the Minotaur. Once...*

Full chronology of all books in the Temple Universe shown on the 'Books by Shayne Silvers' page.

TRY: OBSIDIAN SON (NATE TEMPLE #1)

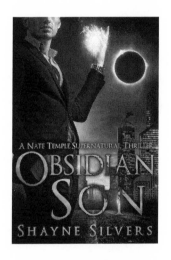

here was no room for emotion in a hate crime. I had to be cold. Heartless. This was just another victim. Nothing more. No face, no name.

Frosted blades of grass crunched under my feet, sounding to my ears alone like the symbolic glass that one shattered under a napkin at a Jewish wedding. The noise would have threatened to give away my stealthy advance as I stalked through the moonlit field, but I was no novice and had planned accordingly. Being a wizard, I was able to muffle all sensory evidence with a fine cloud of magic — no sounds, and no smells. Nifty. But if I made the spell much stronger, the anomaly would be too obvious to my prey.

I knew the consequences for my dark deed tonight. If caught, jail time or possibly even a gruesome, painful death. But if I succeeded, the look of fear and surprise in my victim's eyes before his world collapsed around him, was well worth the risk. I simply couldn't help myself; I had to take him down.

I knew the cops had been keeping tabs on my car, but I was confident that they hadn't followed me. I hadn't seen a tail on my way here, but seeing as how they frowned on this kind of thing I had taken a circuitous route just in case. I was safe. I hoped.

Then my phone chirped at me as I received a text. My body's fight-or-flight syndrome instantly kicked in, my heart threatening to explode in one final act of pulmonary paroxysm. "Motherf—" I hissed instinctively, practically jumping out of my skin. I had forgotten to silence it. *Stupid, stupid, stupid!* My body remained tense as I swept my gaze over the field, sure that I had been made. My breathing finally began to slow, my pulse returning to normal as I saw no change in my surroundings. Hopefully my magic had silenced the sound, and my resulting outburst. I finally glanced down at the phone and read the text. I typed back a quick and angry response before I switched the phone to vibrate.

I continued on, the lining of my coat constricting my breathing. Or maybe it was because I was leaning forward in anticipation. *Breathe,* I chided myself. *He doesn't know you're here.* All this risk for a book. It had better be worth it.

I'm taller than most, and not abnormally handsome, but I knew how to play the genetic cards I had been dealt. I had fashionably shaggy, dirty blonde hair, and my frame was thick with well-earned muscle, yet still lean. I had once been told that my eyes were like twin emeralds pitted against the golden tufts of my hair — a face like a jewelry box. Of course, that was after I had filled the woman with copious amounts of wine. Still, I liked to imagine that was how everyone saw me.

But tonight, all that was masked by magic.

I grinned broadly as the outline of the hairy hulk finally came into view. He was blessedly alone — no nearby sentries to give me away. That was always a risk when performing this ancient right-of-passage. I tried to keep the grin on my face from dissolving into a maniacal cackle.

My skin danced with energy, both natural and unnatural, as I manipulated the threads of magic floating all around me. My victim stood just ahead, oblivious of the world of hurt that I was about to unleash. Even with his millennia of experience, he didn't stand a chance. I had done this so many times that the routine of it was my only enemy. I lost count of how many times I had been told not to do it again; those who knew declared it *cruel, evil, and sadistic.* But what fun wasn't? Regardless, that wasn't enough to stop me from doing it again. And again. Call it an addiction if you will, but it was too much of a rush to ignore.

The pungent smell of manure filled the air, latching onto my nostril hairs. I took another step, trying to calm my racing pulse. A glint of gold reflected in the silver moonlight, but the victim remained motionless, hopefully unaware or all was lost. I wouldn't make it out alive if he knew I was here. Timing was everything.

I carefully took the last two steps, a lifetime between each, watching the legendary monster's ears, anxious and terrified that I would catch even so much as a twitch in my direction. Seeing nothing, a fierce grin split my unshaven cheeks. My spell had worked! I raised my palms an inch away from their target, firmly planted my feet, and squared my shoulders. I took one silent, calming breath, and then heaved forward with every ounce of physical strength I could muster. As well as a teensy-weensy boost of magic. Enough to goose him good.

"*MOOO!!!*" The sound tore through the cool October night like an unstoppable freight train. *Thud-splat!* The beast collapsed sideways into the frosty grass; straight into a steaming patty of cow shit, cow dung, or, if you really want to church it up, a Meadow Muffin. But to me, shit is, and always will be, shit.

Cow tipping. It doesn't get any better than that in Missouri.

Especially when you're tipping the *Minotaur*. Capital M.

Razor-blade hooves tore at the frozen earth as the beast struggled to stand, grunts of rage vibrating the air. I raised my arms triumphantly. "Boo-yah! Temple 1, Minotaur 0!" I crowed. Then I very bravely prepared to protect myself. Some people just can't take a joke. *Cruel, evil,* and *sadistic* cow tipping may be, but by hell, it was a *rush*. The legendary beast turned his gaze on me after gaining his feet, eyes ablaze as he unfolded to his full height on two tree-trunk-thick legs, hooves magically transforming into heavily-booted feet. The heavy gold ring quivered in his snout as the Minotaur panted, corded muscle contracting over his human-like chest. As I stared up into those eyes, I actually felt sorry... for, well, myself.

"I have killed greater men than you for less offense," I swear to God his voice sounded like an angry James Earl Jones.

"You have shit on your shoulder, Asterion." I ignited a roiling ball of fire in my palm in order to see his eyes more clearly. By no means was it a defensive gesture on my part. It was just dark. But under the weight of his glare, even I couldn't buy my reassuring lie. I hoped using a form of his ancient name would give me brownie points. Or maybe just not-worthy-of-killing points.

The beast grunted, eyes tightening, and I sensed the barest hesitation. "Nate Temple... your name would look splendid on my already long list of slain idiots." Asterion took a threatening step forward, and I thrust out my palm in warning, my roiling flame blue now.

"You lost fair and square, Asterion. Yield or perish." The beast's shoulders sagged slightly. Then he finally nodded to himself, appraising me with the scrutiny of a worthy adversary. "Your time comes, Temple, but I will grant you this. You've got a pair of stones on you to rival Hercules."

I pointedly risked a glance down at the myth's own crown jewels. "Well, I sure won't need a wheelbarrow any time soon, but I'm sure I'll manage." The Minotaur blinked once, and then bellowed out a deep, contagious, snorting laughter. Realizing I wasn't about to become a murder statistic, I couldn't help but join in. It felt good. It had been a while since I had experienced genuine laughter. In the harsh moonlight, his bulk was even more intimidating as he towered head and shoulders above me. This was the beast that had fed upon human sacrifices for countless years while imprisoned in Daedalus' Labyrinth in Greece. And all of that protein had not gone to waste, forming a heavily woven musculature over the beast's body that made even Mr. Olympia look puny.

From the neck up he was entirely bull, but the rest of his body more resembled a thickly-furred man. But, as shown moments ago, he could adapt his form to his environment, never appearing fully human, but able to make his entire form appear as a bull when necessary. For instance, how he had looked just before I tipped him. Maybe he had been scouting the field for heifers before I had so efficiently killed the mood.

His bull face was also covered in thick, coarse hair — even sporting a long, wavy beard of sorts — and his eyes were the deepest brown I had ever seen. Cow shit brown. His snout jutted out, emphasizing the gold ring dangling from his glistening nostrils, catching a glint in the luminous glow of the moon. The metal was at least an inch thick, and etched with runes of a language long forgotten. Thick, aged ivory horns sprouted from each temple, long enough to skewer a wizard with little effort. He was nude except for a beaded necklace and a pair of distressed leather boots that were big enough to stomp a size twenty-five in my face if he felt so inclined.

I hoped our blossoming friendship wouldn't end that way. I really did.

～

Get the full book ONLINE!

～

Turn the page to read the first chapter of **UNCHAINED** *- Book 1 in the Amazon Bestselling Feathers and Fire Series - and find out more about the mysterious Kansas City wizard, Callie Penrose... Or pick up your copy* **ONLINE**.

(Note: Callie appears in the Temple-verse after Nate's book 6, TINY GODS... Full chronology of all books in the Temple Universe shown on the 'Books in the Temple Verse' page.)

239

TRY: UNCHAINED (FEATHERS AND FIRE #1)

$\mathcal{T}$he rain pelted my hair, plastering loose strands of it to my forehead as I panted, eyes darting from tree to tree, terrified of each shifting branch, splash of water, and whistle of wind slipping through the nightscape around us. But... I was somewhat *excited*, too.

Somewhat.

"Easy, girl. All will be well," the big man creeping just ahead of me, murmured.

"You said we were going to get ice cream!" I hissed at him, failing to compose myself, but careful to keep my voice low and my eyes alert. "I'm not ready for this!" I had been trained to fight, with my hands, with weapons, and with my magic. But I had never taken an active role in a hunt before. I'd always been the getaway driver for my mentor.

The man grunted, grey eyes scanning the trees as he slipped through the tall grass. "And did we not get ice cream before coming here? Because I think I see some in your hair."

"You know what I mean, Roland. You tricked me." I checked the tips of my loose hair, saw nothing, and scowled at his back.

"The Lord does not give us a greater burden than we can shoulder."

I muttered dark things under my breath, wiping the water from my eyes. Again. My new shirt was going to be ruined. Silk never fared well in the rain. My choice of shoes wasn't much better. Boots, yes, but distressed, *fashionable* boots. Not work boots designed for the rain and mud. Definitely not monster hunting boots for our evening excursion through one of Kansas City's wooded parks. I realized I was forcibly distracting myself, keeping my mind busy with mundane thoughts to avoid my very real anxiety. Because whenever I grew nervous, an imagined nightmare always—

A church looming before me. Rain pouring down. Night sky and a glowing moon overhead. I was all alone. Crying on the cold, stone steps, and infant in a cardboard box—

I forced the nightmare away, breathing heavily. "You know I hate it when you talk like that," I whispered to him, trying to regain my composure. I wasn't angry with him, but was growing increasingly uncomfortable with our situation after my brief flashback of fear.

"Doesn't mean it shouldn't be said," he said kindly. "I think we're close. Be alert. Remember your training. Banish your fears. I am here. And the Lord is here. He always is."

So, he had noticed my sudden anxiety. "Maybe I should just go back to the car. I know I've trained, but I really don't think—"

A shape of fur, fangs, and claws launched from the shadows towards me, cutting off my words as it snarled, thirsty for my blood.

And my nightmare slipped back into my thoughts like a veiled assassin, a wraith hoping to hold me still for the monster to eat. I froze, unable to move. Twin sticks of power abruptly erupted into being in my clenched fists, but my fear swamped me with that stupid nightmare, the sticks held at my side, useless to save me.

Right before the beast's claws reached me, it grunted as something batted it from the air, sending it flying sideways. It struck a tree with another grunt and an angry whine of pain.

I fell to my knees right into a puddle, arms shaking, breathing fast.

My sticks crackled in the rain like live cattle prods, except their entire length was the electrical section — at least to anyone other than me. I could hold them without pain.

Magic was a part of me, coursing through my veins whether I wanted it or not, and Roland had spent many years teaching me how to master it. But I had never been able to fully master the nightmare inside me, and in moments of fear, it always won, overriding my training.

The fact that I had resorted to weapons — like the ones he had trained me with — rather than a burst of flame, was startling. It was good in the fact that my body's reflexes knew enough to call up a defense even without my direct command, but bad in the fact that it was the worst form of defense for the situation presented. I could have very easily done as Roland did, and hurt it from a distance. But I hadn't. Because of my stupid block.

Roland placed a calloused palm on my shoulder, and I flinched. "Easy, see? I am here." But he did frown at my choice of weapons, the reprimand silent but loud in my mind. I let out a shaky breath, forcing my fear back down. It was all in my head, but still, it wasn't easy. Fear could be like that.

I focused on Roland's implied lesson. Close combat weapons — even magically-powered ones — were for last resorts. I averted my eyes in very real shame. I knew these things. He didn't even need to tell me them. But when that damned nightmare caught hold of me, all my training went out the window. It haunted me like a shadow, waiting for moments just like this, as if trying to kill me. A form of psychological suicide? But it was why I constantly refused to join Roland on his hunts. He knew about it. And although he was trying to help me overcome that fear, he never pressed too hard.

Rain continued to sizzle as it struck my batons. I didn't let them go, using them as a totem to build my confidence back up. I slowly lifted my eyes to nod at him as I climbed back to my feet.

That's when I saw the second set of eyes in the shadows, right before they flew out of the darkness towards Roland's back. I threw one of my batons and missed, but that pretty much let Roland know that an unfriendly was behind him. Either that or I had just failed to murder my mentor at point-blank range. He whirled to confront the monster, expecting another aerial assault as he unleashed a ball of fire that splashed over the tree at chest height, washing the trunk in blue flames. But this monster was tricky. It hadn't planned on tackling Roland, but had merely jumped out of the darkness to get closer, no doubt learning from its fallen comrade, who still lay unmoving against the tree behind me.

His coat shone like midnight clouds with hints of lightning flashing in the depths of thick, wiry fur. The coat of dew dotting his fur reflected the moonlight, giving him a faint sheen as if covered in fresh oil. He was tall, easily hip height at the shoulder, and barrel chested, his rump much leaner than the rest of his body. He — I assumed male from the long, thick mane around his neck — had a very long snout, much longer and wider than any werewolf I had ever seen. Amazingly, and beyond my control, I realized he was beautiful.

But most of the natural world's lethal hunters were beautiful.

He landed in a wet puddle a pace in front of Roland, juked to the right, and then to the left, racing past the big man, biting into his hamstrings on his way by.

A wash of anger rolled over me at seeing my mentor injured, dousing my fear, and I swung my baton down as hard as I could. It struck the beast in the rump as it tried to dart back to cover — a typical wolf tactic. My blow singed his hair and shattered bone. The creature collapsed into a puddle of mud with a yelp, instinctively snapping his jaws over his shoulder to bite whatever had hit him.

I let him. But mostly out of dumb luck as I heard Roland hiss in pain, falling to the ground.

The monster's jaws clamped around my baton, and there was an immediate explosion of teeth and blood that sent him flying several feet away into the tall brush, yipping, screaming, and staggering. Before he slipped out of sight, I noticed that his lower jaw was simply *gone*, from the contact of his saliva on my electrified magical batons. Then he managed to limp into the woods with more pitiful yowls, but I had no mind to chase him. Roland — that titan of a man, my mentor — was hurt. I could smell copper in the air, and knew we had to get out of here. Fast. Because we had anticipated only one of the monsters. But there had been two of them, and they hadn't been the run-of-the-mill werewolves we had been warned about. If there were two, perhaps there were more. And they were evidently the prehistoric cousin of any werewolf I had ever seen or read about.

Roland hissed again as he stared down at his leg, growling with both pain and anger. My eyes darted back to the first monster, wary of another attack. It *almost* looked like a werewolf, but bigger. Much bigger. He didn't move, but I saw he was breathing. He had a notch in his right ear and a jagged scar on his long snout. Part of me wanted to go over to him and torture him. Slowly. Use his pain to finally drown my nightmare, my fear. The fear that had caused Roland's injury. My lack of inner-strength had not only put me in danger, but had hurt my mentor, my friend.

I shivered, forcing the thought away. That was *cold*. Not me. Sure, I was no stranger to fighting, but that had always been in a ring. Practicing. Sparring. Never life or death.

But I suddenly realized something very dark about myself in the chill, rainy night. Although I was terrified, I felt a deep ocean of anger manifest inside me, wanting only to dispense justice as I saw fit. To use that rage to battle my own demons. As if feeding one would starve the other, reminding me of the Cherokee Indian Legend Roland had once told me.

An old Cherokee man was teaching his grandson about life. "A fight is going on inside me," he told the boy. "It is a terrible fight between two wolves. One is evil — he is anger, envy, sorrow, regret, greed, arrogance, self-pity, guilt, resentment, inferiority, lies, false pride, superiority, and ego." After a few moments to make sure he had the boy's undivided attention, he continued.

"The other wolf is good — he is joy, peace, love, hope, serenity, humility, kindness, benevolence, empathy, generosity, truth, compassion, and faith. The same fight is going on inside of you, boy, and inside of every other person, too."

The grandson thought about this for a few minutes before replying. "Which wolf will win?"

The old Cherokee man simply said, "The one you feed, boy. The one you feed..."

And I felt like feeding one of my wolves today, by killing this one…

∿

Get the full book ONLINE!

MAKE A DIFFERENCE

Reviews are the most powerful tools in our arsenal when it comes to getting attention for our books. Much as we'd like to, we don't have the financial muscle of a New York publisher.

But we do have something much more powerful and effective than that, and it's something that those publishers would kill to get their hands on.

A committed and loyal bunch of readers.

Honest reviews of our books help bring them to the attention of other readers.

If you've enjoyed this book, we would be very grateful if you could spend just five minutes leaving a review on our book's Amazon page.

Thank you very much in advance.

ACKNOWLEDGMENTS

From Cameron:

I'd like to thank Shayne, for paving the way in style. Kori, for an introduction that would change my life. My three wonderful sisters, for showing me what a strong, independent woman looks and sounds like. And, above all, my parents, for—literally—everything.

From Shayne:

Team Temple and the Den of Freaks on Facebook have become family to me. I couldn't do it without die-hard readers like them.

I would also like to thank you, the reader. I hope you enjoyed reading *WHISKEY GINGER* as much as we enjoyed writing it. Callie Penrose returns in Summer 2018 with book 5, and Nate Temple's book 10 in my bestselling Nate Temple urban fantasy series releases late Summer 2018. Cameron and I might even sneak in Phantom Queen #5 before the year is out.

And last, but definitely not least, I thank my wife, Lexy. Without your support, none of this would have been possible.

ABOUT SHAYNE SILVERS

Shayne is a man of mystery and power, whose power is exceeded only by his mystery...

He currently writes the Amazon Bestselling **Feathers and Fire** Series about a rookie spell-slinger named Callie Penrose who works for the Vatican in Kansas City. Her problem? Hell seems to know more about her past than she does.

He also writes the Amazon Bestselling **Nate Temple** Series, which features a foul-mouthed wizard from St. Louis. He rides a bloodthirsty unicorn, drinks with Achilles, and is pals with the Four Horsemen.

Shayne holds two high-ranking black belts, and can be found writing in a coffee shop, cackling madly into his computer screen while pounding shots of espresso. He's hard at work on book 10 of the Nate Temple Series - coming summer 2018 - as well as Callie's book 5 in the Feathers and Fire series for early Summer 2018. **Follow him online for all sorts of groovy goodies, giveaways, and new release updates:**

Get Down with Shayne Online
www.shaynesilvers.com
info@shaynesilvers.com

f facebook.com/shaynesilversfanpage

a amazon.com/author/shaynesilvers

BB bookbub.com/profile/shayne-silvers

y twitter.com/shaynesilvers

O instagram.com/shaynesilversofficial

g goodreads.com/Shaynesilvers

ABOUT CAMERON O'CONNELL

Cameron O'Connell is a Jack-of-All-Trades and Master of Some.

He writes The Phantom Queen Diaries, a series in The Temple Verse, about Quinn MacKenna, a mouthy black magic arms dealer trading favors in Boston. All she wants? A round-trip ticket to the Fae realm...and maybe a drink on the house.

A former member of the United States military, a professional model, and English teacher, Cameron finds time to write in the mornings after his first cup of coffee...and in the evenings after his thirty-seventh. Follow him, and the Temple Verse founder, Shayne Silvers, online for all sorts of insider tips, giveaways, and new release updates!

Get Down with Cameron Online

f facebook.com/Cameron-OConnell-788806397985289

a amazon.com/author/cameronoconnell

BB bookbub.com/authors/cameron-o-connell

twitter.com/thecamoconnell

instagram.com/camoconnellauthor

g goodreads.com/cameronoconnell

BOOKS IN THE TEMPLE VERSE

CHRONOLOGY: All stories in the Temple Verse are shown in chronological order on the following page

PHANTOM QUEEN DIARIES

WHISKEY GINGER

COSMOPOLITAN - *PREORDER NOW! - JUNE 19, 2018*

OLD FASHIONED - *PREORDER NOW! - JUNE 26, 2018*

DARK AND STORMY - *PREORDER NOW! - JULY 10, 2018*

FEATHERS AND FIRE SERIES

UNCHAINED

RAGE

WHISPERS

ANGEL'S ROAR

BOOK #5 - *COMING SUMMER 2018...*

NATE TEMPLE SERIES

FAIRY TALE - FREE prequel novella #0 for my subscribers

OBSIDIAN SON

BLOOD DEBTS

GRIMM

SILVER TONGUE

BEAST MASTER

TINY GODS

DADDY DUTY (Novella #6.5)

WILD SIDE

WAR HAMMER

NINE SOULS

BOOK #10 - *COMING SUMMER 2018...*

Made in the USA
Coppell, TX
26 October 2019